The Ullswater Undertaking

The Ullswater Undertaking

REBECCA TOPE

Allison & Busby Limited
11 Wardour Mews
London W1F 8AN
allisonandbusby.com

First published in Great Britain by Allison & Busby in 2021.
This paperback edition published by Allison & Busby in 2021.

Copyright © 2021 by REBECCA TOPE

A CIP catalogue record for this book is available from the British Library.

10 9 8 7 6 5 4 3 2 1

ISBN 978-0-7490-2760-5
Typeset in 10.5/15.5 pt Sabon LT Pro by
Allison & Busby Ltd

With thanks to Pat, who almost single-handedly saw me through the horrors of 2020

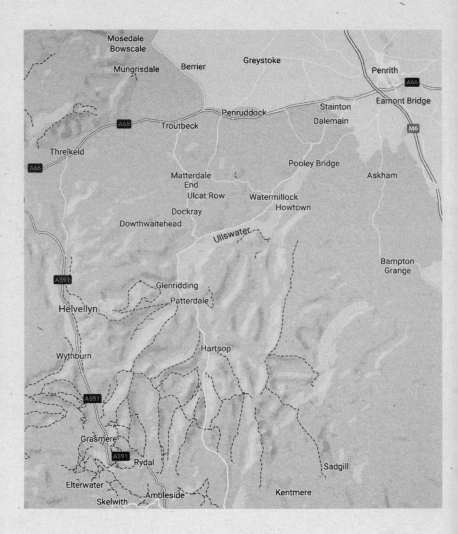

Author's Note

The villages and towns in this story are real but the individual houses and the saleroom in Keswick are invented. I do not entirely vouch for the accuracy of the bus schedules.

Chapter One

Four in the morning in the middle of April was not at all a bad time to be awake, Simmy was discovering. At the age of eighteen days, little Robin was adamant that he had to be fed at this very hour and his mother had no wish to disappoint him. The hours when he was asleep felt like wasted time to her, in the first flush of euphoric disbelief at his very existence. The birth had been ridiculously quick and easy, reaching the hospital in Barrow with barely ten minutes to spare, before sliding him out with scarcely a yelp. 'Classic second labour,' said the midwife knowingly. Simmy had flinched at this reminder, sorry that these would be the first words the new baby was to hear.

A boy! A living, breathing, flourishing boy, weighing nine pounds and apparently pleased to find himself in the world. Christopher, his father, had been almost as incapable as Simmy was of believing he was real. 'Well, the Hendersons are good at boys,' he said. Two more ghosts joined that of Simmy's first baby – the new child would have no Henderson grandparents.

It took them all day to select the baby's name, and

then it seemed destined and obvious and permanent. Not only a subtle homage to the Winnie-the-Pooh books, but other agreeable associations. 'A robin's a lovely little bird,' said Simmy.

'Not to mention Robin Goodfellow,' said Simmy's father, when the decision was conveyed to him. 'That should ensure that he keeps you on your toes. I believe he was actually a hobgoblin.'

'Thanks, Dad,' laughed Simmy.

'Basically it's just a really nice name,' said the new father. 'And we do owe my friend Robin several favours. He worked his socks off trying to find us somewhere to live. He'll think we've named our son after him.'

'"Our son",' Simmy repeated with a soppy smile, quashing the flicker of regret at having the man for ever connected to the baby. She'd forgotten all about Mr Robin Stirling, the estate agent.

Now Christopher was asleep, Simmy was settled into the cosy nursing chair her father had bought her and Robin was placidly suckling. Saturday would be under way before long, and Chris would have to spend a long day auctioning off 750 lots at his workplace in Keswick. The auction house had survived its moment of notoriety the previous year when it sold a piece of Tudor embroidery for a headline-making sum, and was hurtling from one success to another, with income from commissions rocketing up. People from all over the world were spending incredible sums on quality antiques and random collections of memorabilia from house clearances – a situation, Christopher insisted, that would only get bigger and better in the coming years.

Even if the Chinese economy floundered, there were Americans, Japanese, Indians and even newly affluent Africans eager to buy goods that had originated from their countries. They wanted them back and were willing to pay whatever it took.

Outside it was windy. The building was not yet quite weatherproof in some parts, having been built as a large stone barn some two hundred years previously. There had been a very hasty conversion undergone over the winter months, creating an upper storey, staircase and fully fitted kitchen and bathroom. Other rooms were still a work in progress, with walls unplastered and floors uncovered.

Robin the elder, friend of Christopher, had valiantly handled the sale of Simmy's Troutbeck cottage, selling it for more than the original asking price, two weeks before Christmas. It had been on the market a mere ten days. 'Of course, he'll get a good share of the commission,' Simmy reminded Christopher when he showed signs of going overboard with his gratitude. Try as she might, she wasn't entirely able to *like* the man. Giving her baby his name had been an accident, on that first day. She'd been thinking almost entirely about cheerful little birds. And Robin Stirling had not after all found them a place to live. The barn had been – incredibly – just *given* to them by a woman in a rush to escape the area and all it meant to her. As a result they had more money than Simmy had ever thought possible, just sitting in a pathetically low-interest bank account.

Dawn was breaking, pink-tinged clouds racing across

the fells, driven by the wind. Outside was the tiny settlement of Hartsop, a few miles south of Patterdale, itself another short distance from Ullswater and Glenridding. Simmy had never before seen it in spring, and the experience was intoxicating. She was working up a routine of bundling the baby into a sling and walking a mile or two along a rough track that ran alongside the beck to the southern tip of the lake. The first such walk had been on Robin's eighth day, and Simmy had managed almost a mile, feeling light-headed with responsibility for the little life tied on her front, as well as exhilaration at this new phase of her life. She had repeated the walk three more times since then. Christopher worried that she would slip and fall, with Robin altering her centre of gravity. Before they'd moved here he had repeatedly insisted they get a dog. Now, with all this walking, it made even more sense. 'A golden retriever,' he begged. 'Or an Irish setter.'

'I can't cope with a dog just yet,' she always prevaricated. 'Maybe in the summer.'

The walking was growing more important to her with every passing week. Once she had got as far as the pub in Patterdale, taking almost an hour to gather her strength for the return walk and feeding the baby quietly in a corner. She could not see how a dog would enhance this experience. An Irish setter would run across the road and get killed. A retriever would want her to throw sticks for it. A terrier would chase sheep and a spaniel would get under her feet.

It was a precious interlude, which she knew couldn't last.

Her flower shop down in Windermere was still functioning, with young Bonnie Lawson stepping up magnificently and a temporary woman brought in to help. That had been quite a moment, when Verity Chambers had come into their lives. In her fifties, with a broad Cumbrian accent, she was reassuringly compliant and co-operative. She let a girl less than half her age order her about with apparent contentment, never arguing or complaining. 'It's a miracle!' Bonnie insisted. 'I can't get used to it at all. Ben says it's all an act and she's just biding her time before she takes over the whole business.'

'Nonsense,' said Simmy. 'She's just happy to let somebody else carry all the responsibility.'

'But she does talk far too much, most of it total rubbish,' Bonnie added.

Verity knew more than enough about flowers to be an asset in the shop. But when it came to taking orders, with the timing often quite crucial, she was useless. Bonnie forbade her from answering the phone under any circumstances, or from going anywhere near the computer. But she could drive and knew her way around the region, so she could be sent out with deliveries. Bonnie still showed no sign of learning to drive.

Christopher woke shortly before seven to find Simmy and his son dozing together in the chair on the other side of the very large bedroom. Simmy had insisted on sitting by the big new window when she fed the baby because it looked out on a most spectacular view. 'Hey, you two, come back to bed,' he called.

'Not worth it now,' she said. 'Young Sir is dead to the world. I'll go and do us some eggs. My mother's coming later on, when she's finished the breakfasts.'

'I remember.' He got out of bed and joined them. 'Looks like a nice day.'

'I watched the sunrise. It was very pink. Shepherd's warning.'

'April showers, that's all.' He bent over them. 'He's going to look like my dad, isn't he? Same neat little features.'

'Too soon to say,' said Simmy. 'I can see my mother in him every now and then.'

'She'll be pleased about that.'

'She's just pleased, full stop.' Angie Straw's relief at the safe arrival of her only grandchild had been startling to them all. For a whole day, she simply wept, as if a tap had got stuck in the 'on' position. Her husband had walked her round the streets of Barrow in an effort to distract her, but in vain. She had rushed back to the maternity ward to check that she hadn't dreamt the whole thing.

Christopher left home at half past seven for the auction house in Keswick. The drive could take a full half hour if there was tourist traffic on the little road up to the A66. Already, since Easter, the volume of slow-moving cars was growing. The bidding didn't start until nine-thirty, and Simmy never quite understood why he factored in so much time beforehand.

But she was too busy to worry on this particular Saturday. 'I'm going to paint some doors,' she announced. 'Humphrey's going to be here just for a bit, getting everything ready for the dining-room wall. He says I've made a lot

14

of extra work, insisting on it being double thickness. He's calling it the Big Undertaking, which I think he thinks is funny.'

'I don't expect he really minds the extra work. He can see the logic.'

'I can't understand why he ever thought a flimsy partition would be good enough.'

'He's lucky we're not making him build it of natural stone, like the outer ones.'

Simmy grew thoughtful. 'Did we even think of that?' Despite her best efforts, the distractions of pregnancy, timings and inconvenient weather had forced them to take the quick and easy options in many instances. Christopher had shown little interest in the finer details. 'I just want somewhere for us to live,' he kept saying.

Now he said, 'Too slow and much too expensive. Personally, I think you can have too much natural stone. It's not as if we live in the Cotswolds, where it's so much nicer than what they dig out up here.'

'Sacrilege!' she scolded him. 'Anyway, I thought I might do a bit of paintwork upstairs, while Robin has his morning nap.'

'You should let them do it, you idiot. That's what they're for.'

'Not at all. They're builders, not painters. And I *like* doing it.'

Christopher worried that paint fumes would be bad for his baby, or that somehow Simmy's milk would be tainted. The entire Straw family mocked him for such needless worries. Once Robin had convinced them that he intended to live and thrive, they began to entertain very few anxieties. It was as if they'd used them all up before the birth, and now it was perfectly obvious that nothing could go wrong. Even Russell, who had slipped into a state of near paranoia in recent times, appeared to be cured of that condition now. He blithely approved of Simmy taking the child out in all weathers, of putting him near open windows or leaving him for ten minutes in the car. 'That's the way to do it,' he yodelled. 'Bring him up tough.'

Simmy spent forty minutes painting a door frame before Robin stirred. Angie arrived at eleven, to find her daughter and grandson nestled in the new kitchen. The room had been planned to resemble that of an old farmhouse. It lacked an Aga or Rayburn but had an area at one end with easy chairs and a carpet close to a radiator that was not yet functional. Christopher frequently made the point that it was a perfect spot for a dog bed.

'Guess what,' Angie crowed. 'I've just broken a taboo. It was intensely satisfying.'

'Oh?'

'Facial hair on women, to be exact. Have you any *idea* how embarrassing people find that? It's hilarious, especially in these days of so-called gender fluidity. I noticed this morning that I was getting a bit stubbly, and I said to one of the guests, as she was going out, "Wouldn't it be great if society would allow women to grow beards?" Honestly – she didn't know where to look.' She laughed gleefully. 'And your father was fantastic. He came up to me and stroked my chin, and said, "I think I might quite fancy that." Made it all worse for the wretched woman, of course. She's the type to spend half her money at a beauty clinic.'

'She won't be coming back to Beck View in a hurry, then,' said Simmy.

'I don't care. It was worth it to see her face. I'm going to make a habit of it from now on.'

'Don't you dare,' said Simmy.

An hour passed in baby-worship, coffee, idle chat. 'Are you staying for lunch?' Simmy asked, at midday.

'I am – didn't I say? Or we could go to the pub. Your father says he'll come up on the bus this afternoon. We can go and meet him. He was thinking we'd have to fetch him from Pooley Bridge, because that's been the end of the line for the bus since they started those diversions, but it's running normally again now. I left him compiling a long list of stuff to get from the cash and carry. We'll go together on the way home.'

'He won't be staying long, then. Why didn't he come with you this morning?'

'He wasn't ready. He'd spent ages going over maps with one of the guests and was all behind. And there were beds to change for this evening.'

'Poor Dad,' said Simmy regretfully. The demands of the popular bed and breakfast establishment were more and more burdensome, getting in the way of family matters now that Simmy lived so much further away. 'The bus takes ages.'

'He likes it. There's always somebody to chat to. If he really minded, he'd get another car. We don't have to manage with just one if we don't want to.'

'Except you haven't got space for two. One of them would have to live out in the road.'

'So what?'

Simmy shrugged. 'So nothing, I suppose. But I don't think Dad would like it.'

'Lucky he likes the bus, then.'

They were going round in circles, but Simmy was made aware of a shift in the triangular dynamic of her family. She had always favoured her father, joking with him, reading his thoughts, sharing his preoccupations. But since the baby, her mother had grown much closer, with a new softness that surprised them all, including Angie herself. It was, of course, a cliché that the arrival of a baby brought the generations together. The surprise was that the maverick Angie Straw should conform to anything so objectionable as a cliché.

They did not go to the pub but had a simple lunch, while Humphrey and his young assistant measured and marked, and started placing battens for the new wall. 'I love all these smells,' said Angie. 'Paint and new wood. It takes me back to when your father and I had to have the floors replaced in our first flat.'

'It's nice having the builders here, now Christopher's back at work. I might get a bit panicky all day on my own, otherwise.'

'You'll have to get over that,' said Angie briskly. 'The builders won't be here for ever.'

'I know they won't. And they're not here all day every day as it is. I just wish there were a few more neighbours,

I suppose. Proper ones, not second-homers or holiday people.'

'People are people,' said Angie vaguely. 'If you were in a pickle, you could just go to the door and shout, and a dozen hikers would run to your rescue.'

'True,' said Simmy, wondering what that would actually be like.

The phone rang shortly before two. 'It'll be your father with a change of plan,' said Angie. 'He always uses the landline.' This was a slightly sore point between the two households. When the Hartsop house had requested the installation of Wi-Fi and Sky, an inevitable part of the package had been a fixed telephone line. Christopher had queried it, saying they could function quite well with mobiles, and there had ensued a lengthy harangue about signal reliability and system flexibility, which overrode any objections. 'It can't hurt, I suppose,' said Simmy. Like her mother, she actually preferred using the time-honoured instrument, which was always sitting there on its stand, easy to find and easy to use.

But it wasn't Russell calling. It was a strange voice, asking for Christopher Henderson. 'He's not here, I'm afraid,' said Simmy.

'Ah. Well, tell him I called, will you? My name's Fabian Crick – got that? He'll remember me. Tell him I've come to remind him of his promise to me.'

Simmy shivered slightly. 'Promise?' she echoed.

'Right. It was a while ago now, but he won't have forgotten. Your husband, or whatever he is, owes me big time. He made an undertaking, ten years ago now, and I've come to make good on it. You tell him that.'

Simmy said nothing, but before she could end the call, there was a final remark. 'Oh yes – and tell him I'm living in Ullswater now. Just up the road, in fact.'

'Who was that?' asked Angie.

'Um . . . somebody who knew Christopher some time ago. He didn't sound very friendly.' She frowned worriedly. 'And he says he lives just up the road.'

'I dare say Christopher knows quite a few shady characters, one way or another,' said Angie, as if that was perfectly fine with her. 'I'm sure he can handle them. Nothing for you to worry about.'

'I hope not,' said Simmy, eyeing her baby son on his grandmother's lap. 'We need to go and meet Dad from the bus. It's due in ten minutes, isn't it? Then we can all go for a stroll through the village together.'

'Good idea. You'll need to wrap the little one up warm, though. There's quite a nasty little wind today.'

The bus was prompt, and Russell was the only passenger to alight at the Hartsop stop, to nobody's surprise, despite it being a pleasant spring weekend. Tourists might be constantly urged to use buses wherever possible, but the schedules did little to entice anyone to comply. A walk on the fells would be rendered far less relaxing if imbued with worry about missing the only bus back to the hotel or B&B. Hartsop boasted a fair-sized car park at the foot of the Dodd, and almost everyone gratefully used it.

'Hello, my lad,' Russell greeted Robin, who was asleep.

'Enjoying the fresh air, are you?'

'He's due to wake up any minute now,' said Simmy.

Russell nudged his wife. 'Who knew that sleeping could run so beautifully to schedule?' he teased. 'If I remember rightly, we had no such expectations when we had our infant.'

'I don't suppose it'll last,' said Angie.

They all strolled down the winding little road that was the centre of Hartsop, remarking on the bluebells and celandines that grew on any available patch of uncultivated land. There were stone walls separating the few houses from the road, with narrow grass verges fringing them. In April these verges exuberantly sported wild flowers, if allowed to. Above them the dramatic conical hill known as Hartsop Dodd cast a shadow. 'It reminds me of The Old Man of Coniston,' said Simmy. 'Except it has a lot less character. But they both loom over the settlement as if humanity was just a minor intrusion on the grander scale of things.'

'That's my girl,' said Russell cheerfully. 'Seeing the bigger picture. I must say I'm glad you moved here. It's opened up a whole new area for me to explore.'

Angie sighed. 'You're both bonkers. If you look more closely, you can see humanity crawling all over that hill, leaving tracks and scaring the sheep.'

'And I suppose the sheep are only there because of humanity, anyway,' Simmy said.

'Right,' Russell confirmed. 'Without them, the whole landscape would be covered in trees. Once you realise that, it completely changes how you see the fells. They're like someone with a shaven head. It's not natural.'

It was a recurring debate across the whole region – whether or not sheep had always been there, running wild and eating baby trees, or whether they had been artificially introduced, thereby destroying the essential harmonies and systems that nature intended. There were plenty of voices raised in favour of bare uplands, claiming they favoured certain birds and butterflies that would not prosper if there was nothing but trees everywhere. Russell Straw tended to the anti-sheep argument, but he insisted that he remained open-minded on the subject. 'Besides,' he said, 'we all know the sheep aren't going anywhere.'

They went back to the house for a drink, while Russell rhapsodised about the winding road from Windermere, and how it got worse and worse after Kirkstone Pass. 'It's as if someone deliberately set out to play a joke on all these tourists,' he chuckled. 'The stone walls look as if they move in the night, just to trick everybody.'

'A cruel joke, if you ask me,' said Simmy, who was apprehensive about driving down to her Windermere shop along that very road, in all weathers. 'I don't know how they navigate a bus round those awful bends.'

'It's only four or five miles,' shrugged Russell. 'After Patterdale it's almost civilised.'

'Which is the bit that Christopher gets to use,' Simmy pointed out. 'His drive to work is a dream compared to what mine's going to be.'

'Too late to worry about that now,' said Angie. 'But I suggest you make sure you keep your car serviced. Good tyres and so forth.'

The family spent a lazy couple of hours together in the barn conversion, making unrealistic plans for the summer and discussing various memorable guests at the Beck View B&B. Robin woke as predicted and entertained his grandfather for half an hour. The Straws left at four thirty, giving Simmy a full two hours to catch up with some sleep before Christopher came home. On Angie's firm insistence, she took the baby to bed with her, feeling as if she was breaking at least three cast-iron laws. As she drifted into sleep, she remembered the ominous tones of the man on the phone who was intent on meeting Christopher. What had her fiancé promised to do, and what would be the penalty for failing to have done it?

Chapter Two

'So who's Fabian Crick?' Simmy remembered to ask, nearly an hour after Christopher got home. 'He phoned here this afternoon, wanting you.'

She watched his face closely, having no idea what to expect. All she could discern was sheer astonishment. 'Crickers? Is that who you mean? He's dead, as far as I know. Last I saw him was in Botswana, where he was dying of sleeping sickness. A tsetse fly bit him.'

'Seems he recovered and is living right here on your doorstep. He didn't sound very nice.'

Christopher was lost in reminiscence, once he'd got over his surprise at the man's continued existence. 'It must be ten or twelve years ago, at least. We were in an overland group, doing Africa from top to bottom. He was all right, once you got to know him. A bit geeky. Probably on the spectrum, as they say now. Nearly twenty years older than me, but we shared a tent a few times because we were both solo travellers. He was pretty sick by the time we got into the Okavanga and they flew him off to a hospital somewhere. It was all rather a drama.'

Simmy waited for the story to finish, eyebrows slightly raised. Christopher went on in some bewilderment. 'You're telling me he called here? How would he know the number? He can't possibly be living near here. He was in London, I think. Although I remember that his family did live in Cumbria.'

'I'm just repeating what he said. He wants to talk to you about a promise you made – calling in a favour of some sort.'

'Oh God!' Christopher suddenly leant back in the chair by the radiator and stared blindly at the wall in front of him. 'I did, didn't I? Lord help me. He probably wants to kill me, then. We'd better bar the doors and windows.'

Simmy's first concern was for her baby. A threatening man with a grievance against her partner was no joke. 'You're not serious?' she said. 'What about Robin?'

'I don't know. Let me think. Did he leave a number? What did he say *exactly*?'

'I can't remember the exact words. He didn't sound friendly. You made him a promise and he's coming to remind you of it. And he now lives in Ullswater. You don't really think we should worry about him, do you?'

'I thought he was *dead*. He was in pretty poor shape even before the fly bit him. Drugs, smoking like a chimney, eating nothing but junk. The medics that came for him obviously thought he'd barely survive the trip to hospital. He and I had ten minutes together in the tent, and he was raving. Something about an aunt who lived in England and needed to hear an important message from him. Honestly, it was like something from a cheap thriller. I don't remember any details – I didn't take it at all seriously. I mean – you promise anything to a dying person, don't you?'

'Some people do, evidently,' said Simmy, recalling an instance in Grasmere where Christopher had also made a rash promise to a dying friend. 'You especially,' she added.

'Oh? Maybe I do. It's wrong, do you think?'

'It might backfire sometimes,' she said carefully. 'Like it seems to have done with this Crick person.'

'I do remember thinking the aunt sounded interesting and it might be fun to visit her next time I was up here seeing my folks.' Again, his gaze was on the wall. 'He called her "the ultimate entrepreneur" I remember. That caught my attention.'

'Oh?'

'Yeah. The thing is, I'd been doing a bit of dealing before that trip – buying indigenous artwork cheap on the streets and selling it for big profits. I'd been boasting about how easy it was to make money if you just found the right niche. And Crickers picked up the fact that I had people in Cumbria, the same as he did. He connected it all up – that's how his brain worked – and told me I should visit the aunt and see if she had some words of advice for me, and to tell her he was thinking of her in his final days. All rather melodramatic, I admit, but not the sort of urgent message you're making it sound. I thought I might as well do it, if I was in the area – but by the time I got back here, I'd completely forgotten her name, address – the whole thing. And whatever you say, the fact that I was sure he was dead made it seem a bit pointless.'

Simmy thought of wartime soldiers taking considerable trouble to visit the widows of their dead comrades to describe their final moments and wondered whether Christopher was typical of subsequent generations who disregarded such obligations. 'You could have told her all about what happened to him. People like to have the full story when someone dies, you know.'

'I suppose they do,' he said doubtfully. 'But I can't say I saw it like that at the time. She was only an aunt, after all.'

'The fact remains that you ignored your promise to this man, the way *he* sees it. And now he wants some sort of recompense.'

'I didn't ignore it. My plans changed. It was another three years before I came back here. Anybody would have forgotten after that time. I was young and irresponsible, I admit. I'll be able to explain it to him. I mean – he's damned lucky to be alive. And the aunt must have died yonks ago. He probably just wants to rub my nose in it.'

She gave him a suspicious scrutiny. 'Are you trying to make light of it? He sounded as if it's been building up to quite a head of resentment.'

Christopher groaned. 'The honest truth is that I barely even knew the man. It was just my luck that I ended up being the one to watch over him while the medics struggled to get to us. Who knows what might have been happening to him in the past ten years? He might have gone completely round the bend – or the exact opposite. For all I know, he's married with three kids and working in a bank. He might want to come round for a drink and a laugh about those crazy days in Africa. How am I supposed to know?'

She sighed. 'Well, I think we can assume he hasn't been living around here for very long. If he had, don't you think he'd have found you before this? You were in the paper last year – name, job, everything. Before that, the Henderson name was out there when your father died. He obviously hasn't been looking for you until recently.'

'Which phone did he use?' Christopher asked suddenly.

'Um – the landline.'

'So how did he get that number?'

'They still have directory enquiries, don't they?'

'Do they? Did it not occur to us to go ex-directory, then?'

'Not to me it didn't. I quite like being available at the end of a phone.'

'Did he leave a number for me to call back?'

'No, but you can get it with 1471. Nobody's called since then.'

'Good thinking. I'll do that – I'm not sitting around waiting for him to condescend to phone back.' But when he tried to get the number, there was a message: *Caller withheld their number*. Christopher slammed the phone down and snarled, 'Now there's a surprise.'

Robin interrupted at that point with a demand for attention and some food if possible, please. Christopher forgot the phone and applied himself to ten minutes of playtime. 'A whole day tomorrow for more bonding,' he rejoiced.

'We're not going to Hannah's then?' asked Simmy.

'Nope. That can wait till next weekend. I told her

already, it's too soon. We're not ready to take him out into the world yet.'

'I've taken him to the pub at least three times. He'll be three weeks old on Tuesday.'

'My sisters both saw him when you brought him home. They can wait another week. I want him all to myself.'

'You should have put in for paternity leave. It's your legal right.'

'Don't start that again.' They had debated and argued the point endlessly, in Robin's first few days. Simmy had taken so readily to breastfeeding; the baby was so placid and accommodating; Angie and Russell were so attentive; the auction house was so unusually busy – it all made Christopher feel he would be more use as a father in a few more months' time. The rules allowed for him to have two weeks paid leave at any point during the coming year, and it seemed to him sensible to postpone it.

'You're right. Sorry.' Simmy's compliance was genuine. Her days at home with the baby were far less stressful, far more delightful than she had anticipated, partly thanks to the presence of Humphrey the builder and his young workmate. With her habitual tendency to take nothing for granted, she assured Christopher that there would be times when his participation would be indispensable. 'You can have him all day long when he's teething.'

'And all day Sunday, remember. Every Sunday for the rest of my life.'

She laughed and took the baby from him for a feed. Having prepared herself for a total lack of routine, giving feeds whenever the child showed interest, snatching naps when Robin slept and abandoning any thought of housework, the reality was utterly different. The newborn evidently had an active internal clock set to three-hourly intervals. At night this stretched to four blissful hours. He enjoyed his wakeful periods, watching flickering light with as much fascination as he watched his mother's face. 'He must be brain damaged,' said Angie carelessly. 'No normal baby is as good as this.'

'He's just naturally pleased to be alive,' said Simmy defensively. 'The health visitor says he's completely healthy.'

The evening was approaching its early end. Simmy and Christopher often went to bed at nine-thirty, sleeping until Robin called out at midnight. Chris might then go and make a milky drink for them both, which generally ensured that they slept deeply until the 4 a.m. summons. 'Something's supposed to change when he gets to three weeks,' Simmy warned. 'A growth spurt, apparently.'

Christopher shrugged unconcernedly. 'Sufficient unto the day,' he said.

But there was an unfinished conversation hanging over them on this Saturday evening. 'What if that Crick man turns up when you're at work?' she worried. 'What does he look like? What do you think he *wants* from you?'

'He must be late fifties by now, maybe a bit more. I can't really remember what he looked like. Middle height, thin, quite colourless.'

'What work did he do? Wasn't it unusual for a man his age to be doing such a long overland trip?'

'No idea what work he did. He was a bit of a misfit, I guess. There's generally a wife as well – kids just gone off and the parents awarding themselves an adventure. But there are always exceptions. The group had people of all ages. The youngest was a girl of nineteen, and there was a couple in their seventies. And a man and his daughter, I remember. And a gay couple from Belgium. Gosh – I haven't given any of them a thought for years.'

Another detail had snagged Simmy's attention. 'You never told me you did antique dealing as long ago as that.'

'They weren't antiques. Just local crafts. It was lucky chance initially. I was in Lisbon and came across a sort of emporium selling ethnic stuff. I had a few bits and pieces from Tunisia in my rucksack and popped in to see if there was any interest. The bloke almost bit my hand off. Apparently he'd had trouble getting in and out of North Africa, and suggested I do a few trips on his behalf. I stuck to very small items that fitted into my bag or could be sent through the mail without too much hassle. The customs procedures weren't very efficient, so I always managed to get through. Technically, there was probably duty to pay.' He was rambling sleepily, reminiscing without much of a logical thread.

'Anything else I should know?' Simmy persisted.

'Oh – I've no idea. The more I try to remember, the less I can dredge up about him. It was all pretty scary and overwrought, with him being so sick. He was practically delirious at times. It was embarrassing for the tour operator, and highly complicated getting him to hospital. He should never have been taken into the Okavanga in the first place. There were arguments about it. All I can remember now is that some female relative living in Cumbria was expecting

31

him to show up for something important. And he asked me to go instead of him and I said I would.'

'So you made a note of her name and address, right? It was something you both assumed was within your capabilities.'

'Not that, exactly. More that I was planning to come back here to catch up with the family, and he made the connection, geographically speaking. It must have seemed too neat to ignore. Haven't I said all this already?'

'But you promised him.'

'I did. I admit that I did say I'd do it. Whatever it was. It seems like a tremendously long time ago now.'

'Ten years isn't so long, really. *He* obviously hasn't forgotten.'

'Right. And some people take great exception to broken promises.'

'Which explains your first reaction, when you said he'd probably kill you. Which suggests he's quite a scary person.'

'Scary like a zombie's scary. My first reaction was that he'd risen from the dead and was out for revenge. On calm reflection, I doubt if he's more than slightly annoyed. He probably just wants to come and say hi, for old times' sake.'

'Hm,' said Simmy, and fell asleep.

There were visitors just after Sunday lunch, in the shape of Bonnie Lawson and her beloved Ben Harkness, home from university for the Easter vacation. Although they had initially intended to emulate Russell Straw the previous day and come by bus, in the event they were transported by Corinne, Bonnie's foster mother.

'I just had to see the baby,' she explained. 'I'll only stay a minute. I brought cake.' She proffered a creased cardboard box containing a modest-sized piece of fruit cake. 'I made it last week. It's a bit soggy,' she added.

Simmy was fond of the woman and more than happy to drop Robin into her outstretched arms. All the usual blandishments were uttered, and Robin co-operated handsomely. 'I'll go up to Penrith while I'm here,' said Corinne. 'I need to see a man about a trailer.'

Christopher looked up. 'Oh? Taking up antique dealing, then?' To him trailers only meant one thing.

Corinne gave him a blank stare. 'Absolutely not. It's for the sheep.'

Bonnie hurried to elucidate. 'Corinne's got four Jacobs in the field behind her house. They're quite new. She has to get hay and stuff for them, so needs a trailer.'

'I already got the towbar put on,' said Corinne. 'It's all rather exciting.' She laughed. 'So I could collect these two on my way back, if you like. But I don't think I'll be very long.'

'That's okay,' said Simmy. 'They may as well stay the afternoon now. One of us will drive them home again. Are you hungry?' she asked the youngsters when Corinne had gone.

'Not very,' said Bonnie. 'We had a big breakfast. It was more brunch, really.'

Neither visitor was unduly interested in the baby, beyond admiring his new skill of smiling. 'He seems a cheerful character,' said Ben.

Christopher was showing only minor irritation at

being invaded by his partner's friends. It was chilly outside, with flurries of rain, so any prospect of a decent walk had already been abandoned. 'Ben goes back on Thursday, so this is his last chance to see Simmy,' said Bonnie. 'Although . . .' She looked at her boyfriend, eyebrows raised.

Christopher failed to notice the hesitation and busied himself supplying home-made cake. 'Angie left us a huge fruit loaf thing yesterday, and we'll never eat all of it. Plus Corinne brought some as well.'

They ate cake quietly for a few minutes. Simmy noticed glances and even a nudge between Ben and Bonnie and guessed there was something significant waiting to be said. Her first guess was that Bonnie was going to announce that she could no longer endure the ten weeks of term time without Ben and was therefore following him to Newcastle, leaving Simmy with nobody to manage the shop. After that, her imagination ran dry.

'So – what's been happening?' she prompted. 'Did it go all right yesterday? Has Verity been okay?'

'Fine. It's all fine,' Bonnie assured her. 'If you come down one day this week to go over the finances, that's all we need, really. It's gone quiet again now Easter's over.' There had been the usual hectic rush for Mother's Day and Easter. Simmy had dreaded going into labour on Mother's Day, because that had been the day her ill-fated first baby had been stillborn, an anniversary that should not be allowed to taint the first hours of the new baby's life. As it turned out, Robin had waited another nine days to put in an appearance. Simmy had actually managed to juggle orders

34

for flowers, insisting that spending two full days at the shop in the fortieth week of pregnancy was very therapeutic. 'It passes the time very nicely,' she had said.

Verity had been kept extremely busy rushing around with deliveries, and Ben's young sister, Tanya, had done sterling work supplying bouquets and suchlike to customers in the shop alongside Bonnie.

'We did well, didn't we?' said Simmy now. 'Between us, we've kept the show very nicely on the road.'

'How's the auction business?' Ben asked Christopher. 'I meant to go again over the vac, but it's impossible to get there without a car. I see you had some memorabilia yesterday. I was looking through the catalogue online. Looked interesting.'

'Box of old papers,' Christopher nodded. 'Nothing special. We get them a lot. Mostly it's from house clearances – the family just tip everything out of the bureau or whatever and hope there's nothing important amongst it. Nobody's got time these days to have a proper look through. It often goes to someone who wants the stamps, if there are bundles of old letters.'

'Or old photos,' said Simmy. 'Those cartes de visite are quite collectable.'

Christopher snorted. 'Nobody's got them amongst their personal papers any more. They died out a century and more ago. The photos are all from the 1950s now – Auntie Sylvia on the beach, and babies in paddling pools. And dogs. Usually out of focus.'

'I'd love to have bought that box, all the same,' said Ben wistfully.

'You should have said. I could have kept it for you. It

went for eight quid, I think.'

Ben grimaced. 'Don't tell me that,' he said.

'There'll be more. Let me know another time, and we'll do a deal.'

'Thanks,' said Ben. Then, after a short silence, he went on, 'Actually, I suppose this gives me an opening to tell you my news.' He gave Bonnie a look that seemed to Simmy to contain a degree of apprehension.

'What?' Simmy demanded.

Chapter Three

'Well . . .' Ben started nervously, 'the thing is, I've decided
to change my course.' Before anybody could speak, he
rushed on. 'I've done two terms now and I'm absolutely
sure I went for the wrong subject. I know it's embarrassing
and makes me look an idiot, but I can't help that. What I'm
doing is too narrow, too restricting. I was too young when I
made the decision, and never even considered changing it.'
He was addressing Simmy exclusively. 'I feel I'm letting you
down,' he concluded in a quiet voice.

'Me? It's none of my business, is it? What are you
going to do instead? Have you told your parents? Will the
university just *let* you change, halfway through the year?'

'You and Moxon, he means,' Bonnie explained. 'After
all this time, all through the A-levels and everything,
you've both been so proud of him. More than Helen and
David, really.'

Simmy was horrified. 'You can't possibly think I was
pressurising you.' She wanted to throw it back at him, to
explain that she had always taken her lead from what he
showed every sign of wanting. She regarded herself as little

more than a bystander, watching with awe as the young genius forged his way through the educational system. Instead, she felt close to tears and said nothing more.

'History,' said Ben quickly. 'I want to change to history. It fits infinitely better with my interests – and abilities. I like researching and making timelines and that sort of thing.'

'Yes, but . . .' said Simmy. 'Don't those things come into the course you're doing?'

'Not really.' He worked his shoulders, and Bonnie patted his leg. 'It's more than that, if I'm honest. I don't much like university life. I expected to meet people like me, as well as people who knew more and were sharper and quicker . . .'

'He means cleverer,' said Bonnie, with a little nod.

'And didn't you?' asked Christopher.

'Sort of. The trouble is, they're still like schoolkids, trying to devalue their own abilities. And they're so *helpless*. And *timid*. I tried telling a couple of them about what happened to me in Hawkshead, and they almost ran out of the room. I'm telling you, most of them are like six-year-olds. I can't even *talk* to them.'

'So how will a history course be better?' wondered Christopher.

Ben grimaced. 'Good question. I was thinking maybe I could do it through the OU instead. Maybe there'd be a lot of much older students at the tutorials and things, and I might get on better with them.'

'It sounds to me as if you've been horribly miserable,' said Simmy, feeling an overwhelming sympathy for him.

'He has,' said Bonnie. 'It's been awful.'

'Not all the time,' said Ben. 'And I really did go for the wrong course. I've been very stupid, I know now. Letting all those childish adventures dictate my entire career.'

'Childish?' Again, Simmy felt like crying. 'People have died. You were always so clever, and focused. Don't rubbish all that now. It's one thing to feel you don't fit the life there and another to chuck away the actual studies.' She looked from Bonnie to Christopher for support. 'Say something, one of you!'

'I don't think you need get upset,' said Christopher carefully. 'He's trying to explain, and you need to stop being so defensive.' He looked at the youngster. 'And maybe you could be a bit more sensitive in what you say. Things are a bit overwrought in this house just now.' He indicated the baby lying on the sofa fast asleep. 'Even the best of babies creates a degree of stress. Hormones, if I'm allowed to say that.'

'It's probably true,' said Simmy with a short burst of slightly damp laughter. 'Everything gets out of proportion somehow. It's like living in a weird sort of bubble.'

'He didn't mean to say childish,' Bonnie explained. 'He said it much better when he told me.' She gave Ben an accusing glare. 'He got it from that quote in the Bible about putting away childish things. You know?'

She was met with blank looks.

'Anyway, I think he's right – history is much better. I mean, that's what we've been doing for the past two years, when you think about it – isn't it? Researching, checking facts, looking at past influences. Not all the time, I know, but some of the murders have needed that kind of work. So he's not rubbishing anything. Just broadening it out.'

'Thanks, kid,' said Ben softly, giving Simmy a wary look. 'Sorry if I was clumsy.'

'Maybe it's just Newcastle that doesn't suit you,' suggested Christopher. 'What about transferring somewhere else? I mean a real university with all the other things that go with it. Theatres and sports and interest groups and things you'd enjoy. Would the OU even have you, under the circumstances?'

Ben sighed. 'I'd probably have to start again as a first-year in October and just lose this coming term. I'm not sure what all the options are.'

'You mean, you might not go back next week after all?' Christopher made a very adult face, indicating scepticism. 'That does seem like a waste.'

'It wouldn't have to be. I could do a whole load of reading, even write some sort of dissertation, if that helped get me in. I've had good marks for work done at Newcastle. I think the prof could probably swing it for me.'

'Listen, Ben,' said Simmy urgently. 'It's absolutely fine by me, whatever you do. I hate to think I might have influenced you. I never meant to. I still can't get my head round the very idea.'

Bonnie and Ben both gave her looks that said *Duh!* and *Think about it for a minute*. Christopher sat back in his chair, clearly wanting to stay out of it.

Finally, Bonnie spoke. 'Well, it doesn't matter now. The point is, it's all changing. It was already, anyway, with the baby and Ben being away. And Verity . . .' She sighed. 'I don't know what we're going to do about

Verity, I really don't.'

Simmy laughed again. 'You sound like someone my mother's age – d'you know that? What's the matter with Verity? I thought she was doing very well.'

Bonnie repeated a criticism that Simmy had heard before. 'She *talks* all the time. Most of it rubbish. Telly programmes, and the royal family, and whether her new curtains were a good idea. It's mind-numbing.'

'Bonnie thinks it'll have a bad effect on her brain,' said Ben. 'After the highly educational conversations she has with me – and you,' he added politely.

'Oh dear,' said Simmy, thinking there was nothing whatever she could do about that particular problem. All she could suggest was sending Verity out on as many deliveries as possible.

'That's hardly within my control, is it?' Bonnie replied crossly. 'She already does all the deliveries, anyway.'

'Maybe there'll be a nice juicy murder sometime soon. That'll give her something new to talk about,' said Christopher.

'Don't say that!' cried Simmy. 'That's the last thing we want.' She moved closer to her sleeping infant. 'And even if there *is* something horrible, I don't want to know anything at all about it. Do you hear me?' She glared round at the three faces. 'I'm on maternity leave, and that means nobody brings anything nasty or sad or dangerous into this house for at least a year. I mean it, you know.'

'Calm down,' said Christopher. 'Nothing's going to happen to disturb your idyll. I'll barricade the door myself if I have to.'

'My hero,' she smiled, not entirely mollified, thanks to the hovering presence of a man called Crickers.

Robin was stirring for his afternoon feed and Simmy had a moment's indecision as to whether or not she could do it in front of Ben. Angie had talked incessantly about how she would bare her breast anywhere, any time, in order to perform an entirely natural function, and Simmy agreed with her in theory. A friend had bought her a kind of cape, which she was supposed to use to cover her modesty, but Robin disliked being pushed under a curtain of material where he couldn't watch his mother's face as he suckled. In the pub, she had remained in the public bar, but tucked into a quiet corner, where nobody had noticed her.

'Go ahead,' Ben waved at her, realising her dilemma. 'I've seen it all before.'

'Have you?' Bonnie rounded on him. 'When?'

'There's a psychology tutor at uni, who's got a kid about six months old. She carries it around with her and feeds it every half hour, as far as I can work out. She gets a kick out of showing her flesh to the male students.'

'Is that allowed?' demanded Christopher, scandalised.

'I doubt if there's a specific regulation, one way or the other. There have been mutterings, but nobody's quite reached the point of complaining. I mean – who wants to be seen as being that prurient? For a start, it would have to be one of the girls, and they'd be accused of being anti-feminist. When it comes to safe spaces and comfort zones and all that tripe, nobody can quite work out how breastfeeding fits in. It's hilarious, actually. And Simmy's boobs are far neater and more discreet than Ms Sellers' are.'

'Well, don't stare,' said Bonnie.

It was half past four when Christopher drove the pair all the way back to Bowness, where Ben's family lived. Bonnie spent a lot of time there too, although technically she still lived with Corinne, her foster mother, half a mile north of the Harknesses. The streets of Windermere and Bowness merged into each other, confusing visitors and mapmakers.

Simmy enjoyed an hour with Robin, pulling faces at him and marvelling at the energy building up in his little arms and legs. He was so full of life, it seemed miraculous. More often than she would admit to anybody, the image of poor dead little Edith lying limply in her lap would superimpose itself over Robin's healthy little body. He would never know his older sister, but always live in her shadow, however faint and forgotten it might become as he grew up. When people asked her how many children she had, she would be forced to decide, every time, whether or not to include her firstborn, who never lived.

Already she was allowing herself to hope that Robin would not be an only child. Her fortieth birthday, and Christopher's, given that they were born on the same day, was only months away, but somehow it seemed less of a deadline, now she had achieved a living child. The complications that would multiply concerning the shop and finances and logistics if she had another baby were easily pushed aside. How much more difficult could two children be than one? In some ways, it would surely be easier, with them amusing each other as they got older.

43

She dozed on the sofa with Robin on her chest, their breathing synchronised, everything warm and contented. Life was good. Outside there was half an acre of ground, legally theirs, for garden and shed and cars and paddling pools. That alone had made the new home wonderful to her. Granted it was rocky and steep and covered in scrubby, prickly vegetation, but it was so full of potential it made her breathless. When she had lived in Worcestershire with her first husband, they had only had the tiniest patch of garden, almost all of it paved over. In Troutbeck, she had a bit more, which she filled with tall, colourful flowers – but this was her little family's own piece of Lakeland fell, and she loved it.

Humphrey the builder would be back next morning, and countless mornings over the coming months, creating two more rooms upstairs and installing walls, shelves, cupboards and floors all over the building – which was still more of a barn than a house. Robin would probably be crawling before it was all finished. Simmy would be back at the shop, with some other woman doing a share of the childcare. Any hope that that would be Angie was fading. The demands of the B&B were relentless, and tentative hints about retirement fell on deaf ears.

Christopher still wasn't back at six o'clock, when Robin wanted another feed and Simmy herself was feeling decidedly peckish. It was not her job to provide meals, especially at weekends. The freezer was full of easy-cook provisions; they also had bread, potatoes, onions, apples and a cupboard stuffed with rice, pasta and dried fruit. Simmy's preparations had been excessively efficient in the days before the birth, so that now she felt entitled to sit back and let Christopher take charge of the catering.

Then she heard the engine of a car coming through their road gate and into the gravelled parking area that Humphrey had created as a matter of priority. She got up, baby attached, and looked out of the big new window from the kitchen. It was Christopher's car; he and another man emerged from it.

She thought she knew who it was, even before they came in and Christopher performed introductions, blithely ignoring his wife's naked breast. 'This is Fabian, also known as Crickers,' he said. 'I found him down at the junction with the main road, looking lost.'

The man nodded at Simmy with a grin. He was thin, wearing a sleeveless fleece and muddy trainers. His hair was short and flecked with grey. He had poor skin and twitched constantly. 'Nice to meet you,' he said. 'Sorry if I alarmed you yesterday.'

'You did, a bit,' she admitted. 'Excuse me a minute, while I go and sort the baby out. I won't be long.' She pulled at her shirt, trying to cover herself. There was nothing noticeably salacious in the man's expression, not even any embarrassment, and yet she disliked exposing herself to him.

Don't mind me,' he said. 'I spent years in Africa, where the female torso is naked as often as not. It's a thing of beauty, after all.'

'Right,' said Simmy vaguely, and headed up the new staircase.

'I should start something cooking,' Christopher called after her. 'Is it okay if Fabian stays?'

'Fine,' she said, thinking it really wasn't fine at all.

* * *

45

'I was in hospital for six months,' Crickers told them, over the pasta that Christopher had produced. He spoke slowly, as if every word had to be tracked down inside his head before it could be uttered. 'They took me down to Cape Town eventually and bombarded me with every medicine in the book. It was touch-and-go, I can tell you. Since then, I've had to have spinal taps every year to see if there's any sign of it coming back. Well – that stopped a couple of years ago, and they said I was clear. All that from one little bastard of a fly that had probably bitten me months before.'

'We all thought you were beyond help,' said Christopher. 'You couldn't even stand up and you had those lumps on your neck. Not to mention the rash all over you. Like a plague victim, you were.'

'Which is why you thought it was safe to promise me anything I asked,' the man nodded. 'I get it.'

'Really?' Christopher looked uncertain. 'That's very forgiving of you.'

Fabian Crick's expression hardened. 'It's not though,' he said. 'You cost me that house, if you want the honest truth. She would have left it to me if you'd done as you promised.'

'What?' Christopher went pale. 'That can't be true. Didn't you have time to put it right with her?'

'I thought everything *was* all right between us. I gave you that message because it was important to keep her sweet and I trusted you to deliver it. Then I forgot all about it. I was incredibly sick for a while. Couldn't think, had seizures like the worst epileptic fits, and as you see, I've still got this twitch. Damage to the central nervous system – never going to get better, apparently.'

46

'It's not so bad,' Christopher assured him.

'Bad enough, but better than being dead. Anyway, that's the short version of the trypanosomiasis story. Great word, don't you think?' He said it again slowly. 'Tree-pano-somiasis. It's like a little poem, with all those syllables. It took me ages to get it right.'

'I would never have recognised you,' said Christopher, when they'd finished eating, but remained sitting at the table. 'You've lost so much weight.'

'Not to mention going grey and losing most of who I was. They say personalities change when you have this disease – it's probably true. It's a weird feeling, knowing you should really be dead. I'm a medical miracle.'

Simmy was paying close attention, acknowledging to herself that she felt decidedly uncomfortable in the man's company. He looked like a survivor from some extreme trauma – which he was, of course. The constant twitching was unsettling, and the story itself seemed to be a preamble to something more current – and more sinister. She could still hear his voice on the phone, the day before. She had taken an instant dislike to him from that brief conversation and was failing utterly to modify her response. Her resolve to keep life peaceful for at least the first year of Robin's life was already being tested. She could feel the advance of dark forces in the wake of this disagreeable man and was far from pleased with Christopher for so readily admitting him into their home.

'Where do you live?' she asked, rather too directly. 'Did you come in a car?'

'I'm in Glenridding for now. They won't let me drive,

47

on account of the blackouts. I've got a mobility scooter. I followed Chris down from the main road and left it out there.' He waved vaguely towards the lane. 'It'll just about get me back. Three miles, mostly uphill.'

'Blackouts,' Simmy repeated, in a tone that said *Why doesn't that surprise me?*

'I told you – I'm a wreck,' said the man, with a hint of satisfaction.

'Why didn't you go straight to your aunt after you recovered?' Simmy asked, trying to stay with the central point. The accusation against Christopher was rankling.

'One thing after another,' he said vaguely. 'I wrote to her, sent cards. Kept promising to visit.'

'Did she reply?'

'Oh, yes. She sent me newspaper cuttings about Africa mostly. Said my cousin was writing her life story and would probably make a small fortune out of it. Never told me anything very personal. She did say once that she wanted to remember me as I was as a lad, and that she'd heard I was something of an invalid these days. That was a thing with her – she was phobic about illness and disability. We all thought it must have come from things she saw in the war and afterwards. Soldiers with eyes and limbs missing – that sort of thing.'

'You mean she actually said she didn't want to see you again?' asked Simmy incredulously.

'More or less. So I never got a chance to find out who was getting her things when she died. You can't just ask somebody if they'd remembered you in their will, can you? She mentioned it when I was about twenty-five, and that was it. Said my mother had been badly treated, and she'd make sure I was all right when the time came. I guess I took that as gospel, and never bothered to check it out. Then she died and left the house to someone who's not even related.'

'Can't you contest the will?' asked Simmy, who as a general rule did not approve of people doing that. Some perverse spirit made her want to challenge everything this man said.

'No,' said Fabian shortly. 'Nobody would think I had a reasonable claim. I've got two uncles and two cousins who could make an argument every bit as good.'

Simmy charged on with her interrogation, aware that Christopher was trying to say something, but not wanting to let the man off the hook. 'So you're saying that a garbled message delivered by a total stranger after you'd apparently died in Africa would have made her love you best, even if it was rather late by then?' The scepticism was nakedly evident. 'And then you didn't die – and sent her a few postcards, and expected a nice big Lakeland house to fall into your lap as a result? Have I got that right?'

'She had to leave it to someone,' he said sulkily.

'Wait, wait.' She held up her hand. 'This isn't logical. If you thought you were dying, why would it be so important to remind Aunt Hilda that you were thinking of her at the end?'

Christopher belatedly interposed himself. 'It's not illogical at all,' he said crossly. 'Crickers actually *did* love his aunt. She was the primary person he thought of when he was so ill. Of course he would want her to know that. When she never got the message, she thought he didn't care and changed her mind about leaving him the house. Makes sense to me.'

'Thank you,' said Fabian Crick, with a lopsided smile.

'Oh, yes, I see now,' said Simmy, subsiding unhappily. 'Ignore me – it's not my business anyway.'

Christopher gave her a kind look and turned the conversation to Fabian's current situation. 'So what're you doing now?' he asked.

'Not a lot. I came up for the funeral just before Easter and decided to stay for a bit. I've had enough of city life for the time being. It's nice up here, even without any cash. The air seems to be doing me good. I've not had a blackout for nearly a month now. And the family are all still here. I'm catching up with some of them.'

'Are you staying with them?'

'No, no. That wouldn't work. I told you – I've got a little place in Glenridding.' He waved away details of his accommodation as irrelevant. Then he took a deep breath and spoke to Simmy. 'If you've got things to be doing, don't feel you have to stay and listen to me.'

'There isn't really anywhere to go, as you might have noticed. We've got the builders in, finishing the conversion. We only moved in here at the end of February.'

'Brave. With the little'un and everything.'

'We were lucky. It's all worked out beautifully.' She frowned at her own tone. Why, she wondered, did she need to justify herself to this man and make him think everything in their lives was perfect?

'Nice place to grow up, anyway,' Fabian Crick agreed. He turned to Christopher. 'By the way, it's not "Crickers" any more. I never did like that. It's "Fabian" now, okay?'

'Right,' said Christopher. 'No problem. If I remember, it was what you told us to call you on the first day of the trip.'

'Very likely. But that chap's long gone – as I said.'

'But you still want Chris to do something for you?' Simmy challenged, losing patience. 'Isn't that right?'

'Did I say that?' The man narrowed his eyes and his jaw jutted forward aggressively. 'When did I say that?' He looked from one to the other.

'It's obvious, surely. You must have gone to some trouble to track us down. We've only been here a month or two. You called the landline, which is a brand-new number. You were coming here just now, when Christopher coincided with you on the corner. And whatever you might say, you clearly haven't forgotten the promise he made to you ten years ago.'

'Sim . . .' said Christopher warningly. 'No need to be like that.'

'No, no.' Fabian held up his hands. 'She's perfectly within her rights. Fair's fair. Cards on the table. First off, I found you by the simple method of asking my friend in Keswick for your number. Turns out you work with her – Josephine, right? Bet that's a surprise. She and I go back a long way, as it happens. A lifetime, very near. I was a year or two ahead of her at school. Then I left the area, and my parents retired to Morecambe Bay. I used to come back every few months to see Aunt Hilda, and Josie was still living in Grasmere with her mum and dad. Had a bit of a fling, if you must know. Kept in touch with Christmas cards and so forth, ever since.' His delivery

51

was almost as spasmodic as his muscles, words tumbling out in short groups.

'*Josephine?*' Christopher was poleaxed. 'You've got to be joking.'

Fabian shook his head. 'Ask her if you don't believe me. Ever so pleased to see me, she was, when I turned up at Aunt Hilda's funeral. She was there, of course.'

'Why "of course"?' asked Christopher. 'She's never said anything about you or your family to me.'

Fabian shrugged. 'She probably would've, sooner or later. She seems a busy lady, keeping you auctioneers under control.' He opened his mouth to say more, but a sudden twitch seemed to prevent speech.

Christopher filled the gap, holding up one finger. 'Wait. Did she know that you and I were in Africa together? Has she always known that you and I had history?'

'Course not. Come to think of it, there must have been quite a few years when I never sent her a card or anything. She was pretty stunned to see me again, I can tell you that. And I was just as gobsmacked to see that picture of you they've got up in the reception area. "Senior Auctioneer, Christopher Henderson" it says, large as life.'

'Stunned but pleased, apparently,' said Simmy drily, referring to Josephine. 'We're still not getting to the real point, are we?'

'There's no hurry, Sim,' said Christopher, more irritably than ever. 'What's your problem?'

'Sorry.' She got up to make coffee, glancing at the big clock on the wall as she did so. It was well past seven, getting dark outside and wasting the cosy family evening she'd anticipated. Robin was in his pram in the half-finished living room, and she was missing him. Telling herself that was stupid, she produced three mugs of instant coffee and sat down again. Old habits were clinging to life, she realised. No way would she let Christopher hear whatever Fabian's story might be without her. There was something substantial working its way to the surface, if she wasn't much mistaken.

'Okay. I'll try and cut to the chase,' said the visitor, with a placatory look at Simmy. 'I don't always find it easy to order my thoughts. It's the trypanosomiasis at work, you see. I'm never going to be shot of it completely.'

'Take your time,' said Christopher.

'The thing is, there's a few family ructions over my cousin's book. You know the way a person's secrets all come out, once they've died. Old Hilda had quite a life, one way and another. She was a young girl in the Blitz, in Birmingham, spoilt rotten, clever at her schoolwork. She made a bit of a name for herself in various ways, good with money. Never over-endowed with friends, admittedly, but that never seemed to worry her. She liked to be the best at everything. People found that off-putting, I guess.'

'Did she ever marry?' asked Simmy.

'If she did, I never knew about it, and it couldn't have lasted long.'

'Presumably you *would* know? Husbands don't just evaporate.' Again, Simmy felt irritable at the man's vagueness.

'There's a lot of uncertainty as to what she was doing in the sixties,' said Fabian stiffly. 'She kept well away from the family for a good ten years. When she surfaced again, there was no sign of a husband. Mind you, she was a good-looking woman, even when she must have been in her late fifties, which is when I first had much contact with her. By that time, she was pretty well-heeled – dressed nicely and all that. All her energy went into making money and interfering in family matters. My mother died and she made a fuss of me. She was the oldest in the family and my mum was only a year younger. Then there were two brothers after her.'

'Your uncles,' nodded Simmy.

'Right.' He twitched again and seemed to deflate at the same time. 'You won't want to know the whole family history,' he muttered. 'No need for that.' A sly look crossed his face. 'I've heard quite a lot about you, one way and another. I know you've got a hotline to the police and a little gang of amateur detectives.' He raised his eyebrows at Christopher. 'Seems I really did come to the right place.'

'We're nothing like amateur detectives,' Simmy protested. 'Everything that's happened has been pure accident – mostly connected to my work as a florist. I get dragged into the dramatic points in people's lives – births, weddings, funerals, when I'd far rather stay out of them.'

'And who's talking about the police anyway?' Christopher demanded. 'What's all that about?'

Fabian looked even more shifty at these words. 'There are stones that are much better left unturned,' he said cryptically. 'That's the thing with the police – they don't know where to stop. And there's no way of controlling them, either. As I say, it's all very delicate. This cousin I told you about – Uncle Richmond's son. He's doing this book.'

'Yes, you said,' Simmy interrupted.

'There's a few sensitive matters from Auntie's past that he wants to get straight. A bit of a scandal, and maybe people who'd not like to have the whole thing exposed. Uncle Richmond, for one.'

'Did somebody steal a priceless oil painting, or what?' Simmy demanded angrily. 'Is that how Hilda got so rich?'

Both men stared at her as if she'd gone mad. 'What?' spluttered Fabian. 'Where did that come from?'

'She's not getting a lot of sleep,' said Christopher treacherously. Then he heard himself. 'But you were hinting at something of that sort. Don't forget I work with antiques.'

'I didn't forget,' said Fabian, his eyes still on Simmy. 'But it's nothing to do with oil paintings.' He smiled, as if at a secret thought. 'Though you may not be a million miles wrong, after all.'

'So there's nothing going on that would interest the police?' Simmy challenged. 'You can assure us of that, can you?'

Fabian nodded carelessly, and then changed it to a shake of his head, which could have been one of his twitches. 'Nobody's committed any crime – at least not in the past fifty years or so. Even if they had, there'd be nothing in it for the cops. They only care about people tweeting rude things at each other and watching motorways on CCTV, as far as I can see.'

'So – why *exactly* are you here?' Simmy blurted. 'Just to make Christopher feel bad about forgetting his promise?'

'Do you feel bad, mate?' the man asked.

'A bit,' Christopher admitted. 'If it's true that I lost you the house, then I definitely am sorry. But what can I do now? It's too late to put it right.'

'You could maybe give me a hand with my Uncle Richmond,' same the startling reply. 'Because the way things are, he's giving us all a lot of grief.'

'Good Lord!' snapped Simmy. 'This is getting ridiculous.'

Yet again, Christopher seemed intent on defending the visitor. 'Can we leave that for another time?' he asked. 'Maybe you and I can talk it over together. It's getting a bit late now.'

'No need,' said Fabian. 'Have you got a bit of paper?'

Christopher produced a sheet torn from a pad kept beside the phone.

Fabian wrote, in small angular script. 'Here. This is his name. He's got a farm, but I don't remember what it's called. West of here somewhere. If you could help persuade him to get in touch, that'd be doing us a big favour.'

'Us?'

'My cousins – his sons. He's cut himself off from all of us.'

Simmy took the piece of paper and stood over Fabian until he got the message. 'Well, I'll be off then,' he said reluctantly.

'Just one more question,' said Christopher. 'Who did she leave the house to, if it wasn't anyone in the family?'

'Oh – didn't I say? It was my old pal Josephine.'

Chapter Four

After that, there was no getting rid of the man for another hour. Christopher took over from Simmy in the conversation, while she went to make more coffee. The two men had somehow shifted into the living room, and Robin was seriously overdue for his bedtime routine, but Simmy stayed to listen to the rambling family anecdotes that Fabian seemed intent on sharing. He told them about the original family house in Birmingham that was utterly destroyed in 1940 by a German bomb. With it went all the Victorian, Edwardian and art deco possessions. 'Porcelain, pictures, fancy carpets. Not to mention family photographs, letters, diaries. A houseful of precious stuff.'

Christopher gave a soft moan. 'Tragic,' he mumbled.

'Right. But the family all survived and couldn't wait to get cracking on starting all over again. Even Hilda, who was barely more than a child at the time. She never cared so much for antiques as such, but she was passionate about old papers. Anything you auctioneers might call "memorabilia". She bought rare letters and diaries, the oldest books she could find, early photos. All fairly bonkers, in that she didn't care who the things came from. She just seemed to have this compulsion.'

'So when did she buy the house that now belongs to my colleague?' asked Christopher, who persistently tried to turn the conversation back to Josephine.

'Twenty, twenty-five years ago, maybe. Why does that matter?'

'Just trying to get the whole picture.' He frowned. 'Which still is nothing like clear, I'm sorry to say. One minute we're in 1940 and the next you're wanting me to smooth things down between you and your uncle. Maybe I should just ask Josephine to explain it all.'

Fabian mumbled a response that sounded like, 'Do what you want,' and then seemed to slump into a doze.

'God, Chris, he's fainting,' Simmy protested. 'He should have gone home ages ago. It's practically dark. Are you allowed to use one of those scooters at night?'

'I'm going to have to drive him – but there's no way I can get that thing in the car. Maybe he can come back for it tomorrow, on the bus or something.'

'No, no,' Fabian breathed. 'I'll be all right. I'll go now. Thanks for the coffee and everything. I've put my address here, see. With Richmond's name. Just hope that battery holds out.'

Simmy was handsomely excused from further worry by Robin suddenly waking and noticing that his supper was late. Christopher was forced to let Fabian go, having watched him start his vehicle and chug determinedly towards the main road. He went back indoors and followed Simmy upstairs.

'They make those things much sturdier these days,' he said, obviously trying to reassure himself. 'And it's not really dark once you're out there.'

'Has it got lights?'

'I suspect not.'

'He'll be killed,' she said fatalistically.

After he'd gone and Robin was despatched for the night, Simmy and Christopher still had only one topic of conversation. Fabian had left countless intriguing questions dangling for them to pore over. 'How old did you say he'd be now?' Simmy asked.

'Pushing sixty, wouldn't you think? It's hard to be sure. He seemed somewhere around forty in Africa.'

'He's awfully pathetic and I know I should feel sorry for him, but I really don't like him. He's creepy and I'd never trust him.' She clung to her original impression that the man was not to be encouraged. She doubted his honesty and suspected he could easily become an incubus. She was also unsure of his mental competence. His rambling explanation of his family troubles had never reached a clear conclusion. There was obviously a lot more he could have told them. No definite request had been made, on which Christopher could work, even if he wanted to. *Find Uncle Richmond* was not enough on its own – not by a long way.

'You don't have to.'

'I wonder. He's pushed in here, dumped all that family rubbish on us and now wants you to act as a family counsellor with this missing uncle. It's outrageous when you think about it.'

'All my own fault,' sighed Christopher. 'What if I did

lose him that house? It sounds as if that would have turned his life around rather nicely.'

'He never said where it is. Did you notice?'

'It's here somewhere. Ullswater. I remember that much, although technically there's no such place as Ullswater – it's just a lake. It's got to be one of the villages adjoining the lake.' He moaned gently.

'Are you going to track down Uncle Richmond, then? If so, what'll you say to him?'

'I can try and find his phone number, maybe. Or I could just ask Josephine to fill me in on the whole lot of them. That's the obvious thing to do. She might warn me not to touch any of them with a bargepole.'

'Fancy her inheriting the house!' Simmy marvelled for the third or fourth time. It kept hitting her all over again that the apparently unremarkable woman must have hidden and unsuspected depths. 'They must have been really good friends.'

Christopher shrugged. 'That's another thing I can ask her. I'm quite looking forward to hearing all about it.'

Simmy felt another surge of dislike for Fabian. 'Well, don't let them drag you in too deep, will you? We've got a young baby, remember. I need you here every minute you're not at work. And it seems to me you can't possibly have caused him to get written out of his aunt's will. She must have realised what a slimeball he is and changed her mind – probably five minutes after she told him he was going to be her heir. I don't think you owe him anything at all.'

'Well, I beg to differ on that,' said Christopher with a sigh.

'We're going to regret this,' she warned him. 'I can feel it in my bones.'

'Sorry, sorry,' he grovelled. 'But what could I do about it? You saw what he was like.'

'I know. It's not your fault. But what happens now? He's going to keep coming back and it'll be the same thing, over and over again. We've probably got him for life. And we don't even know in any proper detail what he wants us to do.'

'"Us"?' echoed Christopher, with an uneasy smile.

'Yes. You wouldn't know where to start – and you've got plenty of other things to think about. But I've got Ben and Bonnie, and Tanya and even Melanie to call on. It's ages since I've seen her. She might have a bit of spare time.' Melanie Todd was Bonnie's predecessor in the flower shop. She had moved on to work in a hotel, ambitiously climbing a promising career ladder.

'Simmy . . .' Christopher said warningly, before clamping his lips together. There was nothing he could safely say.

Simmy went on blithely, 'If anyone can get to the bottom of this, it's Ben. And Ben's going to like the story. Fabian Crick won't know what's hit him, if I set Ben onto him and his Uncle Richmond.'

'Serve him right,' said Christopher, with another cautious smile.

Over breakfast next day, they went back to the subject. 'I was thinking about it in the night,' said Simmy. 'While I was doing the four o'clock feed. Don't you think that might have just been an opening salvo sort of thing? Checking us out, feeling his way, before he told us anything really important?'

'Could be. I was thinking about it, too. I need to find out from Josephine just what I might be letting myself in for if I contact the uncle. I'll have to tread carefully, or she'll think I'm annoyed with her for giving him my address and number.'

'Aren't you?'

'Surprised more than annoyed. It never occurred to me she might have an interesting past, with boyfriends and dodgy relationships.'

Simmy had refrained from disclosing her own impressions about Josephine. Having met her precisely four times, she was utterly convinced that the woman was besotted with Christopher. She had been working at the auction house for close to twenty years, installing new systems, introducing online bidding, juggling all the buyers and vendors and their complex interactions. Oliver had been the head man for all that time, conducting all the auctions personally, and second to none in his skill at valuations. Right up to the present day, Christopher maintained that Oliver was the object of Josephine's adoring loyalty, a devotion both safe and misplaced, since Oliver never had any interest in women as love objects. On the arrival of a new young man, eager to learn and thoroughly presentable as a junior auctioneer, Josephine's affections had very obviously been transferred. Only Christopher himself remained stubbornly oblivious to the fact.

'Sounds as if she's useful both ways, if you see what I mean,' she said. 'If she's telling Fabian about you, she can tell you about the whole lot of them.'

'She'll probably like that,' he nodded. 'It'll make her feel important. She enjoys being the pivotal person. At least, I think she does. I'm starting to wonder if I know her at all.'

'Well, at least find out why he's living in Glenridding, and what it is he wants to happen next.' She faced him squarely. 'Do you really feel you owe him anything? Have you any intention of helping him with this weird family mystery?'

'I don't know,' he said frankly. 'So far, there doesn't seem to be anything specific I could do, even if I wanted to.'

'He must have been softening you up, testing the water. After all, he probably realises he hardly knows you at all. Everything cuts both ways, remember. That's what Ben would say.'

The Monday following a Saturday auction was always busy with buyers collecting their purchases, involving carriers with vans and trailers loading up the larger items, and the more distant online bidders making various arrangements for the delivery of their goods. While the team was quite capable of handling all that, Christopher needed to be there in the interest of public relations. He was in demand on all sides, for chats with a number of regulars about prices, condition and provenance. New buyers wanted to make themselves known to him. And there would often be disputes to resolve, when someone had gone off with the wrong thing, either by accident or design.

'I'd better be going,' he said, at half past eight. 'I won't be late home.'

Simmy waved as he drove away and went to gather up her baby so she could forget all about lost uncles and unreliable commitments. Humphrey and a youth Simmy hadn't seen before arrived at nine and began quietly getting on with their conversions upstairs, after a brief salutation. 'He's grown since Saturday,' Humphrey said, having paused to admire the baby.

'You're only saying that to please me,' she accused.

'Not at all. His cheeks are fuller. Definitely.'

Robin was lying wakeful in his basket, while Simmy sat with a coffee and watched him adoringly. The peaceful interlude lasted barely half an hour before Fabian Crick pushed himself back into her thoughts. Had he deliberately given her and Christopher just enough to guarantee curiosity, while withholding any specific details? How could anybody talk on a subject for two hours or more and still leave his listeners in almost total ignorance? He had described his great-aunt as a person, dwelling on her younger days and her attitude to her relations. He had also described the Ullswater house, but not disclosed its exact location. There had been implications in plenty, but almost nothing concrete. On the other hand, it could be that Fabian's near-death experience in Africa had damaged his brain somehow and rendered him incapable of sustained logical thought. His rambling presentation of his story supported that theory but did nothing to make the situation easier. The word 'craven' found its way into her head, as a fitting description of him. He had wanted something but had not found a way to fully articulate what it was.

She was going to have to run the whole thing past Bonnie next day and see what happened then. There was no discernible reason not to do so – Fabian had raised no objection when hints had been made about Ben and his skill at solving mysteries. He had made it clear that he was aware of Simmy's little team of amateur sleuths, and – it occurred to her now – there was every chance he had approached Christopher with that knowledge in mind all along.

Robin then occupied the whole of the remainder of the morning by breaking with routine to such an extent that Simmy was thrown into panic. He participated in a little playtime, and then screamed when she tried to put him down at ten; fed heartily at least an hour earlier than usual and then still refused to fall asleep. Could it be the result of his late bedtime the night before, she wondered. He had woken only slightly later that morning, so it seemed an unlikely theory. She wrapped him in the sling and walked as far as the car park at the end of the tiny road that ran through the village. He was quiet but wakeful, wriggling and resisting instead of dozing as he normally did. Back at home, he violently objected to his nappy change and then finally accepted another feed, with a resentful scowl creasing his little face. And still he wouldn't sleep. It was as if the fairies had crept in and left a completely different baby in his crib.

'Growth spurt,' said Angie, when Simmy phoned her in despair soon after midday. 'Weren't we expecting something like this?'

'It's awfully sudden.'

'Hm. So what's changed? Babies are very quick to detect an atmosphere, you know.'

'We did have a visitor last night – but I wouldn't say that did anything to the atmosphere. Robin just won't go to sleep, even in the sling.'

'Take him for a drive. That always works.'

'Yes, but what's the *matter* with him? He must be ill. Something hurts somewhere.'

'Did you eat onions? Or whatever the other things are that they say upset a baby's digestion?'

'I didn't eat anything much,' Simmy remembered. 'Christopher did a very boring thing with pasta and the visitor ate most of it. It did have onions in – but I've had them plenty of times before and Robin's been fine.'

'Well, just keep feeding him and make sure you get a good meal. *Two* good meals would be even better.'

The advice was rather more helpful than Simmy might have expected. Her mother had not enjoyed Simmy's own baby stage and refused to contemplate further children. Could it be that she was secretly reading books or blogs or things on YouTube about the care of infants? It was not entirely impossible and Simmy felt warmed by the idea. 'Thanks, Mum,' she said. 'I expect he'll crash out eventually and sleep for ages. Not that I mind if he doesn't sleep, but he seems so miserable.'

'Are you on your own?'

'No. The builders are here. Humphrey seems to be quite good with babies, actually. I'll go now and make myself a big cheese sandwich.'

'You do that. And don't be shy to summon Christopher

home again. By rights, he ought to be with you all day. It's not even three weeks yet.'

'Thanks, Mum,' Simmy said again, a little more briskly. 'I'll keep you posted. We're coming into Windermere tomorrow. You can give me some lunch, if you like.'

Ten minutes later, as she balanced baby, sandwich and large glass of milk, her mobile rang. It was Christopher. Before he could speak, she was pouring out the day's concerns, while Robin whimpered obligingly as confirmation of his new self. 'He just won't stop whingeing,' Simmy concluded. 'No matter what I do.'

'My mother used to put us in a darkened room and leave us to cry,' he said, with nowhere near enough sympathy. 'Perhaps he's overstimulated.'

'I'll take him for a drive later on, if he doesn't settle.'

'Right. Well, we've got troubles of our own up here. Josephine hasn't shown up for work and isn't answering her phone. It's totally out of character. We've sent Fiona off to look for her. Something must have happened to her. Just when I wanted to have a good talk with her about Fabian Crick. We're helpless here without her. Nobody else knows how to organise the online buyers and their purchases. And there was so much I wanted to ask her about Crickers.'

'Oh.' Cutting through her worries over Robin came the utter certainty that the *something* he had referred to was fatal. Thanks to numerous past adventures, both Simmy and Christopher were far too familiar with sudden, violent death. 'You think she's been attacked in some way, do you?'

'I do,' he said. It seemed, on the face of it, rather a callous act to send the deputy office manager, Fiona Gallagher, to find Josephine. Christopher ought to have gone himself. Or alerted the police and got them to go and see what was happening. Fiona was a quiet, efficient young woman, admittedly, but Simmy's experience of her was also as a shy and even timid person. Given Christopher's apprehensions, it was quite surprising that Fiona had agreed to go. Simmy said some of this to him. 'That's true, but she's got a brother in the police and she said she could cope. She grew up on a farm, apparently, and is fine with blood and so forth.'

'Josephine's probably perfectly all right,' Simmy reminded him. 'We're jumping ahead outrageously.'

'I hope so. I just can't come up with a single explanation that would cover the facts, other than something horrible. She has been known to oversleep now and then, but never for this long.'

The obvious and inescapable assumption had to be that Fabian Crick was involved in some way. The connection was too stark to be ignored. He knew Josephine. He was immersed in a strange family mystery and was not entirely stable in a mental sense. *Has Fabian killed her then?* Was that unspoken question hovering somewhere in the air between Christopher and Simmy?

'I will grant you that a missing manager trumps a wakeful baby,' she conceded. 'But a drop of fatherly concern wouldn't go amiss, all the same.'

'Sorry, love. You don't think he's ill, do you?'

'Not really. He isn't hot and doesn't seem to be in pain anywhere. My mother says it's the growth spurt she's been going on about. I'm sure she's been looking up baby care on the Internet – which is actually quite unnerving.'

'More likely to be your dad, don't you think?'

'Could be. That's even more unnerving.' But she knew better than to belittle her parents to Christopher. He was all too likely to say – *You're lucky to have them*. The absence of his own mother and father was a constant background deprivation, which was now filtering through to another generation. Robin ought to have four grandparents, not two, and everybody knew it.

'Oh – Oliver's here. Damn it, that must mean bad news. He wasn't supposed to come in today. Somebody must have phoned him. I'll have to go.'

'Okay. Keep me posted, won't you?'

Oliver West had been the senior auctioneer before stepping down to let Christopher fill the role. He now described himself as semi-retired and no longer conducted auctions but concentrated on valuations and keeping track of the finances. He had recently acquired a property in the Pyrenees, where he intended to build up a collection of French porcelain. 'One more year and I'll be out of your way,' he said. But if one of his employees was in trouble, he was still the first person the police would go to.

Simmy made herself a substantial lunch and then carried the baby upstairs, where she again broke the rule about taking him to bed with her. The builders had gone off somewhere to acquire more materials and everything was quiet.

Cuddled together, with Robin feeding sporadically, they both fell into a doze. When she woke, she didn't dare move for fear of waking him. The world could carry on in its own wicked way outside – she was doing what nature intended, as well as what she had promised herself. Phone calls would go ignored, knocks on the door unanswered. She would never get these surreal early days back again, with the little bundle of life blossoming before her very eyes, his dependency so inescapable and the trust he placed in her so complete. She knew, dimly, that there would soon be moments when she got it wrong, let him down, went against his wishes and perhaps even hurt him. The early perfection would be spoilt as real life forced itself upon them. She shuddered at the prospect. It seemed such a cruel business, growing up.

But at least he was finally asleep, his head lolling back against her forearm, mouth open. She needed the loo, so began to work her way free of him, leaving him in the middle of the bed. No harm could come to him there. He must be exhausted, she thought, after being awake all morning. Where, she wondered, was Humphrey and what's-his-name? She couldn't remember what they'd said about coming back – or whether they had said anything. Builders were notoriously capricious anyway, in their comings and goings. She had already learnt to avoid drifting around the house in nightclothes, as she would probably have done in recent weeks. Breastfeeding was different – she had warned the men from the outset that they would just have to get used to it. No way was she going to shut herself away for their benefit. She would feed in the kitchen if she wanted to and anywhere else that took her fancy. Humphrey had assured her this was not a problem. 'My missus fed all ours herself,' he said proudly. But the young assistant had flushed and shuffled his feet. 'Be an education for you, lad,' said his senior scornfully.

But she was here on her own now and the usual routine had been shattered. There was no knowing when Robin would wake up – or when Christopher would come home. Things were happening out there, and she was totally isolated from it all. She didn't even care, she admitted to herself. Josephine was not someone she had feelings for, although she still harboured some anxiety about Fabian Crick. He knew where she lived and was quite capable of showing up at any time – even though she could think of no good reason why he should.

Chapter Five

Christopher surprised her by arriving home at half past four, at least an hour before she expected. 'She's dead,' he said, before he was properly through the door. 'Sounds as if it was a knife, but all details are being withheld.' He was obviously quoting an official. 'We've closed early and are staying closed until at least Thursday. Big notice on the gate. Police interviews with all staff will begin imminently.'

He was pale, and as she watched him, he slumped onto a chair that had been left near the door. None of the furniture in the main living space was yet in its permanent position. There was still flooring to be done, as well as more new walls. 'It's . . . *shattering*,' said Christopher. 'She was such a *solid* person. We all relied on her completely. I can't imagine the place without her. The moment we got the news, everyone started behaving like headless chickens. Including me. Fiona called the cops; they called Oliver; Oliver came and told all the staff. They want to know about family, friends – all that stuff.' He started up at Simmy wildly. 'I'll have to tell them about Crickers, won't I?'

'Of course you will. Why – is that a problem?'

'He can't have done it. He wouldn't pull a knife on anybody. Most likely it was just a burglary gone wrong. I don't mean *just* . . .' He shook his head in bewilderment. 'But she did have some decent things in the house. Pictures mostly. She'd got a genuine Stanley Spencer, for one thing. And some nice silver. And about two hundred of those little Limoges boxes. No self-respecting burglar's going to want those. Even Josie was getting tired of them and kept threatening to put them up for auction. She'd have cheerfully handed them over to a burglar without a struggle.' He groaned. 'It wasn't a burglar, was it? That would be too simple. Poor old Josie. What a ghastly thing.'

'It must have happened in the night,' said Simmy, finding herself to be thinking unusually clearly. 'Before she would normally have left for work, anyway. Where does she live, did you say?'

'About a mile this side of Keswick. On the little back road that goes to Threlkeld. Just an ordinary house in a row, set back off the road a bit. I've only been there once, actually.'

'Have you spoken to Fiona?'

He shook his head. 'She didn't come back to work. Oliver came and talked to us all – sent us outside to tell everybody to go home. There were a few people collecting purchases from Saturday still hanging about. We weren't allowed to tell them why – just that there'd been an incident, and the place had to be closed. There'll be all kinds of rumours flying about by now.'

'The truth'll soon be out.' She put a hand on his shoulder. 'She must have been very well known. Had she upset

73

anybody lately? She didn't strike me as especially friendly.'

'She was sharp sometimes. But always totally fair and straight with them all. Even the absolute idiots who bidded for things by mistake or hadn't brought any money with them – she never yelled at them or anything. God – I'm glad it wasn't me who found her. I never want to go through that again.'

Less than a year earlier, Christopher had come closer to violent death than was easily tolerated. Simmy's association with murders, all of them unsought and accidental, filled him with horror and a powerful sense of resistance. More than once, he had made it clear that he blamed Ben Harkness, which was entirely unjust.

'Well, have a mug of tea and try not to think about it,' she advised, waiting for him to take the hint. When at home, almost all kitchen duties devolved onto him since the baby arrived. It took him a while, but he finally got up and went to put the kettle on.

'How's the young master been since I phoned you?' he remembered to ask. 'Everything seems nice and quiet now.'

'He dropped off after lunch and hasn't stirred since. The routine is completely blown. He'll probably keep us up all night now.'

'I'll play with him for a bit – see if that helps.'

'He'll like that,' said Simmy optimistically. She found herself thinking that the benefit might flow the other way – from son to father. Christopher certainly needed some sort of distraction.

* * *

The evening felt like an interval between dramatic events. Robin was still playing ducks and drakes with the routine, and showed no signs of settling down to a reasonable bedtime. A suspension in time, waiting for the police to drag Christopher into their investigation, or for Fabian Crick to show up and persuade them of his innocence. 'How would he have got to Keswick, anyway?' Simmy mused. 'That scooter couldn't possibly have got him there, especially in the night.'

'If he called a taxi, there'd be records and the police would soon be onto him.'

'Yes.'

Christopher ruffled his hair, his expression agonised. 'I can't stop thinking about Josephine. It's going to knock the business sideways, losing her. She's the lynchpin of the whole place. Nobody else understands the inner workings of the software system.'

Simmy's mind was still functioning with surprising clarity. Ideas were firing off in all directions, even as she cradled her restless infant. The afternoon playtime with Christopher had not gone well – Robin had been fractious and unco-operative. 'Is there a rival auction house who thought they could gain an edge by removing your lynchpin?' she suggested.

'Come on – that's a terrible idea,' Christopher scoffed.

The baby clearly took exception to the loss of his place at the centre of their attention. He protested in the only way he knew. 'Right – one last feed, and then we're all going to bed,' said Simmy. 'And that's final.'

'I won't be able to sleep if I go this early,' Christopher

objected. He looked around the half-finished living area as if in search of amusement. 'I could watch a bit of telly, maybe.' The flatscreen TV had been a cheap purchase at the auction. Perfectly good sets went for ten pounds or less at most of the sales. It worked perfectly when connected to the Wi-Fi, but for normal terrestrial channels it was useless. 'We'll have to get a proper aerial put up,' Christopher said, every few days. 'I might want to watch a documentary sometime. I like documentaries.'

Simmy sighed. 'You'll wake me up if you don't go to bed at the same time as me.'

'I'll be really quiet. Once you're asleep, you won't hear a thing. Besides, I've got to do the washing-up, put the bin out, water the ferns and get some meat out for tomorrow. A housewife's work is never done, you know.'

'I think the term is "house husband" in your case.'

'Nope,' he disagreed. 'That's only for people who are married. Which reminds me—'

'Stop!' Simmy interrupted. 'No way am I going to talk about weddings now. There's too much else going on.'

'June the first,' he said, more loudly. 'No ifs, no buts. We can't go on like this. It's not decent. All you have to do is put something respectable on and sign some bits of paper. I'll organise everything.'

'That's a lovely date,' she conceded. 'But it's much too soon. There's far too much to do.'

'Wrong. It'll work beautifully, just you see. Bonnie can do the flowers. Ben can write the speeches. Your father can . . . find something useful to do.'

'Stop,' said Simmy again, more weakly this time. 'It

makes me feel tired just to think about it.'

'But you're not vetoing it?'

'No,' she said, meeting his gaze. 'No, I'm not vetoing it. I'll be very happy to marry you on June the first – assuming I can stay awake long enough to make my vows.'

Tuesday brought grey skies and feelings of apprehension. Christopher's mobile presented him with a text message, requesting his presence at the incident room that had been set up in Keswick no later than ten o'clock. 'Well, that's a first,' he said. 'Fancy summoning me by text.'

'Quick, cheap and efficient,' said Simmy. 'I don't expect they'll keep you very long.'

'Let's hope not. What are you doing today?'

'I'll be in Windermere for most of it. I'm calling in at the shop, and then having lunch at Beck View. I'm quite likely to be there till teatime. I can tell Ben about everything, can't I?'

'Everything?'

'You know what I mean. Fabian Crick and Josephine and the missing uncle. If the girls are busy in the shop, I might even go round to the Harknesses and talk to him there – although Bonnie wouldn't like that. Helen might want to see the baby, though.' Simmy assumed, rightly or wrongly, that everyone in the world was eager to admire young Robin.

Christopher rolled his eyes. 'Why ask me? It's not *my* story.'

'Isn't it? I think it sort of is, actually. It all goes back to that promise you made – your undertaking to Fabian. He'd never have tracked you down like he did, if it hadn't been for that. I admit it's very vague, but he obviously does want something from you.'

'All my own stupid fault, then. But there was always going to be the Josephine connection, wasn't there? When he saw that picture of me in the reception area, he'd have put two and two together even if he wasn't pursuing me for vengeance – or whatever he's doing. Even without that, he might have looked me up for old times' sake. He probably realised that I thought he was dead.'

She gave him a searching look. 'You *do* feel guilty about it, don't you? You say you don't, but you really do.'

'I wouldn't call it guilty, exactly. Uneasy, perhaps. It's more a matter of how *Fabian* feels about it. After Sunday evening, I get the strong impression he was checking me out, testing to see if I was still under a sense of obligation to him.' He frowned. 'And that's what makes it so weird to imagine him killing Josephine. It doesn't fit with anything I thought I'd worked out about him.'

'I know. I was thinking the same thing. Let's hope that by the end of today we'll be better informed. You'll have some idea about the time she died, and how, and all that. I'd better bustle now. I'm not sure I've got any clean clothes. All the washing seems to be baby things these days.'

In the event, she was ready just after nine, the baby strapped into his car seat, a small bag of nappies and spare clothes beside him. Driving with neurotic care, especially on the stretch up to the Kirkstone Pass, she was still parking the cumbersome stroller outside Persimmon Petals in Windermere by nine forty-five. Bonnie came flying out to greet her, peering at Robin's little face and making idiotic chirping noises. 'No need for that,' said Simmy. 'You saw him only two days ago. It's fine with me if you think he's boring.'

'I don't think that. I think he's very sweet, and I want him to be my friend when he's a bit older. It's great that you're so together you can get the two of you here so early. I'm impressed.'

'I impressed myself,' Simmy agreed. 'Especially as we were both wide awake at two o'clock this morning. His routine's got all muddled up, for some reason.'

'Oh, routines,' said Bonnie airily. 'You should hear Corinne on that subject.'

Simmy could well imagine what Bonnie's hippyish foster mother might say. Compared to Corinne, Angie Straw was almost conventional. 'They do make life easier,' she remarked mildly. 'But I wouldn't claim to be obsessive about it. Do you know – the district nurse told me there were apps for monitoring how long they sleep and how many wet nappies there are? And all sorts of other stuff. I mean – *why*? What's the point?'

'Search me,' said Bonnie. 'Come on in, anyway.' She watched as Simmy deftly detached the seat from the rest of the vehicle and carried the sleeping infant into the shop. 'Is he going to wake up?'

'Impossible to say, the way he's been. Is it busy?' She looked round the shop, as if to locate lurking customers. 'Where's Verity?'

'Out on a delivery. It's much as usual. No panics.'

Simmy wasted no time. 'You won't have heard there was

79

a murder yesterday in Keswick,' she began.

'Oh, yes – Ben saw something about that online,' Bonnie said quickly. 'Yesterday sometime. He wanted me to ask you about it.'

'And we want to talk to him, as well. He'll be pleased to know it's seriously complicated.'

'We? You mean you and Christopher? That's a turn-up. He usually wants to stay well clear, doesn't he? Especially after what happened in Grasmere. And I'm sure I heard you say, only two days ago, that you weren't going to allow anything unpleasant anywhere near you and your baby for at least a year.'

'There's no avoiding it, Bonnie. It's somebody Christopher knows. Again. It's finally dawned on me that antiques are just as dangerous as flowers when it comes to arousing strong passions.'

Bonnie giggled. 'Most people would say they're a lot more so. There's money in antiques, but not in flowers. Unless it's a black tulip, of course.' She paused, then asked, 'So who's dead?'

'It's the woman who manages the office side of the business. His right-hand assistant, who is completely indispensable. It's rather a disaster.'

'Blimey! That's not funny, then, is it? Pretty close to home. Who wanted her dead? How did it happen?'

'Too soon to say. There are other complications, which I can't go into now. We need to wait and see what happens today – the police are interviewing everyone as we speak.'

'Blimey,' said Bonnie again. 'That's going to give Ben something to think about.'

'What's he doing today?'

'Nothing much. He's in a real tizzy over whether or not he's going back to Newcastle this week. It's all got a bit awkward. People want to talk to him. I suppose they think it's bad for their image if someone as clever as him doesn't want to stay. They'll have counsellors and whatnot after him.' Bonnie shook her head in exasperation. She knew quite a lot about counsellors after her own badly disrupted childhood. Then she smiled. 'This is perfect timing. A murder's going to help him decide to stay here for a bit. Shall I get him to come up here? Or what?'

'It'll be rather a crowd with Verity as well. But it sounds as if I should talk to him, just in case he commits himself to going back to Newcastle. I could maybe go over to Helm Road and at least tell him the basics now. Assuming there isn't anything you want me to do in the shop? I can come back later, if there is.'

'You need to look over the invoices. The delivery people have whacked on an extra hundred or so, and I can't work out why. And Verity wants to talk to you – something about paying for fuel for the van.'

'Urghh,' said Simmy.

As if catching her mood, the baby began to wake up, jerking his arms and frowning. Within seconds he was wailing at full pitch. A customer walked into a flurry of highly unprofessional activity. 'Sorry,' Simmy said. Hurriedly she carried Robin into the small back room and offered him the breast. He took it suspiciously, still scowling.

'Don't muck about,' Simmy told him crossly. 'There's no time for any nonsense.' And then she heard herself and groaned. Already, then, it was starting. Robin was going to have to learn that he was not in fact the centre of the universe, that there would be times when he would be expected to stay in the background and share attention with other matters. And that was patently unfair, given that he was a mere three weeks old. Of course he had every right to assume he took priority over all else. Furthermore, it seemed evident that he could not just read her thoughts but gauge her unarticulated feelings. He knew when she was agitated or impatient or inattentive. He could sense the loosening of her dedication to his every whim and made his feelings about that very clear. And yet, how many infants successfully maintained this intimate bond for more than a few early weeks? Their mothers had jobs, other children, worries, illnesses – they could not guarantee to be there every second of every day. And the kids survived, didn't they?

But survival wasn't the goal. Simmy wanted her son to be perfectly happy; perfectly balanced and confident and clever and sociable. Perfectly undamaged, in fact. She supposed that every mother wanted the same things, and not a single one ever achieved them.

The feed didn't last long, and when she emerged from the chilly little room, Verity had returned. Without waiting to be invited, she almost snatched the baby from Simmy's arms. 'Doesn't he look like his dad?' she yodelled. 'Same eyes and mouth.' Here, it seemed, was yet another woman who found babies irresistible. Verity had two sons of her own, in their late teens and not much to be proud of, according to Bonnie.

'When did you see Christopher?' Simmy asked, trying to think of any encounter between them.

'When he came in to tell us about the baby,' was the reply. 'The day he was born.' She bent over Robin's face, making exaggerated expressions and cooing. 'Who's a lovely boy, then?' The sheer lack of self-consciousness made Simmy smile, even while hoping the woman didn't have a cold.

'Customer,' said Bonnie, with a hint of relief in her tone. Verity's blatherings were evidently causing irritation.

The man who came in was vaguely familiar, but Simmy couldn't put a name to him. Bonnie, however, was quicker. 'Hiya, Mr Merryfield,' she said warmly. 'Bright and early again, I see.'

It was well after ten. *Merryfield?* Simmy couldn't place the name at all. Bonnie noticed her confusion and hastened to explain. 'This is Corinne's next-door neighbour. He works in Bowness, on an evening shift. This is like 5 a.m. to him.'

Everyone laughed, and the man bought a bunch of spring flowers. When he'd gone, Bonnie embellished her explanation. 'He's rather a sad character. His wife and his mother both died last year and left him on his own. Corinne treats him like a charity case, making cakes and elderflower wine for him. I keep telling her she ought to be careful not to be too encouraging. I bet those flowers were for her. The last thing she needs is a man moving in.'

Verity snorted. 'Doesn't know what's good for her. He'll have a nice big house, mortgage all paid up. Any woman would think she was in clover, landing him. Not bad-looking, either.'

'He's *sixty*,' Bonnie protested. 'And paralysingly boring. And Corinne's got a house already, thank you very much.'

'Huh,' said Verity, and began bouncing Robin energetically up and down. Simmy felt enough was enough, and firmly retrieved him.

By an unspoken agreement, Simmy and Bonnie refrained from any further discussion of the Keswick murder. Verity was not one of their little gang, and never would be. Bonnie was to be admired in the way she calmly put up with the mundane prattle and the predictable comments on the customers. 'She's like your mother, but with about a quarter of the brains,' Bonnie told Simmy after a few days of the woman's company. 'At least Mrs Straw's funny when she's offending people. Verity's just ignorant. And she gets people so *wrong*. She thinks Ninian Tripp is gay, you know.'

Simmy laughed, remembering her brief liaison with the local potter. 'Well, I can assure her he's not. Although I think he'd be quite tickled to know he gives that impression.'

'Well, I suppose it's all good experience,' said Bonnie philosophically. 'And it won't be for ever – I hope.'

'Listen – I think I *will* go down to Helm Road,' Simmy said. 'If Helen's working, I can talk to Ben for a bit.'

'Okay,' nodded Bonnie, with a rueful little smile. 'What're you doing after that?'

'I'll call in at Beck View. I'm making a day of it. The builders are still crashing about at home.' This was an exaggeration, but it was still nice to get away from them when possible.

'Chilly for the little one,' said Verity. 'That little suit

84

doesn't look too warm to me.'

'It's thirteen degrees out there and there's no wind. He'll be fine,' defended Simmy. 'And we'll be indoors anyway.'

Bonnie took a step backwards, so she was at Verity's shoulder before she permitted herself to roll her eyes and pull a face to indicate her exasperation with her workmate. 'Hey – don't forget there's another delivery before lunch. Troutbeck this time. And it's still not finished. They want a sheaf of lilies and lots of greenery. Will you do it?'

Verity squared her shoulders. Her skill at constructing floral arrangements was still hardly more than rudimentary, but Bonnie was making some headway in training her. 'Lilies and greenery,' she repeated. 'Anything else?'

'You could add some of those white carnations, and something blue if you can find it. Keep it simple, okay?'

With a last lingering gaze at the baby, the woman went off into the back room, where they could hear her rustling cellophane and snipping at tough flower stalks. 'Can she do it?' whispered Simmy.

'More or less. I'll probably have to tweak it a bit. At least she knows which flowers are which. And she's very willing.' Bonnie sighed.

'You're a saint,' said Simmy. 'What time's she going to Troutbeck?'

'About twelve.'

'I'll pop back then and let you know how I get on with Ben. It's a shame you can't be there as well.'

'Can't be helped,' said Bonnie, suddenly seeming much more adult. She might look about twelve, but the new responsibility had obviously matured her dramatically. 'Ben's going to be really pleased to see you. And Helen's dying to see the baby.'

Ben must have seen her as she parked outside the Harkness house in Helm Road and unloaded the cumbersome baby seat yet again. He was standing on the doorstep to greet her when she finally got there. 'I wasn't sure if you wanted help,' he said awkwardly.

'No problem – it looks worse than it is. Is your mother in?' she asked.

'Never mind that – tell me all about this murder in Keswick. I'm assuming you and Christopher have some connection with it?'

She wilted at the onslaught. 'Yes, Ben,' she acknowledged. 'You're assuming correctly.'

Chapter Six

They were met in the hallway by Helen Harkness, who commandeered the baby without hesitation and carried him off with infinite care, knowing Simmy was watching her. 'He's very unpredictable at the moment,' Simmy warned her. 'My mother says it's a growth spurt.'

'I'll come and find you if he gets tetchy,' Ben's mother promised, and taking the stairs slowly, she disappeared up to her big first-floor studio, where she worked as an architect.

'How much do you know?' Simmy asked Ben, before he could voice the same question.

'Violent death of a woman in Keswick, foul play suspected. Post-mortem probably already performed and neighbours questioned by police. It's all out there for public consumption. One report said she worked locally, possibly at the auction house.' He gave her a very straight look. 'Which is where I guess you and Chris come in. Who was she?'

Simmy answered succinctly. 'Christopher's right-hand woman, Josephine. Can we sit down before we get into it any further?'

'Sorry. Come on into the dining room.'

Simmy followed him into a handsome room with a large table in the centre. There were seven in the Harkness family, frequently eating together. The table was much used, not just for meals, but homework, card games, jigsaws – and the laying-out of spreadsheets, flowcharts and algorithms when Ben had a murder to contemplate. It had not been very many months since just such an activity had been conducted, with reference to a killing in Grasmere. 'Here we are again,' said Simmy, with very mixed feelings.

Ben sat down and wasted no more time. 'What's her surname?'

'Oh . . . Um . . . I don't know. I don't think I ever knew.'

'Let's see, then.' He tapped the keyboard of a laptop sitting in front of him. 'I've got the auction house website. Here she is – Josephine Trubshaw. Miss or Mrs?'

'I always assumed she was Miss.'

'Trubshaw's a good name – echoes of Concorde and all that.'

Simmy waved this away, knowing better than to ask for her ignorance to be rectified. It was all too easy for Ben – or Bonnie, in recent times – to become badly sidetracked by irrelevancies. 'There's a whole lot more you need to know about, that seems to be connected, but might not be,' she said, thinking of her baby upstairs and the realisation that she had never yet been so far removed from him. What if Helen dropped him? What if a meteor fell onto the roof and crushed everyone on the upper floor?

'Shoot,' Ben invited.

She tried to keep her account brief and lucid, but

nothing about Fabian Crick lent itself to brevity. She outlined the story about Aunt Hilda and Uncle Richmond, before pausing to think. 'Fabian's very strange. Unsettling. Untrustworthy. And quite pathetic at the same time. He uses a mobility scooter to get around because he's not allowed to drive. Imagine that on the roads up there! We can't really believe that he killed her – it wouldn't be physically possible to get there, and he wouldn't be very difficult to resist. Even Bonnie could probably push him over.'

'Hm,' said Ben, paying gratifyingly close attention. 'Not very likely that he'd lie about the car. Too easy to disprove. How old is he?'

'Around sixty, we think. Maybe a bit less.'

'How old was Josephine?'

Simmy flinched slightly at the 'was'. 'Mid fifties, I suppose. He said he knew her ages ago, when they were at school together. Must be forty years nearly. And they kept in touch ever since.'

'That works age-wise, then, more or less.'

'Right.'

'People do keep up with old friends, now more than ever,' Ben said. 'It's so easy these days.'

'Hm. I wouldn't think either of them were natural Facebookers. They sent postcards, apparently.'

Ben laughed. 'I gather that's a thing again. Good business for the post office. Have you heard of an outfit called Postcrossing?'

'No. Is it relevant?'

'Nope. But it's a very interesting phenomenon. Zoe's got well into it.' Zoe was one of Ben's three younger sisters, and the one Simmy had almost never met.

'Anyway, Josephine told Fabian where he could find Christopher, and he phoned on Saturday then showed up the next day. Apparently Christopher made him a promise ten years ago and he'd come to make good in some way. There's something horribly *sneaky* about him. He's scared of the police, as well. And it doesn't sound as if he's got any money.'

Ben was jotting down notes on a big writing pad. 'So Aunt Hilda died, leaving a big house. Haven't we been here before – in Grasmere?'

'Sort of. There's a lot of it about, according to Christopher. But the crucial thing is – she left it to Josephine!' She sat back in triumph, watching his face.

'Oh,' he said. 'So I wonder who gets it now she's dead as well.'

Simmy had not thought to ask herself this question, despite it now seeming glaringly obvious. 'She'll have a relative somewhere,' she said uncertainly. 'Hasn't everybody?'

'You're saying you have no idea. Didn't that strike you right away as the inescapable motive for killing her?'

'Sadly no,' she confessed. 'I hadn't got as far as wondering about a motive.'

'The thing is . . .' he tapped his teeth, as he always did when thinking. 'Unless she made a will leaving it to this Fabian man and his family, they can't possibly expect to inherit it, can they? And if she *did* make a will, they'd be such obvious suspects that they'd never dare murder her. We're assuming it's a highly desirable house, are we?'

'Presumably. Can you find it online? She was called Hilda Armitage. I assume they're all called Armitage except Fabian. He wrote some of it down for us when he was giving us some clues about Uncle Richmond.'

'Leave that for a minute. When did Hilda die?'

'Um . . . I think it must have been about six weeks ago, from what he said. The whole thing feels very recent. Ongoing, in fact. Josephine can hardly have had time to get used to the idea that the house was hers. She never said anything at work – Christopher had no idea.'

'Josephine was probably intending to sell it, then. Make enough to feather a very nice nest in her old age. Did Fabian seem angry about her getting it?'

'Sort of, yes. He blames Christopher, actually. They both believe that if Chris had done as he promised ten years ago, relations between Fabian and his aunt would be so good that she'd have left the house to him. I have my doubts about that. It feels very flimsy – like nearly everything he told us, in fact. It was amazing how little actual hard information he gave us. It was nearly all waffle and self-pity. He stayed for *ages*, but we still didn't really know what he wanted by the end. Just find Uncle Richmond and see if he could be helpful in bringing them all back together. There's got to be more to it than that – Uncle Richmond isn't *lost*, just detached. Out on a limb, not having anything to do with the family, even his own sons. Didn't sound very unusual or mysterious to me – although I think Fabian hoped it would. He'd heard about you, of course. I guess that's really the heart of it, even if I can't work out how.'

'Ten years is a long time. Did Chris remember him?'

'It's not really so long,' Simmy corrected him. 'I can remember my thirtieth birthday as if it was just a few months ago.' She chuckled. 'That's funny – I must ask Christopher what he was doing for his. We were born on the same day, you know.'

'I know. You've told me at least twenty-nine times.'

'Anyway, Christopher never expected to have to keep his promise to Fabian. He only made it because he was convinced the man was dying. He can't remember exactly what it was he was supposed to do, except he said he'd go to Ullswater and see Aunt Hilda. Something about reassuring her that her nephew had been thinking of her right to the end. Christopher thought at the time that he'd easily manage it because his family were all living up here and it didn't seem especially arduous. I think he thought he might get round to it if he had the time – but then his plans changed and he didn't come back here for another year or two, and by then it was all forgotten.'

'So the Crick man survived the sleeping sickness, checked things out in Ullswater and worked up a right old grudge against Henderson Esquire after a delay of ten years.'

'More or less. But at the risk of contradicting myself, it does seem that quite a lot of years went by before he did anything about it. He didn't say where he'd been in the meantime. Or if he did, I can't remember. They thought Aunt Hilda would die ages before she finally did.'

'Seems to be a family pattern – outliving all expectations. How old is Uncle Richmond?'

'Seventy-something, I suppose. Fabian didn't say exactly, but he was a lot younger than Hilda.'

'Well, let's see what we can find, then.' He turned back to the laptop and fell silent. Simmy sat back in the dining chair and tried to recall anything more about Fabian Crick's visit that might be relevant to the killing of poor Josephine. Nothing came to mind, and her thoughts immediately drifted to Christopher and how he would react to his interview with the police. Was there any danger that they might regard him as a suspect? Josephine had nursed a very obvious devotion to him, which some people might think was enough to drive him to lash out at her in frustration. Instead, Simmy had a feeling he had rather enjoyed it, while pretending to think it was all imaginary anyway, and he had always been careful never to wound Josephine's feelings. He would miss her personally as well as an invaluable part of the team at work. The younger members of the staff treated her with wary respect on the whole, despite her schoolgirl yearnings. She was extremely good at her job – brisk, polite, knowledgeable. The more she thought about it, the more Simmy discovered she knew about the woman.

'Here we are,' Ben announced. '"Miss Hilda Armitage, long-time resident of Jasmine House, Ullswater, has died at the age of ninety-one. Well known as a keen collector of Victorian porcelain, memorabilia and other objects . . . a colourful life . . . da-da-da . . . acute business sense . . . a rare female entrepreneur in a male world . . . The deceased leaves two brothers and three nephews, and other more distant relatives. Measures have been taken to safeguard the valuable contents of the house, until issues of inheritance have been resolved."

The local paper, five weeks ago. I'm surprised you didn't see it.'

Simmy snorted. 'I was a bit busy at the time, trying to organise hot and cold running water in the house, making sure Bonnie would be all right in the shop and a thousand other things. And that must have been just around Mother's Day, which was even more of a palaver this year than usual.'

'I wonder what Josephine did with the porcelain and memorabilia,' mused Ben.

'She hasn't sold it, or Christopher would know about it.'

'It's rather vague. Doesn't say what sort of entrepreneur Hilda was. Did Fabian tell you that?'

Simmy shook her head, and Ben returned to his keyboard. 'Must be here somewhere,' he muttered. 'Let's try directorships . . .' He fell quiet while the Internet worked its magic. 'Got it! She was founder and CEO of an outfit called Avicat. Short for Aviation Catering. You'd never guess, would you? She supplied meals for long-haul flights.' He scanned the screen. 'High quality, aimed at business class and above, supplied to eighteen frontline airlines. Founded in 1982, when the market must have been expanding exponentially. Good for Aunt Hilda!' He turned to Simmy. 'Must have made a fortune.' He looked again and discovered that the whole business had been sold nine years earlier, for a very handsome figure.

Simmy peered over his shoulder. 'Why couldn't Fabian tell us that? It's obviously not a secret. He must have deliberately decided to say as little as possible. I'm telling you – it was hopeless trying to get any hard facts out of him.' She spent a few minutes going over everything again, with a few added details. By the end of it, she was almost certain that Ben knew everything that she did, and there was a feeling of relief as a result.

Ben made copious notes, and then doodled as he let his thoughts run free. 'So why does Fabian want to build bridges with this uncle? After all, the house is lost to the family now, whatever happens. Even if they all knew Josephine, I can't see what they could gain by her death. From what you've told me, they're all a lot more fixated on their aunt.'

'It's early days,' she reminded him. 'We've got no idea how everything fits together.'

'True. What if the family sent Fabian round to you on Sunday as a sort of smokescreen? He'd bone on about Africa and aged relatives while one of the cousins popped over to Keswick with a knife.'

'We don't know for sure it was a knife,' she said with a frown.

'It's an educated guess, listening to what the police have put out in their statement. What does Christopher think was used?'

'He said it was most likely to have been a knife,' she conceded ruefully. Ben nodded his silent satisfaction.

'See what you can find out about Richmond,' Simmy urged him, pointing at the laptop. 'While we're here.'

'Ooh, families!' Ben sang cheerfully. 'I do love all these connections, don't you? With any luck, all this is going to go back a century or so, and we can delve around in all sorts of history.'

'You're really not going back to Newcastle, then?'

'I'm not sure. It's all up in the air. Mum and Dad aren't too chuffed about me doing history at all, for some reason – they think I've let myself in for a whole lot of complication.'

'They're probably right. But better to do it now than later, I suppose.' She looked at her watch. 'Gosh – it's quarter past eleven already. I should rescue your mother from Robin, pop back to the shop and then get to Beck View for lunch. We've probably only got another fifteen minutes. Less, actually.'

Ben shrugged. 'I can carry on without you, now. I'll email anything interesting and print it out as well. I'll start a file.'

'A dossier,' said Simmy, remembering earlier episodes, where the schoolboy Ben had assembled impressive quantities of information and insight concerning local killings.

'Bonnie says I shouldn't call it that any more,' he said. 'For some reason she thinks it's a nasty word.'

'Does she?' Simmy repeated it to herself, thinking of the way her father would analyse individual words, unpicking them and tracing their origins. 'I suppose it sounds like "doss" or "dosser".'

'Right. Something like that,' he said absently, his attention back on his screen. 'This is going to be a lot of fun,' he went on enthusiastically. 'So many hidden connections. I can't find a single thing about Fabian Crick, though. I've just done a search for him.'

Simmy had got up to leave but remained standing near the door for several more minutes. 'I'm not surprised. I doubt if he's computer literate, or even that he's got a job worth mentioning. Come to think of it, he never said a word about any kind of work. Christopher might remember what he was doing before he went to Africa, I suppose.'

'The police are going to be all over him, of course. Once they find out about his aunt leaving the house to Josephine, they'll want to check up on the whole family.'

'You think?' The idea made her wince. 'Surely only if Christopher tells them about him.'

'Which he will – obviously. How could he not?'

'He won't want to. He's already got a bit of a reputation for dropping people in it after the Grasmere thing. And we both think it's completely impossible that Fabian attacked Josephine.'

'Yes, you said. Even so, he's the key to it. Got to be. There's a clear chain, connecting you to him, and him to her.'

'You make it sound far too simple. It doesn't feel simple at all to me.'

'No, well, you're right, I suppose. But it's somewhere to start. The police are going to think so, too.' He tapped his front teeth thoughtfully. 'It would help to know more about the victim. How well did Christopher know her?'

'Less well than he thought, probably. He'd only been to her house once and doesn't seem to have much idea of what she did outside work.'

'So we've got two dead women, from different generations, then. And Uncle Richmond, who suddenly feels like a bright scarlet herring to me. Or perhaps I mean he's a smokescreen. Did you not get a feeling that Fabian was throwing him at Christopher as some sort of punishment?'

Simmy struggled to keep up. 'Say that again.'

'There's no hint of a credible reason why he was brought in, unless we're missing some big piece of the story.'

'I expect we are. Obviously we are, given what happened to poor Josephine.'

'What if there's no connection? What if we're looking at two quite different matters?'

'I thought you didn't believe in coincidences.'

'Sometimes I do,' he said, to her irritation. 'So let's get back to Aunt Hilda. Ninety-one years old. That's wild. Just think – if she knew her grandparents, they'd go back to about 1860 or so. They'd remember times that seem impossibly distant to us now.' He sighed happily. 'Just confirms what I've been thinking about history. It's all so fabulously *rich*.'

It made Simmy's head hurt to scan back through the centuries like that. The past had never held very much interest for her, other than the enjoyment of her father's tales of local celebrities like John Ruskin and Fletcher Christian. And they tended to feel more like fairy tales than actual historical reports. 'If you say so,' she said. 'Josephine must have had a feeling for history, I suppose, with all her collecting.'

'You mean she and Aunt Hilda were both collectors?'

'I told you that already. But I'm a bit vague as to exactly what they collected. Hilda liked stuff they call "memorabilia". I'm never too sure what that means.'

'Old letters and diaries, basically. Photos. Postcards. Personal writings, you might say. Notebooks. You remember Chris talking about that lot at Saturday's auction. A box of papers from a family, all chucked in together. You can get a lot of information into one big cardboard box.'

Simmy thought of her own very small packet of documents. Passport, birth certificate, car insurance. Three or four letters she'd kept from her father, and a few of the nicest cards people had sent for various birthdays. In total they would easily fit into a shoebox. 'Right,' she said uncertainly. 'All very old-fashioned. That stuff all exists on people's phones now, I guess.'

'For our sins,' muttered Ben. 'So what did Josephine collect?'

'China, apparently. Lots of little Limoges boxes, Christopher said. I can't remember what else. No mention of memorabilia.'

'Hm. So why in the world did Hilda leave her the house? That's got to be crucially important.'

'No idea.'

Again, the youth tapped his teeth. 'I can think of several theories that would connect all this up together. Might be these collections did overlap somehow. Could the two women have been fighting over something? Or' – he looked up excitedly – 'what if someone else, a third party, wanted this thing, whatever it might be, and assumed they'd get it when Hilda died. But instead she gave it to Josephine, which meant she had to be bumped off, so they could nab it.'

Simmy took a deep breath. 'That's a theory, yes, but I can't see one single shred of evidence to lead you to think it might be right. And quite a few details that make it extremely unlikely. This isn't like you, is it? Starting from the wrong end, you used to call it. What changed?'

He gave a rueful grin. 'Can't get anything past you, can I? The thing is, since I decided to abandon the forensic studies, I've been trying a whole new approach. Not just to things like this, but everything. Bonnie says I get too bogged down in the minutiae, picking people up on tiny mistakes, agonising over small problems, and forgetting the big picture. So this time I thought I would try to see it from the other end, so to speak. Start with motives and relationships and personalities and see if it works that way.'

'And does it?'

'Too soon to say. We still have to have some hard facts, and they seem pretty scarce so far. The other thing I never gave enough attention to is *context*. What else was going on in people's lives – what their priorities were, what they *wanted*. I'm trying to think more like a historian, see?'

'I do see,' she agreed. 'And I suppose now you put it like that, you've been drifting in that direction for a while now. Ever since last summer when you were with your relatives in the Cotswolds.'

'Right. I learnt a whole lot about families and their complicated histories when I was down there. And this looks as if it might be more of the same.'

Simmy leant back. Complicated families were well outside her experience. The Straws had all been boringly lower-middle-class, working in offices or factories for generations. On her mother's side, Angie stood out as a stark aberration. Everyone else was as dull and dutiful as the Straws. Not a whiff of adultery or secret love children, no embezzlements or bankruptcies. But Ben had a very different experience – he had come to realise that the family his mother came from was far from immune to lurking secrets and tangled motives. And as for Bonnie Lawson, the very mention of families made her flinch.

And then Helen was coming downstairs with Robin, who was bleating anxiously, and Simmy rushed to collect him. She watched apprehensively as Ben's mother took the steps with agonising care. 'Don't want to fall,' she laughed. Simmy could see that she was finding it difficult, startled to observe how much worse the arthritis had become since their last encounter. She went up a few steps and took the baby.

'Stairs are the worst thing,' panted Helen. 'It's my knees. They won't bend, and they hurt. It doesn't seem fair, when for years it's just been my hips. Hips are a lot easier to deal with.'

'Are you booked for replacements yet?'

Helen blew out her cheeks in exasperation. 'They don't know where to start, now I'm in such a state. This last winter was ghastly. Every day's worse than the last. And I'm not even sixty yet! I'll be in a wheelchair for twenty years at this rate.'

'We keep telling her to go private,' said Ben from the dining-room doorway. 'Start with the knees this year, and when they're working nicely, go back for the hips. Probably less than a year from start to finish, and she'd be a new woman.'

Simmy winced away from the prospect of four major operations for poor Helen, however quickly or slowly they might be performed. Like caesarean births, or heart bypasses, the mere fact that they were common did not reduce the deep physical trauma of any surgery. There was a kind of conspiracy to pretend that the whole thing was routine and nothing to get excited about. Simmy herself found even a minor thing like removing an appendix dreadful to contemplate. *But I'm just a wimp*, she reminded herself.

'I'll give him a quick feed, if that's all right, and then get out of your way,' she said. 'Thanks, Ben.'

'For what?'

'Oh – reassuring me that my brains haven't melted, I suppose. I wasn't sure I'd be able to function now I've got a baby. I wouldn't say I was altogether back to normal, but at least I can follow a logical thread.'

'I had five,' said Helen mildly. 'And still managed to do a decent day's work after the first few months were behind me. That's all nonsense about motherhood rotting your brains. The opposite happens, if anything. You get more focused, more observant – and you're always having to keep one step ahead. I pity the poor things who never even have one.'

Simmy smiled and said nothing. She and Christopher had already decided to let nature have her own way when it came to contraception. If another baby came along quickly, that would suit them very nicely, they agreed. Privately, Simmy envisaged them as a proper family of four by the end of the next year. Which reminded her – 'Oh, by the way – we're getting married in June. Only small, but you two are invited, of course.'

'Great,' said Ben carelessly.

'That'll be nice,' said Helen, with little more enthusiasm that her son. 'Make everything official.'

Some people disliked weddings, Simmy remembered. She wasn't madly keen on them herself, as it happened. And she'd done it all before, with Tony. 'That's the thing,' she said. 'It still works better in a lot of ways. We really should all have the same surname.'

'Of course,' said Helen. 'Let us know when it's all fixed.'

After that, there was nothing to do but give Robin a swift snack and head back to Windermere, which was less than five minutes' drive away.

Chapter Seven

Bonnie was busy when Simmy got back to the shop, with a small impatient queue of customers. There was an air of suppressed panic, emanating chiefly from a large woman who was muttering relentlessly at the back of the queue. 'Shouldn't leave a slip of a girl like this in charge. How's she meant to cope? All I came in for was a quick bunch of tulips. I've got to be in Bowness in exactly five minutes from now. I'll be getting a parking ticket at this rate.' A man in front of her felt compelled to make sympathetic grunts and nods, while casting embarrassed glances all around.

Simmy parked Robin at the back of the shop, in his bulky carry-seat and mentally rolled up her sleeves. 'Who's next?' she asked brightly.

The only man in the queue took a step sideways. 'Better deal with this lady first,' he said gallantly.

Bonnie was wrapping a large sheaf of lilies, freesias and gypsophila, refusing to be hurried, her face very pink. The customer was a young woman who was obviously itching to help, her hand hovering near the cellophane, making Bonnie's task more difficult. 'Right then,' said Simmy to the large woman. 'Tulips, did you say? What colours?'

'Red and pink, please. A dozen. No need for any fancy wrapping. Just let's get on with it.'

'We haven't got any pink,' Bonnie said softly.

'Let me see what I can find,' said Simmy with a broad, insincere smile.

Five minutes later, the shop was empty except for Bonnie, Simmy and little Robin, who was curled up in his portable chair, a white milky dribble trickling from his mouth. 'That woman's never going to come back,' said Bonnie with a sigh. 'Don't you hate people who are in a rush?'

'Can't win 'em all,' said Simmy. 'The man was nice.'

'Verity's going to be back soon. Quick – tell me what you and Ben worked out.'

Simmy's mind went blank, much to her alarm. 'Er . . . he's checking everybody on the Internet. He thinks there's an obvious connection between Fabian turning up and Josephine being killed.'

'Who's Fabian?'

'Oh Lord, Bonnie. I can't go right back to the beginning again. You'll have to ask Ben. And I should phone Christopher and find out what happened this morning. He was due for a police interview at ten o'clock. The auction house has closed for a couple of days, out of respect for Josephine. Plus, I suspect nobody's sure how to carry on without her, anyway. She was the one they all relied on.'

'Surely it's all on the computer? All the buying and selling and prices and so forth?'

'There's always something that isn't, though. Little details that never got logged, because they were all in Josephine's head, and everyone knew to ask her if they were stuck.'

'Like what?'

Simmy shook her head irritably. 'Oh, I don't know. Why are you being so . . . *picky*? Asking about things that are obvious. The point is, they're going to be lost without her.'

'Sorry.' Bonnie pantomimed excessive meekness, designed to make Simmy feel awful. 'I just wanted to try and get the whole picture. I've never been to one of their auctions, remember. I can't really imagine what it's like.'

Simmy responded precisely as she was meant to. 'No,' she moaned. 'I'm the one who's sorry. It's been a bit of a busy morning, and my head isn't working like it should. Helen says motherhood gives you focus and sharpens your wits, but it's not working for me just at the moment.'

'Well, don't worry about the shop. You caught me at a bad time just now. It's never like that usually. Thanks for rescuing me.' There was a hint of resentment in the girl's tone, or at least impatience, which Simmy fully understood. Just when Bonnie had wanted to demonstrate how effortlessly she was coping, fate conspired to show things at their most dysfunctional. 'I should have ordered more pink tulips,' she accused herself.

'I shouldn't leave you to do the ordering. I can easily manage that myself. There's plenty I can do, if we're organised about it. I can park Robin with my mother for an hour or so, two or three days a week, and we'll muddle through like that until September or thereabouts.' Again, the mention of a date reminded her. 'Oh – and we're getting married in June. I keep forgetting to tell people.'

'Wow!' Bonnie was visibly taken aback by this news and greatly cheered. 'Who's doing the flowers?'

'You, obviously. It'll just be small.'

'Small! I can already think of at least fifty people who'll absolutely have to come. Chris's family for a start must be a dozen or more, counting the children.'

'It'll be a weekday. Children will be at school.'

'Even so – Melanie, Ninian, Ben and his family, me, Corinne, Verity – *loads* of people.'

'Ninian?'

'Why not? He's a good mate. And you'll have people from where you used to live, old friends.'

Where Ben and Helen's reaction had seemed a trifle lukewarm, Bonnie's was definitely excessive in its enthusiasm. 'Stop it,' Simmy begged. 'It's just a formality, really. Nothing to make a great song and dance about.'

But Bonnie wouldn't be repressed. 'Moxon's going to want to come. You know how he loves you.' Detective Inspector Nolan Moxon had crossed paths with Simmy many a time in her accidental involvement with successive murders. He had worried about her, admired her, lost patience with her, always with an avuncular air of concern for her welfare. It was highly likely that he would want to come to her wedding, she acknowledged with a resigned smile.

'He'll be welcome,' said Simmy.

'When in June? It's not long, you know.'

'The first.'

Bonnie squawked and opened her mouth to protest, when Simmy interrupted her. 'Let's not talk about that now. I really do have to phone Christopher and get over to Beck View. And Robin must need a new nappy by now.'

'I won't say anything about the murder to Verity. She'll be silly about it. There's another order just now, so I can send her out again this afternoon.'

'Is she terribly hard work for you?' Simmy asked worriedly.

'I told you – it's good for me. She could be ever so much worse. And it's not her fault if she's so ordinary. Anybody would be compared to you and Ben.'

'Me? I'm as ordinary as they come.'

Bonnie merely laughed at that.

'Sorry I went to see Ben without you. I remember when Melanie got upset because she always seemed to be left out of the most interesting bits of the murder investigations. It just seemed to work out that way, but I was always sorry about it.'

'Don't worry – I'm not going to be left out. I'll make him tell me every detail this evening.' Bonnie's eyes sparkled. 'And there'll be a whole lot more by then, anyway. I'll be more up to speed than you.'

Simmy didn't doubt it. A lot could happen between lunch and dinner, in her experience.

Christopher had a lot to tell her when she phoned him. 'They didn't reveal any details, obviously, but reading between the lines, it looks as if poor Jo was killed somewhere around midnight on Sunday. She's got a cat, and I guess somebody saw her letting it out – something like that. They wanted every little fact about Fabian, going back umpteen years, trying to figure out the connections. I ended up telling them practically everything he told us Sunday night. Uncle Richmond – the lot. I have to admit they were quite clever about it. Caught on a lot faster than I expected.'

'Were they friendly? I mean – they don't think you did it, do they?'

'God, Sim – you don't mince your words, do you? There's certainly no evidence against me, is there? Luckily, they seem to have cottoned on to my links with the Moxon man, through you, which gives me a bit of kudos. At least they were careful not to be too unpleasant.'

'Kudos,' Simmy repeated thoughtfully. 'Haven't you got that anyway? Prominent local figure with respectable credentials and so forth.'

Christopher laughed. 'I'm not sure selling second-hand junk counts as respectable. They've all seen *Lovejoy*, don't forget. They've got a very warped idea about what goes on at auctions.'

'I saw Ben,' she interrupted. 'Helen was thrilled with the baby. But her arthritis is terrible now. She can hardly move, poor thing.'

'Oh dear. She's not very old, is she?'

'Not at all. It's awful bad luck.'

'So – what time will you be home? I'm back already. Should I go and get some shopping?'

'Good idea. Get lots of meat for the freezer. I feel horribly carnivorous. Is Humphrey there?'

'He is. They've made brilliant progress already today. We've got a corridor halfway along the upstairs landing now. It looks great.'

'Gosh! I should be back by three. I'm excited to see what they've done.'

She heard a knocking sound coming down the phone. 'What's that?'

'Somebody at the door. Bloody hell – it's Fabian back again. What does he want?'

Simmy didn't like to think and said nothing. Christopher went on, 'He doesn't look very happy. I can see him through the window.'

Simmy struggled with visions of the man wielding a knife in his rage at her fiancé. Because, whatever her good sense told her, and the apparently impossible logistics, she found herself perfectly able to view him as a murderer. 'Don't let him in,' she said urgently.

'Too late. He's just walked through the door.'

Simmy was sitting in her car outside her parents' home as she spoke to Christopher. Beck View was a large handsome house with five bedrooms and an adequate garden, situated on the main road running down to Bowness. The Baddeley clock tower, which marked the boundary between Windermere and Bowness could be seen from the front gate, not many yards away. She remained gazing blankly at the traffic, reminding herself that Christopher could not possibly be in any danger. There were two burly builders upstairs who would fly to his defence if necessary. And

Fabian was undeniably weedy. There really was nothing to worry about, even if the beastly man did look cross and marched into someone else's house without invitation. She unloaded the baby yet again and carried him into the house, forcing herself to concentrate on her parents and set aside any worries about her fiancé.

Lunch with Angie and Russell was generous and Simmy ate well. 'Eating for two,' said Russell, with a smile. 'Got to keep up your strength.'

'Two clichés in two seconds,' said his wife, raising her eyebrows. 'That's your ration for the day.' Both the Straws were very resistant to popular idiom and general misuse of language. They would never say 'hopefully' to mean anything other than 'optimistically'. They avoided 'devastated' and used 'seated' where everyone else said 'sat'. Russell was by far the more pedantic, but Angie entirely approved of the basic principle.

Simmy let her thoughts settle comfortably on the family chit-chat, encouraging tales about B&B guests, their dogs and fatuous demands – and avoiding any mention of a killing in Keswick or an unwanted visitor in Hartsop. Russell's latest anecdote was about a man who insisted on being told the precise provenance of every item of food, including the teabags. 'I thought it was very rude,' said Angie.

And then, with a faint feeling of reluctance, Simmy told them of the decision to arrange a wedding. 'Very small,' she added firmly.

'Good,' said Russell. 'Do we have to get you a present?'

Chapter Eight

She was back in Hartsop before three, having left her parents with all the work that she had helped with throughout the previous year. The fact of her baby excused her now. She had no idea what she would find when she got home but persuaded herself that it would be nothing nasty. Presumably Christopher would be there, most likely having managed to send Fabian packing. She supposed the builders were still on site. He might, however, be needed by Oliver or the police. Much depended on what had taken place between him and Fabian.

What she did not expect was a note, left conspicuously on the kitchen table, which said: *Gone up to Ullswater with Fabian. Shouldn't be long.*

'What?' she said aloud. She looked at Robin, asleep in his seat. 'What's going on?' The idea of Christopher complying with some crackpot scheme orchestrated by Fabian Crick was outrageous. Completely out of character. And potentially dangerous. What would the police think? And what was there to do in Ullswater?

The only answer she could think of was that they must

be visiting Aunt Hilda's house. If they'd gone to Fabian's rented place, whatever that comprised, he'd most likely have said 'Glenridding' not 'Ullswater', although locally the terms appeared to be almost interchangeable. She desperately wanted to follow the men and find out what they were doing. But she couldn't because she had a baby to think about. She started to call Christopher on the phone, and then killed the call before it could connect. Instead she phoned Ben Harkness.

'Any progress?' she asked, with a strong sense of self-control. She wasn't going to complain about her man going off or the frustration arising from having to consider the baby before making any sort of move.

'Plenty,' he said excitedly. 'I found Uncle Richmond quite easily. He's got two sons, an ex-wife and lives on a farm near Workington. The wife might be dead – she hasn't lived with him for about twenty years, as far as I can see from the voting register.'

'Wow!' Simmy applauded. Then, 'Well done.'

'It's perfectly simple when you know how to go about it. But lots of people give up when they realise they don't even supply proper phonebooks any more.'

'Have you found out anything else about him?'

'Like what?'

'Well, what does he *do*? I mean, is it a proper big working farm?'

'Have a heart,' he protested. 'It's not dairy, but I haven't traced the exact nature and number of his livestock. Although he did achieve a brief week or two of fame four years ago when he dug up a piece of Roman treasure in a field. That's quite an interesting story, but not pertinent, as far as I can see.'

'Was he metal detecting?'

'No, funnily enough. He was just digging for some reason and there it was.'

'Couldn't that be why Fabian's looking for him? He probably thinks there's money sloshing about.'

'There isn't. It wasn't a treasure trove and he just got a modest finder's fee.'

'It's a nice bit of background, even so.'

'I can't say I've got any sort of feeling for the actual man. I couldn't find a picture of him. You only get random snippets from searching newspapers, but it's a start.'

'So it would be easy enough just to go and find him,' she said slowly. 'If we wanted to.'

'Assuming you'd be up for a drive to Workington. Which might be a bit of a hassle with the baby. And why would you?'

'I don't know.' She was trying to straighten her thoughts. 'But you know what – Christopher's told the police all about the Armitages and their connection to Josephine. So they'll be tracking Richmond down, the same as you've just done.' She felt herself shiver. 'That feels a bit treacherous, actually. They're not going to like it, are they?'

'Nobody likes the intrusions that go on when there's a murder investigation. And the chances are pretty good that one of the family did it – or knows who did. Did Chris say any more about how she was killed, by the way?'

'No. They won't have told him that, will they?'

'Who found the body?'

'A woman from the auction house called Fiona. I suppose she'll know if it was a knife or a gun or—'

114

'A garotte,' said Ben with slightly too much relish.

With a jolt, Simmy remembered that her fiancé had gone off with a man who was at best unreliable. But before she could convey this worrying development to Ben, the boy read her mind.

'That's where we need Christopher,' he said urgently. 'He can surely find out a whole lot more about the entire family just by asking Fabian Crick, and I bet he's gleaned quite a bit today as well. If this promise he made to Fabian means anything, then he's working blind unless he gets more actual facts. Although that might turn out to be totally irrelevant now Josephine's dead.'

Simmy spluttered. 'I'm not sure I followed that last part, but let's hope he's doing exactly that as we speak. Finding out about the family, I mean.' She quickly described the note and the anxiety it caused her. 'I'm quite scared,' she admitted. 'Everything's completely different now from how it was on Sunday. There's a murderer out there.'

'I wouldn't worry about Chris. It doesn't sound as if the Crick chap's very tough.'

'He might have hidden skills, like judo or something. He might have a *knife*.'

'Don't get in a state. If he's only in Glenridding, you can go and see for yourself, can't you? Has he gone in the car? If so, you'll easily find it, won't you? It's a small place.'

'Not that small. There are quite a few houses. And what about the *baby*,' she wailed. 'I can't strap him into his blasted seat again and take him with me, if there's a chance there'll be trouble.'

'Calm down,' said the youth, who was half her age.

'Take some breaths. Nothing's going to happen to any of you. Why would it? We already decided there's virtually no chance that the Crick man killed Josephine. He's probably a lot more scared than you are, thinking the police might be after him.'

'If they are, it'll be thanks to Christopher, and that might make him mad.'

'It sounds to me as if Christopher went perfectly willingly. It might even have been his idea – trying to get more information. Anyway, we found Uncle Richmond. That's a step forward. Next step ought to be to go and talk to him, don't you think?'

'In theory,' she agreed cautiously, trying to keep pace with Ben's zig-zagging thought processes. 'But really it's got to be Christopher, not us. All we can do is tell him the address. He'll probably think phoning is the best he can do – if he does anything at all. It's probably much more sensible to stay out of it.'

'Pity,' said Ben. 'We might have had a nice day out.'

She snorted, but then admitted, 'I've never been to Workington. It always sounds like somewhere dark and industrial. Even my father barely knows it.'

'Steel furnaces, yes. But plenty of Roman history and some pretty bits. Blighted by a huge number of wind turbines, in some people's view. They are terribly dominant, it must be said. Seabirds slaughtered in their thousands, apparently. Interesting place to live, I should imagine.'

'Well, I can't just drop everything and drive forty miles,' she repeated. 'And it wouldn't make any sense to do that anyway.'

'Not until we get a bit more information,' he conceded.

'And anyway, we just said we should leave it to Christopher.'

'I know we did. We don't wanna do that, do we? Because we're hooked now, and there's been a murder, and it's a very weird story, which we'd really like to get to the bottom of.'

She giggled. 'Stop it, will you. I'm not supposed to be getting into any more madcap amateur detecting. I've got a *baby*.'

'Too late to worry about that. Christopher's already up to his neck in it, and you're not going to want to leave it all up to him, now, are you?'

'I might. Except he's already said he wants you to lend a hand. Doing what you do best. Which you've already done, I suppose.'

'Thanks to you coming here and explaining the whole thing to me. Which you did not have to do.'

'I wanted to,' she realised with a sigh. 'I really want to know who murdered Josephine.'

'Hey!' He sounded bewildered. 'What's come over you? The Simmy I know would be delighted to have an excuse to back off and forget the whole thing. Surely having a baby doesn't change a person as much as that? And if it did, I'd have expected you to get *more* risk-averse, not less.'

'It's nothing to do with the baby. It's Fabian, and the hold he's got over Christopher. I want it all settled properly, so we can just get on with . . . well, raising the baby, I suppose.' She was grabbing passing thoughts as they happened. 'And there's something about justice and truth and making the world a better place for Robin, if that doesn't sound too pious.'

'I see,' said Ben.

* * *

They left it undecided, dependent on what Christopher had to say when he came home. Which he did fifteen minutes later. Simmy had lost track of the time, thanks to Robin's confusing behaviour. He had slept almost the entire day, feeding with less gusto than previously and developing a number of spots on his face. When she picked him up for closer examination, he was suddenly wracked with sobs. 'Hey!' she told him. 'There's no need for that.'

But the baby clearly thought otherwise. For the first time since he'd been born so reassuringly alive, Simmy experienced a stabbing terror that he was going to die, just as Edith had done, after all. Here in her arms, he would expire from one moment to the next. He was, after all, only three weeks old. What was that in a lifetime? If he died now, it would hardly be different from being stillborn. A flickering little spark of life stubbed out after a mere handful of days. She rocked him and then held him tightly against her cheek, crooning wordlessly, utterly incapable of soothing him or guessing what the matter was. She walked around the house, vaguely wishing that the builders hadn't gone. Humphrey might have some suggestions as to what to do. She hadn't realised till then what a comforting presence he had been in the past weeks. He and his little crew of assistants had become such familiar fixtures that she was never entirely sure of their movements. In and out, back and forth, on their own mysterious schedules, they worked diligently and made impressive progress when they were in the house, and more than that she left unexamined. But they weren't here now and now it was incredibly nearly six and she needed help. She must have spent over an hour doing just about nothing but try to settle her infant – with very poor results.

Robin screamed more loudly, and Simmy clutched him more tightly. They were bound together in an agony of distress. It was terrible, and before long mother and baby were both in tears.

'Good Lord, what's all this?' came a voice that contained an outrageous hint of amusement. 'You're squeezing the poor kid half to death.' The new father prised the squalling bundle from her arms and balanced him on his own forearm, peering into the furious little face. The howls stopped as if a switch had been flipped.

Simmy sank exhaustedly onto a chair. 'That was awful,' she moaned. 'I couldn't think what was wrong. It's been going on for ages. I thought he was going to die.'

'Babies don't just die,' Christopher assured her. 'They're incredibly tough. And anyone who can make a noise like that obviously hasn't got much wrong. I could hear him from the road.'

'I don't believe you. And look at those spots!'

'Didn't we read something about milk rashes? I expect that's all it is.'

'Oh.' She heaved a sigh and wiped her face. 'This must be a reality check or whatever they call it. It's all been so smooth up to now. I thought I understood him – what he wanted and how to give it to him. And then he just started screaming at me.'

'Well, he's all right now. He was picking up on your panic, presumably, and you got into a vicious circle between you, winding each other up. You've been doing the opposite until now – relaxing each other. Sort of,' he finished humbly. Simmy could see he didn't want to sound as if he knew better.

'Thanks,' she said. 'You saved our lives.'

'Rubbish.' He smiled. 'You know what? I was planning on digging over that potato patch before it's too late. It won't be dark for a while yet. I've always wanted to grow potatoes.'

'You've been saying that for weeks. Get on with it if you've got the energy.' She spoke affectionately, even playfully, challenging him as she had done thirty years earlier. 'But you won't leave supper too much longer, will you? And I am desperate to know what you've been doing with Fabian this afternoon.'

He yawned. 'You know what? I'm too knackered for digging. It's been quite a day. Quite a *week*, come to that.'

'And it's not half done yet.'

'Indeed. So now I'm going to do a big pan of scrambled eggs, with bacon and black pudding and sautéed potatoes. It'll take precisely twenty-five minutes. You go off somewhere cosy and feed the young master, and then we'll eat. All sorted.'

She looked at him in a sort of wonder. Here was the Christopher she had almost forgotten. She was transported to an evening on a beach in North Wales, bathed in westering sunshine, Christopher was cooking sausages on an open fire he'd made himself. He must have been barely seventeen. His father was sceptical – the sausages would taste of smoke and be raw inside, he insisted. The younger Hendersons were running in and out of the waves, squealing and pushing each other. The three Straws were passively observing the much larger family. It was perhaps the last day of the annual seaside holiday that they'd all shared every summer for years. And it was, as it turned out, the last of such holidays. Christopher and Simmy had discovered each other as sexual beings, instead of semi-siblings, and the parents were alarmed.

The sausages turned out beautifully. So did the baked beans that he had gently warmed at the edge of the fire. For good measure he had toasted slices of white bread as well. 'Enough for everyone,' he announced proudly – which was in itself a miracle. Ten people ate the little barbecue meal with relish, and muted astonishment at this sudden show of competence by the eldest Henderson son.

'You're a marvel,' she told him now. 'An absolute marvel.'

'Rubbish,' he said again. 'Now go away while I cook – and then I'll tell you all about my very weird afternoon with Fabian Crick. And after that I'll fill you in on everything the police asked me this morning.'

It all happened more or less as he'd planned, apart from Simmy having to eat with one hand because Robin was slumped over her shoulder. He had accepted the feed with reasonably good grace, burped gratifyingly and then remained wakeful. She could feel him turning his head, just under her ear. 'He's listening to what I say,' she laughed.

'Of course he is. But he's going to find what *I* say a lot more interesting.'

'Go on, then,' she invited.

Christopher plunged into a lengthy account of his

121

afternoon. 'Fabian began by explaining in much more detail about the family situation ten years ago. It's rather more than he said on Sunday, which makes it even more embarrassing for me. Apparently at that time Aunt Hilda had recently had an operation for cancer, and everyone was worried about her. Fabian had been very attentive, and they'd got very close. He did talk about her quite a lot on the trip, which is how we worked out the Cumbria connection. Then when he was delirious and dying, he made a massive production of how he'd never said goodbye to her when he left for Africa. They'd had a bit of a tiff, apparently. Honestly – it was all so melodramatic, I think I simply dismissed it as the ravings of a disordered mind, or whatever they say. But now he insists it ruined his chances of inheriting the house, because she never got the message I was meant to deliver. By the time he'd recovered from his sleeping sickness, she'd found a new friend in the shape of Josephine.'

'And she survived her cancer.'

'Right. And then this cousin decided he was going to write her biography, and they immersed themselves in old diaries and so forth, before she finally died this year. She was very keen on the whole project, according to Fabian. And he was totally sidelined.'

'Sounds to me as if he's got an awfully good reason to be furious with Josephine.'

'I know. And now the whole family's under police scrutiny, which isn't going down at all well with any of them.' He sighed. 'It is rather a mess. He's living in a dark little room at the back of one of those ugly little houses behind the grassy bit in Glenridding. The bit where nobody ever goes. And he's got no money. Just state benefits. You've got to feel sorry for him.'

'Oh dear. I don't think I can manage that. He's just too *creepy*.'

'He's not so bad as that. He came all down here again today on that scooter, you know. It takes some nerve, on that road.'

'And back again, presumably. Why did you go there anyway?'

'In the end I managed to ram it into the car, with all the seats folded down and the boot flap hanging open. It weighs a ton. Lucky I didn't damage my back. Getting it out again was just as bad.'

'You idiot. Answer the question. Why go there at all?'

'Mainly I think he wanted me to see how wretched he is – to make me feel even worse about letting him down. But he's got a stack of old photo albums – and some not so old. I remember he was mad keen on taking pictures on the trip. But then, everyone was. It took him years to get them all printed out and put into albums. Being Fabian, he had no intention of storing them all on a computer. Anyway, he's got pictures going back to the late sixties – all the family were there. Aunt Hilda was a striking woman, all right. In fact, she looked familiar, but I couldn't place her. Everyone else is there, except Uncle Richmond. Apparently he never lets anybody take his photo.'

'Hang on a minute. Can we try and think through what would have been different if you *had* delivered the message? She would have assumed Fabian was dead –

right? So she'd have changed her will then, if he'd been her main beneficiary before.'

'Well, no, because she'd have made enquiries, and discovered that he hadn't died after all. We're talking about ten years ago, not a hundred. She could have contacted people in Botswana and been told there was no record of his death.'

'Okay. And then she'd have wondered why he didn't get in touch and tell her he was alive and still loved her.'

'Not necessarily, because I would already have told her that. I'd have said he was terribly ill, probably dying, and his last thoughts had all been of her. So she'd have rested on that for quite a while.'

'How long? Surely she'd have expected him to surface eventually and make up the lost time?'

'He says he did send a few postcards but didn't say much. It was three years at least before his brain got working again. It sounds as if he more or less forgot about her. And without my assurances, the cards must have seemed very cold and distant.'

'So – because you never visited her, she didn't know about the illness and just thought he was swanning around the world ignoring her completely, apart from a few rubbish postcards.'

'Exactly.'

'I see,' she said, just as Ben had said to her a little while earlier.

The early evening became bedtime, with further sporadic discussions about the Armitage family, interspersed with domestic and parental matters which they shared amicably. Simmy found herself treading carefully, aware that her fiancé's feelings were fragile. The shock of Josephine's death had come on top of the remorse over letting Fabian down, and then been compounded by the stress of his police interview. And, she reminded herself, being a new parent was every bit as destabilising for the father as it was for the mother. There was a risk that Robin would lose his place at the centre of all their attention by the ill-timed murder. She tried to voice this worry.

'We mustn't let it swamp everything else,' she said. 'Robin's got to come first.'

'I don't think that's going to be a problem. He knows exactly how to make sure he gets his rightful due. Look at him!' The baby was lying on the sofa, propped against a cushion, alertly watching the world that consisted entirely of two people. Both those people were squatting a few feet away, like slaves before a pharaoh.

Then he slowly sank into a deep sleep and the parents were left to talk about other things. 'I forgot to say that Ben's found Uncle Richmond. It took him about two minutes, by the sound of it. He's got the address of his farm in Workington.'

Christopher groaned. 'I should really hate that boy.'
'Why?'
'Because he makes me look old and slow and brainless.'
'No, he doesn't. You haven't had time for finding disaffected uncles, and he has. Besides, you've been unearthing plenty of stuff yourself, as well as heaving Fabian's blasted scooter in and out of the car.' That, she

found, was quite a sore point.

'But now the whole Richmond thing is fairly pointless anyway. The police will want to talk to him, presumably.'

'Will they, though? We don't know that he ever had anything to do with Josephine or Aunt Hilda's house, or any of it.'

'True. In fact, I get the impression he's never been included in family stuff. Although his sons are. One of them is writing the biography. So he's got to be at least vaguely relevant. Otherwise, why would Fabian bring him up in the first place?'

'Probably because he's a nasty little man who thinks he can make you do what he wants. He's a leech. He'll be after you for money next.'

'I won't give him any, I promise. And he is upset about Josephine. And he definitely can't have killed her. Pity, in a way,' he snorted. 'He'd be better off in prison.'

Simmy laughed. 'Maybe he ought to make a confession, then. When they find out it's all lies, they might lock him up for wasting police time.'

Robin stayed wide awake through the final stages of supper, and then found himself being put to bed at the new time of eight o'clock. 'We'll have to try and keep him awake more in the afternoons, so he gets tired earlier,' said Simmy. 'We won't have any evenings to ourselves if he goes on like this.'

'I expect it'll settle down,' said Christopher unhelpfully.

They were still talking about Fabian when they went to bed. 'I liked the sound of Uncle Ambrose,' said Christopher.

'Did I mention him?'

Simmy was losing interest. 'I don't think so. What about him?'

'He's an archivist. Probably knows Oliver, actually. Or did. He's a bit doolally now, apparently. Had a head injury a while ago.'

'Did somebody bash him?'

'What?'

'You said he had a head injury.'

'Oh – no – he fell off a motorbike that he'd just bought. Something much too big and powerful for a man in his sixties. A typical story. It took Fabian a good twenty minutes to tell that part.'

'Ambrose is a wonderful name,' Simmy said ruefully. She found herself wondering if that would have been a better choice for her baby.

'That's what I thought. It must be due for a revival any day now.' He had obviously read her mind. 'But we don't want our child to be that sort of pioneer, do we? Names can damage a person's whole life.'

'I wouldn't say that,' she argued. 'Speaking as somebody called Persimmon. It makes you memorable and it probably builds character.'

Christopher just laughed, and went on, 'Anyway, Ambrose spends all his time reading old books and collecting Edwardian postcards. Fabian hasn't much time for him. The cousins both live in Keswick, so they must have known Josephine as well.'

Simmy yawned. 'This is all going round in my head until I've got confused. Can we talk about something else? Or just go to sleep. I think Fabian's just a silly little man who's made a complete mess of his life, hoping to blackmail a good-natured acquaintance into sorting things out for him.'

'Meaning me? Good-natured, am I?'

'Aren't you?'

'Not always. Right now, I want to call his bluff and text him Richmond's address, phone number and email – if Ben managed to find all that. Then I don't want to see him ever again. It was stupid of me to waste time today listening to him, when I should be thinking about Josephine and how in the world we'll ever manage without her.'

'Yes,' said Simmy. 'I feel exactly the same. Now let's drop it.' She patted her pillow and pulled the duvet over her shoulder. Then she said, 'Did you say happy birthday to Robin today? He's three weeks old now, you know.'

'Happy birthday, Robin,' said Christopher obediently. 'And please don't keep us up all night.'

Chapter Nine

Wednesday morning started at four-fifteen, courtesy of baby Robin. 'Are we back to the old routine, then?' Simmy asked him in a whisper. Christopher hadn't woken as she slipped out of bed, gathered the baby and went to her favourite spot beside the window. It was going to be a bright day, she noted from the clear sky. There were moon shadows on the fells, everything utterly still. Before long the birds would anticipate the sunrise with their reassuring chorus.

The peaceful rhythm of the suckling baby sent Simmy's thoughts wandering freely. She felt almost culpably contented, largely, she realised, thanks to Christopher. They were going to get quietly married and try for a second baby. He was taking on the disaster of Josephine's death with a much better attitude than on previous occasions. She was almost tempted to use the word 'maturity' about him, except that it felt patronising to do so. The willingness to talk at such length about all the theories and details and implications was different from earlier responses, and very much to be welcomed. Where once her 'team' had comprised herself, Ben and Bonnie, now she felt as if she and Christopher were the pivotal pair, working in a harmony that exceeded all her hopes.

All the same, he was definitely shouldering a degree of responsibility towards Fabian, which Simmy found unnerving. Perhaps, she thought suddenly, it was fatherhood that had changed him. Didn't men generally feel an obligation to set a good example to their sons? Did Christopher feel he should do the right thing because anything else would make him vulnerable to critical judgement from Robin, as he grew up? If seemed fanciful, looking at the helpless, trusting infant at her breast, but the idea persisted for all that.

Which inevitably took her to consideration of the murder itself. There was still no indication that it was linked to Fabian Crick and his family, and yet it seemed impossible that it was not. The central connecting figure was Christopher Henderson, employer of the victim. On one of Ben Harkness's flowcharts, all the lines would radiate out from Christopher. *Logic*, she adjured herself. Where was the logic? It could quite easily be a coincidence, with no earthly sense in casting suspicion on Fabian or his relations. Josephine had probably been killed by someone after her antiques. The little Limoges boxes could have a value, after all. The old chestnut of 'A burglary gone wrong' could well apply here. On the other hand, Josephine just might have discovered that Aunt Hilda had a terrible secret and suffered the ultimate fate as a direct result at the hands of one of her relatives.

She crept back to bed at five, to the sound of soaring

birdsong just outside. The sun was risen, and another day had begun, but she hoped she could postpone it for another hour or so. Robin had obligingly gone back to sleep, and within moments his mother did the same.

She woke again at seven, to find Christopher standing by the bed with a welcome mug of tea. 'Gosh, thanks,' she smiled. It was still a novelty to be waited on. Her first husband had never acquired any such habit, always the last to get out of bed. Even when Simmy had been annihilated by the death of their baby, Tony had been equally useless, so that neither of them made tea or did anything to show care or concern for the other. 'I had a dream about Josephine and Aunt Hilda,' he said. 'They were both shouting at me – really angry they were.'

'Oh dear. Guilty conscience,' said Simmy thoughtlessly.

'Maybe,' he acknowledged with a wince. 'But I thought I'd got past that. And shouldn't it be Fabian shouting at me? How did I annoy Josephine?'

'Dreams aren't always logical. Don't let it worry you.'

'I'll try not to.' He leant down to kiss her. 'Not long till we make it official,' he said.

For a moment she couldn't think what he meant. 'Oh – getting married, you mean. Right. Is that how it seems to you – official?'

'Sounds horribly conventional, doesn't it? I'm thinking of Robin, mainly. It's supposed to be better for a kid if its parents are married, apparently.'

She had no answer to that; certainly she didn't want to argue. But it left a small niggling question in her mind

131

about the real meaning of marriage in modern times. Commitment was the aspect she most favoured, 'forsaking all others' was the part of the wording she valued, like any jealous female since the dawn of time. She had heard enough women of all ages voice the unhappy truth that men were not naturally faithful. You had to make them promise and threaten them with an array of painful penalties if they defaulted. Even good-natured men like Christopher.

'Right?' he prompted her, after several silent seconds.

'Absolutely.' After all, he was the one eager to sign the contract, make the vows, label himself as a husband. 'Aren't I lucky!' she sighed. It was not difficult to banish the wicked little notion that the reason men often seemed to favour marriage was that it gave them a kind of ownership. As Robin's married father he gained a lot more rights than he might otherwise claim. And the ring on Simmy's finger would count for something, too.

She finished the tea and rolled out of bed. Robin was in his cot, waving his arms and squeaking. 'New nappy?' Christopher asked.

'Knock yourself out,' said Simmy cheerfully.

The procedure completed, he picked up the baby and took him to the window. 'So what're we doing today?'

'It looks sunny out there. Maybe we should go to Workington.'

'Pardon?'

'To find Richmond. Ben will have to come as well. The police won't want you again, will they?'

'I doubt it. But why don't I just tell Fabian where his

uncle is and let him get on with it? Isn't that what we said last night?'

'Oh.' She pulled on her clothes and watched her menfolk thoughtfully. 'That *would* be the sensible thing, I suppose.' She felt a ridiculous stab of disappointment at the idea. 'Ben won't like it, though. He wants to be involved, right in the middle of everything.'

'I don't think it's a very good idea. I can't imagine what we'd say to the man, for a start. And I think I really ought to check in with Oliver and see what we're going to do from tomorrow. We can't stay closed after today if we want to hold the sale as usual next week. It doesn't feel right just to stay at home, or even to go waltzing off to the coast on a wild goose chase. Obviously we'll all go to Josephine's funeral, whenever that is, but in the meantime we need to keep functioning. Thursday and Friday are the days for people to deliver stuff for sale. The girls will need supervising, so we should assume I'll be going in tomorrow.'

'Poor Josephine,' Simmy sighed. 'I feel as if I hardly knew her, which was bad of me. I should have tried harder to be her friend. Did she *have* any friends? Who's going to be most shattered at losing her?'

'Good question. I don't think any of us knew her really well. She was just one of those people who are always there, keeping everything running smoothly, dedicated to the job, part of the furniture. All those clichés. Oliver was always very fond of her, in a jokey sort of way. He also took her for granted and paid her quite badly. If you feel bad about her, how do you think *I* feel? I was a pig to her at times.'

'Even though you knew she adored you?'

'That was more or less of a joke as well. Embarrassing, to be honest. But she kept it under control pretty well – and it's really just another cliché anyway. She was very schoolgirlish, in some ways.' He was speaking jerkily, ideas tumbling over each other. 'It was Oliver before me, you know. She was a serial adorer. One crush after another. For all I know, Fabian was on the list as well.'

'How sad. Why couldn't she just find a suitable man and marry him? She seemed quite motherly to me. Cuddly, with that nice wide bosom.'

'More like grandmotherly. I can't imagine what she must have been like as a schoolgirl.'

'I can,' said Simmy. 'Frizzy hair, good at hockey, friendly. Something must have gone wrong somewhere.'

'Oliver, probably,' said Christopher carelessly. 'She must have had designs on him for decades, living in perpetual hope. Then when I showed up, she transferred her affections. We did have some fun at first, chatting about antiques and computers. She taught me an awful lot.'

'Poor woman,' Simmy sighed again. 'You've all exploited her, in one way or another.' She gathered up the bag of dirty nappies and started to leave the bedroom. Then a thought struck her. 'Maybe she did know something the family wanted to keep secret,' she said suddenly.

Christopher stood frozen on the spot, staring at his baby son as if it had been he who'd spoken. 'What? Where did that come from?'

'I'm not sure. It's all smoke and whispers, but don't you get a sense that Aunt Hilda is very much at the heart of it all? Ben always says we should ask "Why now?"

and the answer to that is very likely to be Aunt Hilda dying.' To her own ears she was speaking entirely lucidly, impressively so, in fact.

'That's possible – but so are lots of other things.' He put the baby down on the bed and started to get dressed. 'And I would very, *very* much like it if we could talk about something else.'

'So would I, but I doubt if we'll get far. This is such a huge thing – and every time we try to escape from it, Fabian pops up and sends us right back again.'

'We won't let him do that. I can't see that he's got any reason to, either. If we've got any sense we'll just sit back and leave it all to the police.'

Simmy groaned. 'Do you know something? Every time there's been a murder, since I've been living here, somebody has said exactly that. Usually me. And it never happens. Either Ben or Bonnie or someone keeps it rammed against our faces so we can't focus on anything else. *My* face, I should say. I've learnt not to fight it. And this one is so close to home, we've got no choice. We have to see it through to the end, like it or not. Do you see?'

'I don't know,' he said helplessly. 'This is all going too fast for my poor brain. I still don't follow what you said about Hilda.'

She tutted impatiently. 'It's not so very complicated. Ben would get it.'

To his great credit, Christopher did not rise to this. 'I never pretended to be as clever as Ben,' he said mildly. 'It just strikes me you've made a few too many leaps. Nobody says there's a deep, dark secret to be found. And even if there was, don't they say that a dead person's private business always comes spilling out? Papers come to the surface, connections get made at the funeral, the bank discloses confidential details.'

Simmy was easily diverted. 'Did Josephine go to Hilda's funeral, I wonder?'

'I have no idea.' His grown-up calm began to crack slightly. 'But I'm sure young Mr Harkness could find out.'

Robin, perhaps detecting an incipient atmosphere, began to make his presence felt more loudly. Simmy took him from his father and carried him downstairs to the kitchen. 'Just sit there while I have breakfast,' she told him, strapping him into his little chair. 'You can watch me,' she added generously.

Nothing had been definitely decided concerning the day's movements. Simmy felt guilty at having compared Christopher to Ben, and to make amends she directed their attention back to the matter of getting married. 'Can we even call it a wedding?' she wondered. 'If it's just a register office and a pub?'

'Technically, yes, I suppose so. And whatever we say, my sisters will turn it all into a big event. Nobody in the family has got married for ages.'

'We should have done it before now,' she worried, thinking perhaps it was her fault they hadn't. 'Why didn't we?'

'We were too busy. And it was winter. And things kept happening.'

'Yes,' she said. 'And they still do. So we're not going to Workington to look for Uncle Richmond, then?'

'I already said, I can't see any sense in doing that. I can just give Fabian the address and leave it to him. I've had enough of his whining about having no money, or car, or anywhere to live. Even if it is my fault, he's had time to get his life back on track by now, hasn't he?'

'Stop! We're talking about getting married, remember.'

And they did. They speculated about the chances of a little honeymoon, and whether they should veto any suggestion of presents. They told cautionary stories about weddings they had seen and hated. They worried about how Angie might behave and whether Bonnie would go overboard with the flowers.

'It's really going to happen, then?' Simmy smiled, meeting his gaze. 'I'll really be Mrs Henderson.'

'Not necessarily – you could revert to Straw. But I'd quite like you not to be Brown any more.'

'If I'm married to you, I want to have your name. It might be old-fashioned, but to me that seems axiomatic.'

'As Ben would say,' he supplied with a grin.

'As Ben would say,' she agreed.

Still no decision had been made as to what to do with the day, and Christopher was becoming restless by ten o'clock, clearly worrying that he was wasting time. He was moving around the kitchen, collecting plates and dumping them in the sink. Simmy watched him, thinking he was changing into a different man in ways she found entirely satisfactory. There was something deeply relaxed about him, despite his present behaviour, as if contentment had filled him to his very bones. None of the usual stress of new parenthood appeared to be afflicting him. The balance between home and work felt manageable and secure. He paid attention to her and the baby, and was still eager for them to get married. He even co-operated in talk about mysterious murders, although that made him anxious. As far as Simmy could tell, the anxiety was mostly superficial and nothing to do with the essential facts of her and Robin and the new house.

He spent a few more minutes playing with the baby, then wandered around the outside space that was destined eventually to become a garden, moving stones about and pulling up a few plants that he believed to be weeds and marking out the increasingly postponed potato patch. When Simmy inspected his work, she protested at what he'd done. 'Those are foxgloves,' she cried. 'Why did you pull them up?'

'They're weeds, surely? Everything here's a weed – by definition. Nobody's ever tried to turn this patch into a garden. Besides, haven't I heard somewhere that foxgloves are poisonous?'

'Not according to my father. He insists that hardly any wild plants are poisonous. Or not enough to worry about, anyway.' She was kneeling at the foot of the stone wall that marked their boundary, trying to replant one of the ill-used foxgloves with her bare hands. 'You've torn off most of the roots. It can't possibly survive.'

'I'm sure there are lots of things you have to avoid when you've got a small child,' he persisted. 'Deadly nightshade. Hemlock. Aconite. I mean, Sim, it's only a few months since that bloke was killed with a poisonous plant.'

'Which no child would be fool enough to eat,' she

snapped. 'They've got *instincts* to protect them.'

'Hm,' was all he said to that. Then he looked up. 'Why don't we all go up to Keswick? It's a lovely day for a drive, and I could go and find Oliver and see what he thinks we ought to do tomorrow. Pub lunch by one of the lakes, and home for tea.'

'Okay,' she said slowly. 'But can't you just phone Oliver? What are Robin and I supposed to do while you chat to him?'

'Shopping?'

'I don't think so. It's too awkward with the buggy and everything.'

'Right.'

'Oh, Chris – I don't want to be a drag. A day out would be lovely. I'm happy just to sit somewhere sunny and watch the world go by. You can park me and Robin by the river somewhere and go off to talk to Oliver. Just don't take too long over it.'

'Better idea,' he announced. 'We all go to lunch somewhere together. He'd be fine with that. He's always saying he'd like to get to know you better, and he's sure to want to see Robin.'

'Really?' Oliver was a bachelor in his late sixties, plumply debonair in his dress and universally affable in a detached sort of way. 'Has he ever actually *met* a baby?'

Christopher just laughed.

It was all readily arranged, and soon after eleven the little family set off northwards to Keswick. 'I wish we had a dog to complete the picture,' said Christopher, as he did every day or so. It was a campaign that Simmy knew she was going to be unable to resist for much longer. The putative animal was gradually gaining ground in her imagination, despite her best efforts.

In the car, they yet again began to talk about the murder. 'With everybody knowing each other, we ought to find out more background – the wider family, and who knew Josephine best,' said Christopher. 'I feel at a disadvantage, only having been here a few years. This all goes back decades. Maybe we should ask Oliver – he's very much part of the social network round here. Everybody knows him, after all.'

'Do you think he knows Fabian and Hilda and all the rest of them?'

'I wouldn't be surprised.'

'Well, we can assume that Josephine did know the whole family. And I agree with you we ought to see if we can find out a bit more. We could start with Uncle Ambrose.'

'He's an old man.'

'And that's another thing. Ben found out that Richmond is only about seventy. That makes him miles younger than the rest of them. His sons must be a lot younger than Fabian.' She tried to order her thoughts. 'Did you say they all grew up together – Fabian and his cousins and Josephine?' This struck her as potentially rather important.

'That's right. Fabian told me what she was like then. Top of the class in history, as well as brilliant at maths. And then when they were in the sixth form the four of them started a little business together – backed by Aunt Hilda, who always took a shine to Josephine. It was a family full of boys, and she became a sort of honorary niece, apparently.

Fabian never took his A-levels but dropped out after a year. He didn't say what happened after that.'

'Aha!' said Simmy. 'That does sound significant. I wonder if he'll explain all that to the police.'

'I wonder whether they'll ask him for that sort of stuff.' He looked at her with a grin. 'That's where your Ben turns up trumps – especially now he's got this passion for history. Not that it always works out that way. I mean – not every crime stems from something in the distant past.'

'But you think this one might?' She wracked her brains for any evidence to suggest this. 'That would rule out a panic-stricken burglar, then?'

Christopher shrugged. 'I guess so. I can't say I find that a very likely theory. But it must appeal to the cops – makes it nice and simple.'

'They've had two days already and haven't questioned Fabian yet. Seems a bit remiss.'

Christopher pointed out the turning into Threlkeld, which offered an alternative route to his workplace. 'I usually go this way now,' he said. 'It actually goes past Josephine's house if you carry on into Keswick.'

'Oh,' said Simmy. 'I'm still very hazy about the geography up here. I always stick to the way I know.'

'Well now's your chance to learn,' he said.

She had no recollection of ever going into the village of Threlkeld and was surprised at its size and relative normality. Very few obvious signs of tourism, but the trappings of an ordinary settlement in the shape of school, church, pubs and food shops. 'I had no idea it was so nice,' she said.

'Too late now.'

'Pardon?'

'You're going to say we should have come here to live, instead of Hartsop.'

'Am I? It's very close to the busy road.'

'It stretches quite a way back, so you'd probably barely even hear the traffic. The school's the other end of the village, and there are lots of nice, sensible family houses.'

'Are you trying to sell it to me?'

'Just teasing,' he laughed. But the more she looked, the more she liked it. There was even a modest war memorial decorated with flowers. She counted four women pushing baby buggies. And for good measure there was a perfectly self-respecting fell rising up to the north. 'Blencathra,' said Christopher. 'One of the very best, in many people's eyes.'

'A long way from Windermere.'

'A good road, though. Except for having to go right through the middle of Ambleside.'

'I bet it snows dreadfully. It's high up here.'

'The road's kept clear right through the winter.'

'Prone to flooding.'

'Like everywhere else in the area.'

'Stop it,' she said. 'We've got a beautiful house already. Or will have, when Humphrey finishes.'

'Yes, we have,' said Christopher.

Chapter Ten

The auction house was much less deserted than expected. The big double gate stood open and there were several vehicles in the yard. 'I thought you were closed today,' said Simmy.

'So did I. That's Jack's car, and Pattie's. I guess they just couldn't keep away.'

'What about Fiona?'

'Wait here and I'll go and see what's what. Nobody's meant to deliver stuff until tomorrow, so there's not a lot to do. I can't think why anybody's shown up.'

'Same reason you have, I expect,' she said.

Christopher got out of the car and headed for the main entrance. Simmy watched him go with a pang of resentment. Women everywhere had to share their menfolk with workmates, she supposed. And vice versa, although that never seemed to be quite the same. The fact of Josephine's naked devotion had been only a part of the whole sense of Christopher living a separate life at the heart of a group of people that were very like a family. Considerably more than his actual family, in fact. His two brothers seldom put in an appearance, and his sisters were superficially attentive but certainly not a part of his daily life. Now here were 'Jack and Pattie' showing up beyond the call of duty, united, no doubt, in the trauma of losing their manager. And Christopher had trotted eagerly into their midst to share the grief.

But then two people came out and made for the car with broad smiles and Simmy managed to open her window, after turning the ignition on. One was a ginger-haired young woman in her twenties, who Simmy thought was Pattie. Despite her many visits to the business, she was still hazy as to exactly who was who. This particular person had been barely glimpsed in the background, generally with a clipboard in her hand. The other was Oliver, whose beaming expression felt oddly inappropriate. 'Can we see the baby?' asked the girl, already peering through the back window next to Robin's seat. 'Is he awake? Can we take him out?'

Blimey, thought Simmy. *Some people.* 'Not while he's asleep,' she demurred. 'If he wakes up, I'll have to feed him.'

Oliver was standing beside the passenger window, still smiling. 'Chris says we should get some lunch, so I've booked us a table upstairs at the Merienda. They know me there. Lovely cakes.'

'Okay,' said Simmy, trying not to feel bulldozed. 'Thanks.' It occurred to her that he was trying to say that he would be paying for the meal, which meant she ought to be grateful.

'Pattie, come away from that baby,' he told his employee. 'You'll wake it up.'

So it *was* Pattie, Simmy thought with relief. 'I'll bring him up here again in a week or two,' she promised. 'When he's a bit more sociable. He's not terribly interesting at the moment.'

'Oh, no – I *love* them at this stage. All floppy and warm and smelling so heavenly.' The girl gave a little frisson of ecstasy. 'And it's all over so terribly quickly.'

Simmy felt she'd been ungracious. 'I'm sorry he's asleep. Maybe we'll come back after lunch. Will you still be here?'

Pattie glanced at Oliver and then at the main building, as if lost for an answer. 'I don't know,' she said. 'Everything's . . .' Her enthusiasm for the baby suddenly evaporated, along with every other cheerful thought. Her face drooped and she was clearly at a loss for words.

'I asked her to come in and have a go at the financials,' Oliver explained. 'We generally send out payments for last Saturday's sale on a Wednesday, you see. We still do it the old-fashioned way, posting cheques to everyone. Josie always said it was simpler than keeping track of hundreds of people's bank details while making sure nobody steals them. Trouble is, it's quite labour intensive. How were you getting on?' he asked Pattie.

'More than halfway,' she told him. 'People have been popping in to talk about Josephine, which slowed it down.'

Simmy concluded that Oliver had not been on the premises all morning, since he seemed unaware of Pattie's progress. 'What's Christopher doing?' she asked.

'Who knows? Jack wanted him for something, and there's a bloke from Leicester or somewhere with about twenty pictures he wants valuing. Just turned up with no warning at ten this morning apparently.' He raised his eyebrows at Pattie, as if she was somehow responsible. 'I got called in as backup.'

'Happens all the time,' Pattie murmured.

Simmy was pleased to see no hint of apology on her face. 'I suppose it's what you're here for,' she said with a little laugh.

'Among other things,' Oliver agreed tightly.

Simmy was losing patience. 'What time did you tell them for lunch?'

'Twelve-thirty. We need to go soon. Do you need anything – for the baby, I mean?'

'What?' She could not imagine what he might have in mind. 'No, thanks. He's asleep,' she repeated, thinking that this could not remain true for much longer. 'When he wakes up I'll have to find somewhere to feed him. I don't suppose that'll be a problem for the Merinda, or whatever it's called.'

'Merienda. Have you never been there?'

'No. I don't come to Keswick much. It's out of my usual stomping ground.'

'Of course. You've got the shop in Windermere. I was forgetting.'

She found herself liking this man less and less with every passing minute. He ought to be much more upset about the murder of his faithful and long-serving employee, for a start, instead of making such a palaver about lunch. He ought, too, to remember not to refer to a person's precious baby as 'it'.

146

Before she could confirm that she did indeed have a shop in Windermere, Christopher emerged from the main door. He was very much not smiling. He was looking back over his shoulder at a man behind him, with a scowl.

'Hey, Chris – don't upset the customers,' Oliver muttered, too quietly for Christopher to hear him. He then went briskly to see what the trouble might be. Pattie remained beside the car, still eyeing the somnolent Robin as if tempted to disobey Simmy and rouse him into wakefulness. Simmy was twisted awkwardly in her seat, watching the baby as well as everything else that was going on.

Within a couple of minutes, Christopher was back in the car and starting the engine. 'Bloody prat!' he snarled, with another scowl at the offending customer.

'What did he do?' Simmy asked.

'Wanted me to give him a signed statement to the effect that two of his pictures are genuine Russell Chathams, from the 1980s. Lithographs.'

'And aren't they?'

'They might well be. I'm not qualified to judge. I surprised myself by having heard of the bloke at all. But as it happens, I have. He died not long ago – lived most of his life in Montana.' He was driving as he talked, heading into the centre of town, apparently on autopilot.

'I've never heard of him. Are his pictures valuable?'

'Very much so. Jack Nicholson collects them, among other people. They're pretty nice. Clever. Not like most of those wild west people, trying to make paintings look like photographs. The point is, what makes him think I'm going to risk my reputation on validating something just so he can make a profit?'

'Outrageous,' said Simmy, ratcheting up her role as loyal supporter. 'What was he thinking? Incidentally, where's Oliver? Shouldn't we be waiting for him?'

'He said to go ahead. He's trying to smooth ruffled feathers. I'll be in for a bollocking, I shouldn't wonder.'

'Will he say you should have signed the validation or whatever it is?'

'He might.'

'Outrageous,' she said again.

This time, Christopher laughed and patted her leg. 'That's my girl,' he said. 'I'll let you tell him.'

Oliver initially took charge of the lunch, treating it as a real occasion, insisting on wine and apologising for the limited menu. 'They actually do a much better spread in the evening,' he explained. But Simmy and Christopher ignored him, being far too much engrossed in the fact that there was nowhere to feed the baby, who had woken up hungry and cross. 'I'm going to just sit here and do it, and eat with one hand,' Simmy said. 'Whether people like it or not.' She awkwardly manipulated her clothing for minimal exposure and tried to stay calm. There were only a few other people present anyway, and they all discreetly averted their gaze.

'You'll soon get used to this,' said Christopher. 'I'm sure it's easier these days than it used to be.'

'I thought I *was* used to it,' she moaned. 'But this isn't like the local pub.'

'We need to talk about Josephine,' Oliver began, looking rather pink. 'And how we're going to get along without her.'

'Isn't it a bit soon?' Christopher demurred. 'We haven't even had the funeral yet. They don't know who killed her, or why. It's only been a few days, after all.'

'Yes, of course. Of *course* that's all true. But you and I are running a business, remember. And like it or not, poor Josie was the one person who held it all together.'

Christopher pouted a little at that, indicating a level of disagreement. 'I think we'll find it's all there on the computer if we look. Everyone's got their own job – logging stuff in, tracking the bids, despatching stuff to the online buyers. We all know the system, if we put our heads together. You especially – after all, you started the whole business in the first place. It must be second nature to you after all this time.'

'It *was*. But I have to confess there are aspects of those confounded databases that floor me completely. I never have been too great at numbers, if I'm honest.'

Simmy listened to this with some impatience. Here was the head of the company and senior partner, who had performed the central auctioneering role for twenty years before handing it over to Christopher, claiming ignorance as to how his own business worked. 'It's not so much numbers as logic,' she corrected him. 'Surely the databases are basically just lists of buyers and sellers, and hammer prices? All logically arranged so anybody can understand them.'

149

Oliver widened his eyes in shock at such straight talking. Christopher cleared his throat. Robin smacked his lips and burped lavishly.

'There are guide prices, reserves, commissions, fees on top of all that,' Christopher said. 'It's really not at all simple. Everything has to be inputted, then checked and rationalised. Fiona can do most of it – she's the one who records every lot as it's sold and tallies up who owes what at the end of the sale. But she doesn't have the same grasp as Josephine had.'

'Well, it sounds to me as if you're getting much too bogged down in all that, when you should be thinking far more about what happened to Josephine. Did you get any sense of what the police might be thinking when they interviewed you? What possible motive can there be, for a start?' Simmy was channelling Ben, as she often did, bringing the men back to the central point.

Again, Oliver looked startled, as if a menial was stepping over a line. *But I'm the boss* seemed to be the unspoken subtext. *You shouldn't speak to me like this.*

'Well?' she challenged him with a bold look. 'Surely that's the most important thing?'

'Well . . .' Oliver echoed, glancing at Christopher for rescue. 'I don't quite see . . .'

Christopher attempted an amused laugh. 'Hey, Sim – it's not fair to attack him with a baby at your breast. Gives you an advantage. Here – he's had enough for now. Pass him to me for a bit.'

She understood that he was exaggerating his parental role for Oliver's edification, for which she was grateful.

Without a murmur she handed Robin over and buttoned herself up, trying to order her wits at the same time.

Oliver straightened his shoulders. 'I wouldn't say that *motive* is the most important thing, no. It comes very much second to who did it. Who killed a harmless middle-aged woman who never hurt a fly and deserved nothing but admiration?' The words came out in a stream that sounded rehearsed to Simmy. Probably he had said them several times already.

'I didn't mean motive specifically, but the whole business. All the same, it would be useful to know whether anybody had anything to gain from killing her. Christopher has told me she had a nice collection of antiques, but we don't know if any of it was taken. What did Fiona say she found there, when you sent her to look for Josephine?'

Oliver swallowed. 'I haven't asked her for details. All I know is that she couldn't get in because the door was locked but went round the back and saw Josie in a room there, when she peered through the window.'

'So she called the police?'

'Not immediately. She tried the back door and found it wasn't locked or damaged. Josie most likely never bothered to lock it – people don't around here. Fiona wasn't very clear, but I assume she felt she ought to go in, in case she could save Josie somehow. She did say there was rather a lot of blood.' He spoke faintly, his head turned away.

'Which must have been completely congealed by that time,' said Simmy, having learnt more than she really

151

wanted to about how blood behaves when it leaves its rightful channels.

'Simmy!' Christopher was yet again attempting to silence her. 'We're trying to eat.'

'I know – but surely we all want the same thing? If we talk it through, we might find a clue that's been missed. You two have both spoken to the police – you must have some idea of what they're thinking.'

'Not much of an idea, actually,' said Oliver. 'They're very skilled at not giving anything away.'

'Well, they probably don't think it was a burglar,' said Simmy. 'Even if it's a lot easier to imagine a drug-crazed teenager lashing out at the householder who hears a noise while they're taking stuff. Something random like that, with no real malice behind it. Don't you think?' She was voicing her thoughts as they occurred, trying to remain conciliatory towards the man who Christopher clearly respected. Oliver had, after all, always been very generous and patient with his new partner, who had been welcomed into the business with no discernible reservations.

'The police didn't confide in me,' Oliver said tightly. 'They probably have me on their list of potential suspects, in fact. I've known Josie for twenty-five years, near enough. Like you, they seem to think that should give me special insight into why she was killed, at the very least.'

'I know how that goes,' said Christopher. 'Being in the spotlight just because you knew the victim. At least you didn't find Jo's body. That takes things to a whole new level, believe me.'

'Poor Fiona,' Oliver sighed. 'We really ought not to have

sent her to the house like that.'

'That was mostly me,' said Christopher. 'You hadn't shown up at that point.'

'But I agreed to it, on the phone,' Oliver reminded him.

'Well, it doesn't matter now. What's done is done,' said Christopher. 'Nobody could have known what Fiona was going to find.'

'Never crossed my mind,' Oliver agreed. 'Not in a million years.'

'Well, perhaps that wasn't true of everybody,' said Simmy softly. Both men gave her startled looks but said nothing. Again, she understood that she had crossed a line, but the knowledge only made her impatient. She wondered if it would be sensible to introduce the subject of Fabian Crick and his relations. The conversation was drying up, with the food suddenly occupying more attention than anything else. Oliver tucked determinedly into a steak, which was very much too rare for Simmy's sensibilities. Then, the last of it gone he said, 'Of course, you can't ignore the wretched Armitage bloke. He was probably feeling pretty murderous when Josie turned him down.' He looked from face to face. 'I don't suppose you know him, do you?'

It seemed to Simmy then that the case was solved, just like that. 'You mean one of Fabian Crick's uncles, do you?' she said quietly. 'Or someone else in that family? Or Fabian himself?'

'What do you mean – turned him down?' Christopher demanded, a second later.

'Ah. I see you do at least have some idea of the connection. But no, actually. I wasn't thinking of anyone named Fabian. I was talking about Richmond Armitage. The one who lives in Workington. The one who wanted to marry our precious Josephine.'

Chapter Eleven

'But he must be twenty years older than her,' said Simmy. 'At least.'

Both men looked at her, eyebrows raised. 'So what?' said Oliver brusquely. Again, Simmy had the sense that she'd shown insufficient respect, that she was coming across as insolent. 'Actually, I believe it's somewhat less than that. Jo was a fair bit older than she looked.'

'We know about Richmond,' Simmy said. 'He's Fabian's uncle, Aunt Hilda's brother. Fabian has asked Christopher to find him, as it happens. We know he lives in Workington and has two sons. Are you saying you think *he* killed Josephine?'

'Slow down a minute,' Oliver complained, swiping a melodramatic hand across his brow. 'I never said anything of the sort. Are we even talking about the same people? Hilda, you say? I do remember her. But who's Fabian?'

'I met him in Africa, a million years ago,' said Christopher. 'He's just resurfaced, in the past few days. Now he lives practically next door to us, in Glenridding. He's been telling us about his family. Josephine told him where he could find me. He's been here at the saleroom recently, renewing an old friendship with her. The whole family knew her from schooldays, according to him.'

'Does Richmond go to your auctions?' Simmy asked, still trying to complete the circle of acquaintance and work out how everyone connected.

'What?' Oliver barked.

'It's a simple question.' She glimpsed Christopher grimacing, as he sat beside his boss. However hard she tried, she was never going to manage to be sufficiently tractable in her dealings with Oliver. The man was too pompous and self-important to be treated with deference.

'No, no, I wouldn't think so. Of course I can't know everyone who's there. I don't follow every transaction. But I do know who the regulars are – I remember their bidder numbers and their little habits.'

'But you brought his name up. You obviously know him.'

'Years ago now, he used to drop in to see Josie. His wife had gone off or died – I don't remember. Josie liked him well enough, but he was totally uninterested in antiques. He couldn't tell a Moorcroft from a Poole, or a kelim from a bearskin. Josephine used to talk about how uselessly ignorant he was.'

In Simmy's mind, the circle was not so much closing as growing convoluted swirls, that linked to other circles. 'You said he wanted to marry Josephine? When was that? Is it a recent thing?'

'No, it goes back a while. A *long* while. She used to get the girls in the office to say she wasn't there when he phoned her, once he got too pressing. It wasn't far off being stalked, at one point. It's probably twelve or fifteen years ago or thereabouts that it started. She'd have been hitting forty, and he was a well-set-up farmer approaching sixty. He was scouting around for a new wife. I never really understood what her problem was. It would have been a good move from her point of view. He wasn't in Workington, though. That must have happened more recently.'

'You think he could have killed her, then?' This time Christopher butted in. 'Like Simmy said?'

'I wouldn't dream of making such a slanderous accusation.' He forced a laugh. 'And it wouldn't be very convincing, anyway. He might have done it all those years ago, but it's a bit late in the day now.' He looked from one face to the other. 'I think we should all be very careful in what we say. You've both got your teeth into this. I hadn't realised.' He sat back, his eyes narrowed. 'And it's a dangerous game to be playing. Haven't you got better things to do?' He looked meaningfully at the baby.

'Don't worry,' said Christopher. 'As Simmy said, we all want the same thing. And we're all a bit overwrought, with everything that's happened.'

'That's true,' Oliver managed a forgiving smile. 'Pity poor Fiona, trying to revive a murdered woman slumped between all those filing cabinets.'

Before Simmy could pick him up on this new detail, Christopher interrupted with some comment about coffee. Then Oliver's phone rang and he turned away for a brief conversation. Simmy felt weak. She was discovering how little affection she felt towards Oliver. She did not like being snapped at for making perfectly reasonable remarks. Luckily, her baby son was impressively telepathic and began an insistent whimpering on Christopher's shoulder, bobbing his heavy head up and down, and stiffening his back.

'He's bored,' she said. 'Nobody's paying him any attention.'

This was handsomely rectified, not only by the doting parents, but a strange woman who crossed the room to croon and exclaim over the adorable little darling. Oliver sat back, giving an eerie impression of a neglected baby himself. The meal was obviously over, and they took their leave after a few more minutes. Christopher made a token objection to having it paid for by his partner, but Oliver was adamant. Simmy could see that it fed his self-image nicely to be seen as a man of largesse and tried to convey to her fiancé that he did no good by protesting.

In the car, with Robin far from happy to be squashed back into his uncomfortable seat, Simmy remembered her promise to Pattie. 'Can we go back to the auction house for a bit?' she asked. 'If that Pattie person is still there, she can play with Robin.'

'Fine by me,' Christopher agreed. 'Oliver won't be there, which is just as well. Seems to me you've had enough of him for one day. And I dare say the feeling's mutual. You didn't make much effort to charm him, did you?'

'Sorry,' she muttered. 'But he's not my type of man. Much too pleased with himself. Do you *like* him?' she wondered. 'I've never heard you say anything against him.'

'He's been good to me, so I feel grateful to him. The fact

158

is, we don't coincide much. He only comes in a couple of days a week now. I know he hasn't given up with business completely, but much of what he does is outside. He goes all over the place, doing valuations mostly. He's in big demand as an expert, spotting fakes and all that.'

'You mean pictures?'

'Not so much. More along the lines of ivory and tortoiseshell, I think. It's illegal to buy anything made since 1947, so there's big business in making things look older than they are. Oliver's got a very good eye for that. He's been asked to give opinions on old documents as well. There must be similar clues, I guess – rubbing cold tea into things, and using the wrong ink.'

'That doesn't sound very scientific,' she teased.

'No, well – it's completely beyond my pay grade. I can spot hairline cracks and the wrong sort of screws, but it doesn't go much further than that.'

'And Oliver cares, does he? I mean, he thinks the rule about ivory and so forth is a good one?'

'I couldn't say how he feels about it. But it's bad for business if a lot of wrong stuff gets through. Undermines confidence, so it gets to the point where nobody's going to touch even the genuine things. If you press me, I'd say what he really likes is the reputation of being an expert. Does wonders for his image – and pays pretty well, if it's something important. I gather he's darn good at it. Those Hitler diaries would never have got past him, if anybody had asked his opinion.'

They were at the auction house, which was showing little sign of life. 'Most of them have gone home, by the

159

look of it,' said Christopher. 'But Pattie's still here – that's her car.'

Simmy extracted Robin from his seat and followed Christopher into the reception area, feeling self-conscious. She could see the main saleroom through a glass-panelled door and thought back to the handful of times she had attended a sale there. The shelves and tables were almost empty now, waiting for fresh deliveries of goods the following day. 'Why are there things there already?' she asked.

'Left over from last time. Some of the regular vendors have an arrangement to let stuff go through again. Officially they're all meant to take it away, but we make some exceptions.'

She wasn't sure she quite followed this explanation. 'You mean if nobody bidded for it?'

'Mostly, yes. It's not exactly that simple, but you don't need to know all the details.' He was speaking over his shoulder as he peered into first one office and then another. 'Where is everybody?' he called.

The man who functioned as a general dogsbody appeared at the main door, through which Simmy and her family had just entered. 'Hello again,' he said chirpily. 'Didn't think you'd be back so soon.'

'Pattie wanted to see the baby when he was awake,' said Christopher. 'Oliver's gone off for now. Back to normal tomorrow, then?'

'Seems like,' nodded the man, who Simmy remembered was called Jack. 'Won't be like normal without Josie, though.' He sniffed with a sudden naked emotion. 'Poor old girl. What a thing to happen. What a thing, eh?'

His gnomish little face contorted and Simmy wondered whether everyone had overlooked him in the general confusion. 'Had you known her a long time?' she asked.

'Man and boy,' he said, with an attempt at a smile. 'Must be close on forty years.'

'Don't tell us you went to school with her as well,' said Christopher, a trifle impatiently.

'Lived in the same road. Her dad and mine were best mates. She's ten years younger'n me, but yeah, we went to the same school. Everyone did. Big comprehensive, where else are we going to go?'

'Right,' said Christopher. 'Have you seen Pattie anywhere?'

'It was Josie who got me this job, you know. I'd been knocking about doing this and that, nothing regular, and then one day she said she could have a word with Oliver and see if he'd take me on. Been here ever since.' He sighed. 'Won't be the same now.'

'Pattie?' Christopher prompted.

'Upstairs with the pictures, last I saw her.'

'I'll go and call her, then.'

Simmy was carrying the baby on her shoulder instead of lugging him in his seat – which he had been keen to escape. It was by far his favourite position, whichever parent adopted it. It gave him a good view of the world, while being warm and secure. For Simmy, the little head against her neck was bliss. It made her feel connected to him as no other arrangement did, other than feeding. Sometimes she forgot he was there, having a free hand

and no cumbersome equipment.

'Seems a contented little chap,' said Jack, who was hovering behind her. 'Looks like his dad.'

'Do you think so? Most people say he takes after Christopher's father.'

'Hm,' said Jack vaguely. 'Here's Pattie, look.'

The girl came rattling down the little staircase from the upper level where pictures were displayed. Simmy had never been up there and had little idea of what it was like. The building was a converted warehouse, as most auction houses seemed to be. There were odd additions such as half-floors and small side rooms, but almost all the action took place in the huge central space. 'Is he awake?' Pattie demanded eagerly. 'Can I hold him?'

Simmy was still not comfortable with handing him over to anyone but Christopher and her parents. Helen Harkness had given her no choice and had in the process forced her to relax a little. But she had never met this Pattie person before and could have no confidence that she wouldn't drop him or squeeze him too tightly.

'Course you can,' said Christopher firmly, and plucked little Robin out of his mother's grasp. 'We only came back so you could have a bit of baby-worship.' He handed the infant over, and Pattie seized him joyfully. Simmy was left with a cooling place on her neck and a clamouring inner voice saying *What if she's got a cold? Or something worse?*

'Did you have a good lunch?' Jack asked, still hovering.

'Pretty good. Oliver's cut up about Josephine, of course. It's going to be bedlam here tomorrow, with everyone trying to figure out the system.'

'It'll be fine,' said Pattie, not looking up from Robin's little face. 'Josie wasn't nearly as indispensable as people keep saying. But we will need a replacement, of course. We can't do everything with one person missing.'

Christopher gave a small laugh. 'Looking for promotion, then?'

She did look up then. 'Well, somebody's got to be manager. I've been here as long as any of the others – except Jack,' she added with an expression that said it certainly wasn't going to be him.

'What about Fiona?' Simmy asked.

'She's got different skills,' said Pattie tightly. 'And the others are all part-time. They only work twenty-five hours a week, when you average it out. Even less in one or two cases.'

Simmy was unsure who 'the others' were, exactly. There was a stout woman who sat beside Christopher while he conducted the auction, and a small gang of boys who helped to find lots for the buyers at the end of the sale. 'Well, good luck then,' she said doubtfully, aware that she could be missing some powerful office politics.

Robin was treacherously enjoying his new friend. He gazed into her face and worked his mouth as she talked. 'Look – he's copying me!' Pattie cried. She put her tongue out, and miraculously the baby did the same. 'What a clever boy!'

'They do that,' said Simmy.

'Do they?' asked Christopher, who was every bit as impressed as Pattie. 'I haven't seen him doing it before.'

'My mother does it with him.' She was exaggerating, in a confused attempt to diminish Pattie's triumph. Angie had in fact only once managed to get Robin to open his mouth when she opened hers right in his face. 'We should get him home,' she went on. 'He must be tired by now.'

'Well, thanks for bringing him,' said Pattie with a frank smile that made Simmy feel churlish all over again, as she had done with Pattie before lunch. 'He's an absolute treasure. You're really lucky.'

'I know,' said Simmy, taking the baby back. 'I still can't entirely believe it.'

'Every baby's a miracle,' said Pattie simply.

For the first time, Simmy noticed a gold cross hanging round the girl's neck. Suddenly everything fell into place. She was religious – something that seemed unusual and even slightly embarrassing in modern times. It transformed her into a whole other person – still irritating, but somehow innocent and well-intentioned. She really did believe that every baby was a miracle, precious in the sight of God, and to be cherished accordingly. The aura of blithe confidence made sense, too. But where did that leave the violent killing of her colleague? And did she really imagine she could step into Josephine's shoes and run the business as it had always been run?

'Thanks,' Simmy said. 'I'll bring him again in a few weeks' time. He likes you,' she added generously.

Christopher took her arm gently, as if approving of her words. 'Better go,' he said. 'See you tomorrow, Pat. Don't expect it'll be much fun. Where did Jack go?' he wondered, looking around.

'Oh, he sloped off five minutes ago. You know what he's like.'

Simmy wondered whether the patronising look Pattie had given the man had been the cause of his withdrawal. Had she hurt his feelings? Was there some sort of history between the two of them? She found herself brimming with questions to ask Christopher in the car.

Chapter Twelve

But there was a new distraction when they got back into the car. Simmy's phone was poking out of her bag and reflexively she switched it on to check for messages, once she'd secured Robin back into his seat. There was a text from Ben. *Where are you? What's happening? I have info about Hilda you should know.*

She replied briefly saying they were driving home from Keswick and she would call him in an hour or so. 'Ben says he's found out more about Hilda,' she reported, as Christopher turned onto the sweeping A66, which was one of Simmy's least favourite Lakeland roads. It felt alien – too new and brash and hurtling for the region. Once they'd left it for the much smaller lanes down to Patterdale and Hartsop, she felt more at ease. Christopher was an erratic driver, never seeming to fit his speed to the conditions, causing Simmy to look for excuses not to ride with him more than necessary.

'Oh?' was all he said.

'What's the matter? Why are you so quiet?'

'Nothing much. Oliver was awfully pompous, wasn't

he? I've hardly ever seen him in that sort of context. He's always very businesslike at work.'

'He was okay,' she argued, aware that she was contradicting herself. 'He's the sort of man who's uneasy around babies and female flesh. Has he ever had a serious relationship?'

'That's what everybody wants to know. We all assume he's gay, but there's never been a sign of a paramour. If that's an acceptable word. He's away a lot, of course. He might have someone tucked away in a town flat somewhere. My guess is he hates to seem like a stereotype, but really he is. Those soft grey waistcoats and girly fingers – did you notice? All ideal for handling delicate antiques and confirming his image as an expert. But there's more to him than that. He's no fool.'

'I didn't notice the waistcoat or the fingers,' she admitted. 'But it was a perfectly nice lunch, and you obviously need to stay on the right side of him.' And she went on to quiz him about relationships between the saleroom staff, and whether Pattie stood any chance of stepping into Josephine's shoes.

'Fiona wouldn't like it,' he said. 'But Pattie does have a point. Fiona's fine with the *things* and coping with the stressful days when everyone's running round in circles, but she wouldn't make a good team leader. I can't imagine her issuing instructions or trying to teach anybody how to do something. She's quite driven, I suppose, but only on her own narrow business. She doesn't do idle chatter and seems uninterested in anyone else's lives.'

'Was Josephine interested in other people's lives?'

'Oh yes! She knew the names and birthdays of everyone's spouse, child and mother-in-law. Not just the staff but most of the vendors and buyers as well. And she had a phenomenal memory for past sales – prices, who bought what, all that stuff. Sometimes it felt as if she imbued the things with a character – a soul, if you like. She'd go all wistful about a bronze figurine we sold twenty years ago. Or if a stray plate showed up, she'd agonise because it could have been matched up with a set that went for six quid back in 2009, because it wasn't complete. All that sort of thing. She lived and breathed the place. We all wondered whether she had any life at all outside the auction house.'

This was a new angle on the woman, and Simmy took time to absorb it. 'She did, though, if she took so much interest in people's lives. That must have extended beyond her workplace, surely? And what was that about filing cabinets?'

'Say again.'

'Oliver said she was slumped between the filing cabinets – something like that.'

'Did he? Sounds unlikely.'

'It's definitely what he said.'

Christopher had nothing more to offer on that topic, so they returned to the question of Josephine's social life. 'She did keep up with Fabian, after all,' said Simmy. 'And she had a cat.'

Christopher laughed. 'Another stereotype, then.'

'You could say that. Maybe anybody who works in the same job for decades turns into a bit of a type. They get stuck in the same routines and are surrounded by the same people every day. Doesn't that sound sad? A wasted life.'

Christopher nodded. 'That's what I envied about my dad – going to all those different houses, no two days the same. The stories he came home with! It was life's rich tapestry, all right.' Kit Henderson had been a carpet fitter for much of his working life.

'What about you? You're not trying to tell me you'll be wanting to move on one of these days, are you? Take up car maintenance or become a postman?' She was fleetingly concerned that this really might happen. For herself, she had no great argument with a modest number of routines, if they meant she always knew where the next loaf of bread was coming from.

'Definitely not car maintenance. All that horrible oil! And I don't think a postman's pay is enough to tempt me.'

'I wonder about Aunt Hilda,' she went on, thinking of Ben's message. 'She must have been open to change and risk, the way she made such a success. Building up a business and then selling it, and going on to something new. It takes courage, especially for a woman.'

He made a sound that suggested disagreement. 'I'm not sure we can believe all of it. I mean – we've only got Fabian's word, and he could have been exaggerating. Wouldn't she be a sort of female Richard Branson, if it's all true? We would have heard of her.'

'It is true. Ben found most of it online. And she was obviously special if the nephew's writing her biography. Anyway, Ben wants me to call him. It sounds as if there's more to tell us.'

'You mean after you've fed Young Sir, and checked the

post, and listened to whatever Humphrey might have to say, and had a cup of tea?'

'I thought you could do most of that – and I can speak on the phone while feeding. I factored some of that in anyway when I told Ben it might be an hour before I get back to him. I doubt if Robin will want anything for a while, anyway. He's spark out, look.' She twisted round to inspect the baby on the back seat. His head flopped awkwardly, almost touching his chest. 'That seat's terrible,' she said. 'He'd be much better off in a carrycot, like in the olden days.'

'Tell that to the health and safety police. They'd fine you just for thinking it. What if the car rolled over? What if we were in a head-on crash and he shot through the windscreen. What if – um – a horse fell on top of the car?'

'Shut up,' said Simmy.

The plan to call Ben was comprehensively thwarted, first by the hassle of unloading a crochety infant from the car, then by Humphrey as predicted by Christopher. The builder tousled his own hair, grinned sheepishly and admitted he had taken it onto his own initiative to decide which way the new door into the third bedroom should open. 'I know people have their own ideas about that sort of thing,' he said. 'I've made it open outwards – gives you more space inside the room, see. But might not be to your liking?'

'Couldn't it have waited an hour or two?' Christopher asked crossly.

The builder shrugged. 'Not really. Everything else depended on it. We've done the panel, look. And no way could we start painting till the door was sorted. Still haven't got the proper stones for the fireplace downstairs, and the rest is done for now.'

For now echoed in Simmy's head and made her feel tired. If the work went on much longer, Humphrey would begin to feel like one of the family, exploited in small ways such as baby-minding and answering the phone. And when he finally left, she would miss him. 'You don't have to do all the painting,' she said, not for the first time. 'I'd quite like to do some myself. I started the door frames – did you see?'

'Opening outwards is fine,' said Christopher, before looking at Simmy and adding, 'Isn't it?'

'What did we decide for the others?' She went along the new corridor and opened the door to the main bedroom. 'Inwards,' she discovered. 'I don't remember even thinking about it until now.'

'Inwards is the usual way,' Humphrey said patiently. 'But this is a small room, look. And there's often trouble with carpets, if you want a nice tufted one. The door can catch it you don't set it high enough.'

'It works all right in our room,' Christopher said. He operated the new door. 'It *does* feel peculiar, pulling it instead of pushing. Won't it be even more of an obstacle like this?'

'I can change it,' sighed Humphrey. 'I had a feeling you wouldn't like it.'

Simmy forced herself to think about doors and paintwork and carpets, telling herself she ought to find it all exciting and comforting and properly domestic. 'Does that mean replacing the door frame?' she asked.

'No, no. Just a bit of cutting. The door will have to be set higher, see, and new holes made for the hinges, and . . .' he tailed off with a helpless expression.

'Doesn't look especially arduous to me,' said Christopher. 'And I still can't see why it couldn't have waited. What have you actually done that's so dependent on which way the door opens?'

Simmy didn't wait for any more. Robin was downstairs in his little seat, wanting attention. The men were being all too annoyingly male about the whole business. Humphrey was in the wrong, and everybody knew it, including him. He'd been impatient and cavalier, for no convincing reason. Christopher was right to make him change it, given that they would have to live with the damned door for the next twenty – thirty – *fifty* – years. Children would burst out of the room sending each other flying when the door hit them. It might even knock them downstairs, since the room was quite close to the top of the staircase. Whatever Humphrey had been thinking, it was wrong. But she didn't want to listen to her fiancé telling him so.

She had only been downstairs for a minute when someone knocked on the front door. For a moment, she wasn't sure what the sound was. Then she found herself weirdly wishing they had a dog, which could warn them of impending visitors. 'I'm a very peculiar person today,' she muttered to Robin. 'Had you noticed?'

Four men stood quietly outside, only one of whom she recognised. 'Sorry about this,' said Fabian Crick. 'This

172

is Uncle Ambrose, and these are my cousins Keith and Petrock. They're Uncle Richmond's sons.'

'So all we need now is him to show up and we'll have the complete set,' said Simmy. She was cross, curious, suspicious and bewildered all at the same time. 'Christopher!' she shouted, much too loudly. 'Can you come down here?'

In her arms, Robin started to scream, even more loudly than his mother's shout.

There was nowhere for so many people to sit. Uncle Ambrose was as small as Fabian, and they perched together on the two-seater wooden settle that Christopher had got from the auction house. Keith and Petrock found chairs in the kitchen and carried them through to the main room. Simmy and Robin bagged the only armchair and Christopher had to make do with the bottom step of the staircase. Robin nuzzled and whimpered, wanting a feed. Even Angie, thought Simmy, might baulk at baring her breast in front of a roomful of strange men.

'We won't stay long,' said Fabian in a maddeningly Uriah Heep-ish tone of voice. 'We just thought you might want to meet everyone.'

'I can't imagine why,' said Christopher, who was showing signs of wishing Simmy had slammed the door in all these faces. 'This is an invasion.'

Humphrey came sliding down the stairs as unobtrusively as he could, stepping over Christopher, and bobbing his head vaguely at the assembled crowd. He was clearly chastened and thoroughly out of his depth. 'See you tomorrow,' he mumbled, and fled.

Fabian twitched and stammered out his explanation. 'No, but – the thing is, we all knew Josephine, and we'll all be attending her funeral, when it happens, and we all want to help find who did such a terrible thing.'

'And you're probably all of interest to the police,' said Simmy. 'Except perhaps Ambrose.' The old man was evidently far too frail to thrust a knife into anybody. He looked confused and daunted by the way events were swirling around him. 'Why have they brought you with them anyway?' Simmy demanded of him directly.

'They wanted me to tell you what I know about Richmond and Hilda. Isn't that right?' he appealed, not to Fabian, but to the cousin named Petrock, who was by far the biggest member of the family and looked as if he was probably the most intelligent. He nodded.

'We know where Richmond is, and how he was keen on Josephine,' said Christopher. 'Fabian asked me to act as a go-between, but now I can see that was a ploy to keep me involved. You could easily go and talk to him yourselves if you felt like it. I honestly feel there's no more to be gained by talking to any of you. Simmy and I are more than happy to leave the whole business in the hands of the police.' He made a swishing motion, as if wanting to sweep the whole family out of the house.

But Simmy felt entirely otherwise. Of all her initial emotions, she found curiosity rising to the top. Inconvenient and outrageous as this visitation might be, she did want to know more. At first glance, she found old Ambrose to be an appealing character, and the silent Keith seemed to have something about him she thought might be worth discovering. And Petrock was almost charismatic, drawing deferential glances from all sides. Both Fabian's cousins looked to be at least twenty years junior to him, which hardly fitted with Implications that they all grew up together. 'You'll have to put up with me feeding the baby,' she announced, as Robin's demands grew more insistent. It was five o'clock, she realised – far too many hours since the last feed. 'I'm not going out of this room to do it.' She ignored Christopher's obvious opinion that this made an ideal excuse to eject all the visitors immediately.

She had also underestimated the Armitages. Not one of them even blushed. Keith, who was wearing a suit and tie as if he'd just come from an office somewhere, was the only one who shifted his seat slightly and made a show of looking away.

'Get on with it then,' Christopher urged Fabian. He looked to be on the verge of ordering all these men out of his house but did not quite have the balls for it. 'It's been a long day and we've got things to do.'

'Aunt Hilda,' said Fabian. 'Petrock wants to tell you about her.'

Again, everyone looked at the large cousin . . . nephew . . . brother. Simmy was suddenly reminded of Ben's text, sent hours ago and undoubtedly waiting eagerly for a proper response in the form of a phone call. She was gripped by an agreeable sense of things coming together, at the same time as reproaching herself for forgetting poor Ben.

'I'm writing her biography,' said Petrock in a tone that

implied he wanted awe and admiration at such a feat. 'She was a remarkable woman in every way and deserves to have her achievements recorded.'

Nobody responded to this, but simply waited for more.

'Her early life in the thirties was typically middle class. Big house, plenty of cash, servants and dogs – all that. She was eleven when war broke out and everything changed.' He leant down and picked up a briefcase that was propped against his leg. 'I've got the manuscript here, actually.' He proffered a thick wad of printed pages. 'I could read a bit, if you like.'

Nobody responded, but he rested his work on his knees, as if waiting for his chance. Christopher spoke first. 'Fabian told us all about everything going up in flames,' he said. 'Tragic.'

'You speak as an auctioneer of antiques,' said Petrock understandingly. His accent had a hint of American or Canadian, which only enhanced his appeal for Simmy. Something oddly formal in his delivery also piqued her interest. She would not at all object to a short reading from his opus. He went on speaking. 'The first chapters go back over earlier family history, to give a proper context,' he explained. 'It wasn't only the material possessions that were lost. Her father – our grandfather – became very mentally unstable. Bipolar, in all probability. His mother was German, you see. Throughout the First World War she was ostracised and tormented, but clung on and prospered in the following years. But it left scars that bled down the generations, so when another war broke out, it was a personal catastrophe for our family.'

'Did you know her? Your German great-grandmother?' Simmy asked, keen to get as much of the picture as she could. On the stairs, she heard her fiancé sigh.

'No, no. She died before I was born. But of course Hilda and her brothers did,' He waved at Ambrose.

'And her sister,' said Fabian stiffly. 'You always leave my mother out.'

'Sorry, Fabe. You have to admit she is a bit shadowy.'

'Stick to the point,' said Keith.

'Right. Yes. Except there isn't precisely a *point*, is there? I just want these good people to understand that our intentions are honourable, and that it's little more than coincidence that they've become involved in our story. It's a chain of connection, so to speak, from Josephine to them, with us Armitages in the middle.'

'There is a point,' Keith argued. 'Explain about what Josephine was saying.'

'Oh, that.' Petrock turned his chiselled features towards Simmy. 'I believe Keith means me to tell you that my aunt left all her papers to Josephine, along with the house. Thousands of old letters, notebooks, one or two diaries, along with financial statements, theatre programmes. It's mainly the letters, though.'

'Filing cabinets!' said Simmy suddenly.

Petrock blinked. 'Well, yes. Four of them, to be exact. We helped her move them to her house. You wouldn't believe how heavy they were.'

'She died beside them,' said Simmy, enjoying the sense of a picture coming together, despite the horror of a violent attack on an innocent woman.

Again, nobody spoke for too many seconds. Robin made a particularly embarrassing slurp, which drew at least two pairs of eyes to her breast.

'Did she?' said Keith.

'Is it possible she was trying to protect something in them?' Christopher asked. 'Was there anything of actual value inside?'

'Apparently not,' said Petrock with a sigh.

Simmy was visualising the pattern as more of a circle than a chain. One of Ben's flowcharts would probably give it a different shape again, with side-shoots and satellites and big question marks. 'Well there's certainly no sign of a point yet,' she said, easing Robin off the nipple and switching him to the other side, without any conscious thought. It was no more of a process than kicking off shoes would have been or rubbing an itch. Her lack of self-consciousness made it all the easier for the men to accommodate it. But she was faintly aware that it put her in competition with Petrock as the focal point in the room. As the only female, she knew she possessed a definite power.

'If there *is* a point, then it's the family papers,' said Keith. 'All those letters from after the war. Even Petrock doesn't know what's in most of them.'

Petrock shook his head. 'I've seen the ones that matter. I've quoted them in the book.' This appeared to be his cue, and with no further invitation, he flicked through until somewhere close to halfway through the typescript. 'Here – listen to this.' Taking a breath, he began to read. '"Hilda's thirty-fifth birthday was spent on the golden sands of the historic island of Santorini. She was accompanied by

178

three friends, all of whom shared her passion for sunshine and good food. Indeed, the hotel invoice still exists, which makes it plain that regular cocktails were consumed prior to three-course dinners, frequently involving shellfish and other expensive fare. That same month she enrolled on an art appreciation course in Hampstead, but only attended three lectures before dropping out. It was believed in the family that this was due to one of the class drawing attention to her identity as the main individual in a recent – and wholly spurious – story in the media concerning her past. Hilda felt bitterly towards this treacherous classmate for many years afterwards."' He stopped, looking round brightly, as if at a class of eager pupils. 'You see how rich a life she led. And almost every week has some sort of written record. It's taken me two years so far, and it's far from complete.'

'Phew!' said Simmy. 'Two years sounds like very good going. Do you have to juggle it with a job as well?'

'Indeed I do. Luckily, I find I can work on the train. I have a fifty-minute commute twice a day.'

'Wouldn't you say he's rather too free with his adjectives?' said Uncle Ambrose in a mild tone.

'I didn't notice,' said Simmy diplomatically. 'I was too involved in the story.'

'He'll never find a publisher for it,' said Keith. 'Can't see why he's bothering, personally. Fabian thinks the same.'

'Well, if that's all,' said Christopher, standing up, suddenly looking much more forceful. 'We really have quite a lot to do.'

'We haven't talked about Richmond,' bleated Fabian. 'I thought that's what we came for.'

'Whatever gave you that idea?' asked Keith, who seemed to be speaking for everyone, while revealing little of himself.

'Oh, we know plenty about him already,' said Simmy, feeling reckless. 'I gather he wanted to marry Josephine?'

The effect was gratifying. Fabian twitched feverishly, Keith took a long deep breath and Petrock put a dramatic hand to his chest. 'Who told you that?' he demanded.

'Why? It's not a secret, is it?'

'It's old news, anyway,' said Keith. 'He'd given up years ago.'

'It would be interesting to meet him, all the same,' said Simmy, still enjoying a sense of mischief.

'We've lost sight of Hilda again,' said Fabia, with shameless inconsistency. He looked round at all the faces. 'The simple fact is that Petrock needed Josephine's help with his book. She knew how to find archive stuff on the Internet and kept proper notes for him.'

'And me,' piped up the aged Ambrose. 'I understand archives as well, don't forget. Better than anyone, including the wretched Miss Trubshaw. Not that anyone ever asked for my help,' he added bitterly.

'It wasn't a matter of archives,' said Petrock. 'We only wanted to get back to the sixties and seventies – not the Dark Ages.'

'So – who killed her then?' asked Christopher loudly and suddenly. 'Isn't that why you're here – to persuade us that it was none of you lot? Or are you oh-so-subtly trying to point the finger at the absent Richmond? Is that what all this is about?'

Nobody said anything, until Robin detached himself from his mother and emitted one of his prodigious belches.

Chapter Thirteen

It was a shameful seven o'clock before Simmy managed to find time for a proper conversation with Ben. He had texted again by then, clearly losing patience. A whole day had passed without any communication between them, and for him, in the middle of an absorbing murder, this was intolerable.

'Where've you been?' he began, like any controlling husband.

'Where do you think?' she flashed back, irrationally and unfairly.

'Sorry. But seriously – you haven't just been at home all day washing nappies, have you? You told me you'd gone to Keswick.'

'Nobody washes nappies any more. At least, I don't. We did go to Keswick, as it happens and had lunch with Oliver, and saw one or two people who work at the auction house, and when we got home we had a deputation led by Fabian to try to persuade us that none of them killed Josephine.'

There was a short silence, then, 'Right. Okay. I see. Busy day.'

'Yes.'

'So – did any of them kill Josephine?'

'Hard to say. Right at the end, Fabian said, "Well, we can't vouch for Uncle Richmond, of course, but it does seem extremely unlikely that he could be the one." He was trying to sound all casual and offhand as he said it, but it was very obvious that they wish we'd find a way to meet him.'

'So who came? Go back to the beginning.'

She did her best to identify and describe the four men who had barged into her unfinished home. She found herself remembering disappointingly few significant details. 'Petrock's by far the most substantial one. He's writing a book about Hilda. He even read us a bit from it. I didn't think it was bad, but Chris says it's a mess. Keith was the quietest, didn't seem at all sure why he was there in the first place. And Uncle Ambrose is sweet. A right old pet. He's an archivist and says Petrock uses too many adjectives. You'd like him.'

'This isn't useful,' Ben told her sternly. 'I need to see you really to put a better picture together. And what happened in Keswick? Don't forget that's where the murder actually happened. It could easily be the most important area to investigate.'

'It all connects,' she said urgently. 'Uncle Richmond wanted to marry Josephine. If we take Fabian and his cousins at face value, they might well have been trying to tell us they thought it was him, but didn't dare say so outright. They said they came to persuade us that it wasn't any of them, and that they thought Aunt Hilda was the main person to focus on.'

'Where do the police come in? Had they all been interviewed? Where is there the slightest morsel of evidence?'

'I don't know. Not one of them even mentioned the police. That's odd, isn't it?'

'They sound worried. Do they know about me and Bonnie and all the other murders we've been connected with? Do they know about you and Detective Moxon? Was the whole business just one big smokescreen? What did Christopher think?'

Christopher was at that moment giving Robin his bedtime bath, expecting Simmy to join them for the final stages, which went much more easily with a second pair of hands. 'He's a lot more *engaged* than usual,' Simmy said in a low voice. 'It's probably because he knew Josephine and cares about what happened to her. But he's also feeling guilty about that promise he made to Fabian, the idiot. The man has some hold over him that seems unreasonable to me.'

'Might there be more to it than he's told you?'

'It's possible, but I don't think so. If there is, he's forgotten what it is. Fabian's incapable of saying anything directly, which doesn't help. He comes at everything sideways and changes the subject until you don't know what he's talking about. I'm not sure he's quite right in the head.'

'Which we're doing now,' said Ben. 'We're missing a whole lot out. We've been here before, charging along without any idea of where the police investigation has got to. Isn't that where Chris could be useful? What happened yesterday when he was interviewed?'

Simmy hesitated, trying to think. 'Just the obvious questions. He gave them Fabian's name, as someone who knew Josephine, as well as the rest of the family.'

'*Did* he? Would that be a normal thing to do? Why would the police ask *him* to list all her acquaintances? That should be Oliver or the people next door, surely?'

'He probably thought it would be helpful to make them realise that she'd grown up locally and knew a lot of people from the distant past. He was probably thinking that's the sort of thing you'd approve of.'

'Me? Why would he care what I thought?'

'Or perhaps it was just that Fabian's sudden appearance coincided so totally with the murder, that it would feel wrong not to say something. That's probably it. I mean – it *was* odd, the way it happened. And then, at the same time, we could give Fabian a pretty good alibi for Sunday night.'

'And there lies the crux of it,' said Ben heavily. 'You might well have been set up for that very reason. Which Christopher might have figured out and concluded that he ought to name Fabian, as a sort of self-protection. Anyway,' he burst out, 'why can't you just go and *ask* him? Get all this cleared up, before we go any further.'

'We've got to put the baby to bed first. Look – can you get here tomorrow? We can talk it all through then.'

'Not easily. You need to come here. Again. There's a whole lot I have to show you about Hilda. She really was quite a woman. The papers were full of her at one time.'

'You definitely won't be going back to Newcastle this week, then?'

Ben groaned. 'Don't let's get into that. It's all a real mess just now. We can't guarantee that I'll be here beyond this weekend. As things stand, I'm in disgrace with just about everybody.'

'So a nice complicated murder is just what you need to distract you.'

'Precisely,' he said.

They left it that Simmy would drive down to Bowness at some point the next day. 'Make it early, if you can,' he urged. 'There's a lot we need to catch up with.'

After Robin had been left snugly in his cot, Christopher and Simmy slumped together on their small sofa and reviewed the day.

'We need to get the marriage licence and book the registrar,' he said. 'Do we know how to do that?'

She understood that he was conceding superior knowledge to her, since his own first marriage had been conducted on an island in the Caribbean. 'I can't remember,' she admitted. 'It was so long ago. It might be different now.'

'I went to a wedding last year. It was in a register office. As far as I could tell, the couple pretty much wrote the whole thing themselves. It was all over in about three minutes, and the word "contract" seemed to feature prominently. I thought it was a bit soulless.'

'I'd be happy with the classic wording. Although I suppose I might feel a bit of a hypocrite, making the same vows that I didn't stick to the first time.'

'Which ones did you break?' he asked her, with a teasing smile.

'"As long as you both shall live", I suppose. We were meant to stick at it for our whole lives.'

'Maybe it's knowing that so few people can manage it that makes them loosen up on the wording, then. But for myself I can honestly promise you the full list – if I can remember it all. I'm more than happy with "forsaking all others".What else is there?'

'"To have and to hold" is nice.'

'You and Tony got married in church!' he realised. 'Why did that never occur to me?'

'You should have been there. My oldest friend, and all that. Your parents didn't come either, although we did invite them. Frances wasn't very well, if I remember rightly.'

'And I was off in Costa Rica or somewhere. I don't remember even being told you were getting married.'

'And then you got a wife of your own, not much later.'

'I was twenty-six and she was twenty. We were like two silly children.'

'I was twenty-five, which felt quite old at the time. We did well to last as long as we did, I suppose. We just made it to ten years.'

'We split up the week after our second anniversary. I have no idea where she is now.'

'You are properly divorced, I hope? What if she shows up when they do that bit about anybody knowing good cause, or whatever it is?'

'No worries. She married someone else about eight years ago now. I'm sure they're very happy. Second time around works pretty well, as far as I can see.'

'The triumph of hope over experience,' said Simmy with

a little shiver. 'And I can think of quite a few which were just as hopeless as the first time.'

'Nonsense! We should look online and find out what the procedure is. June 1st is definite, right? I'll email my relations and let them all know. Get the show on the road. Which pub are we going to afterwards?'

'Where's the register office?'

'Um – good question. Penrith I guess, or Carlisle.' He fished his phone from his pocket and began a search. 'There's one at Kendal. Maximum ten people. Looks quite sweet.' He showed her the pictures. 'Handy for Angie and Russell.'

'But quite a way for your people. Ten isn't many. Does that include you and me and the registrar?'

'Doesn't say. Presumably not. How many do we want? Angie and Russell, Hannah, Lynne, Bonnie, and my brothers. That's seven – nine if the wives insist on coming. I'll have to choose who'll be the best man and make the silly speech afterwards.'

'You forgot Ben. And Helen. I invited them both already.'

'I thought maybe they'd be okay with stepping aside. The whole family can come to the party afterwards.'

'He probably will settle for that. Thanks for including Bonnie at least. She'd be the only non-relative.'

'Bridesmaid. You have to have one to hold your bouquet or something.'

'It sounds lovely,' she said, suddenly flushing with excitement. 'Cosy, informal. And then a big party at a pub somewhere.'

'You know what people will say, don't you? They'll try and persuade us to do the whole thing in a posh hotel. Storrs or the Belsfield, probably. Make a twenty-four-hour event of it.'

'Luckily for us there's nowhere near enough time to organise anything like that. And I think hotel weddings are horrible. Ever since . . .' she tailed off.

'Ever since that poor boy died at the wedding at Storrs. Yes, I remember. I think they're fairly grim, as well. I'm just warning you about my sisters and what they'll say.'

'I'll set my mother onto them. She'll soon put them straight. She's going to think we've got the perfect plan if we do it like this. Quick little ceremony in Kendal, then up the road to Windermere or maybe Troutbeck. Oh – we didn't count Robin!' She giggled. 'He brings it up to ten.'

'I don't think that's likely to be a problem.'

'Except he'll probably bawl through the whole thing. And I'll have to feed him while promising to love you for ever, or whatever we decide to say.'

'I hope you'll love me for ever, whatever you promise,' he said, with an unusual sentimentality. 'I really do like the idea of being married to you, Persimmon Straw . . . Brown . . . whichever. It makes me go all squishy inside to think of it.'

'So that's all right then,' she said comfortably.

Robin woke them at one-fifteen and again at four forty-five. 'Short night,' said Christopher, aiming at a philosophical tone. 'Is this still the growth spurt?'

'Probably. I can take him to be weighed on Friday, and

woe betide him if he hasn't gained at least four ounces.'

'Friday's tomorrow now,' said Christopher pedantically. 'Another week almost gone.'

Simmy ignored this remark and concentrated on her baby. She could feel the weight of the entire western culture screaming at her that her milk must be drying up, that the solution quite obviously lay in a full bottle of formula and it was little short of perversity to insist on exclusive use of the breast. She had been almost completely unaware of this doctrine until her second encounter with a health visitor. The woman had pursed her lips, smiled insincerely and said that of course breast was best. Except when . . . and proceeded to list numerous instances where salvation lay in a bottle. Simmy did not possess a bottle and had no intention of getting one. She knew that it would represent a malign temptation, not very different from how a litre of Jack Daniel's would to a recovering alcoholic. It was all her mother's doing of course. Angie had conceived a burning passion for breastfeeding forty years before and clung to it ever since. And nobody would lightly flout Angie Straw's edicts.

Fortunately, Robin was on her side. When she changed his nappy, the old one was heavy with wee. There was obviously plenty of fluid going through his system. Anyone could have a wakeful night without causing panic. 'He'll probably sleep all morning now,' she murmured, suspecting that Christopher had gone back to sleep.

Nobody stirred again until eight, when Christopher emerged from sleep in a panic, remembering that he was going back to work that day. Simmy never got her morning tea, and breakfast dwindled to a slightly overdone slice of toast. 'I need to eat more than this,' she complained.

'You can get yourself a bowl of cereal, can't you?' was the unsympathetic answer. 'You're not an invalid.'

He was right, of course. 'We're running low on bread,' he went on. 'And a few other things.'

'I could do a supermarket order and get them to deliver,' she said doubtfully. Neither of them really liked this means of provisioning themselves. It made more traffic on the winding lanes and removed any interest or pleasure from the shopping process. 'Or maybe I should pop down to the shop in Troutbeck. They've got the basics, at least.'

'Blasphemy,' he quipped. 'How dare you consider anything other than St Tesco or Sainsbury?'

'I want to go there anyway,' she said. 'I thought the Mortal Man would be nice for our post-wedding bun fight. Troutbeck's fairly easy to get to, and I do have sentimental feelings about it.'

'It would be perfect,' he said slowly, savouring the suggestion. 'That's a brilliant idea.'

After he had gone, she indulged in twenty minutes of mindless domestic ease, the baby asleep, birds singing outside, no builders yet arrived and no really crucial need to be anywhere.

And then she remembered Ben, and the lack of bread, and the pressing urgency of the wedding plans, and Robin's abandonment of a perfectly fine routine, and went upstairs to get herself dressed.

* * *

190

At ten she phoned Ben and said she could probably be with him by eleven, with luck – rather later than they had agreed the evening before. 'Sorry about that,' she said. 'Today's a bit disorganised, and everything's later than it should be. But I can't come tomorrow because it's the baby clinic.'

'Does that take all day?' he asked as if that really might be a possibility.

'No, but it's going to be traumatic for both of us. We won't want to do anything else.'

'Well, there does seem to be a lot to discuss,' he said diffidently. 'That's if you want to stay involved. I mean – you could just drop the whole thing, I guess.'

'I don't think I could. Fabian Crick isn't a person you can just drop. He's sort of sticky – like chewing gum on your shoe, if that isn't outrageously rude. It's all far too close to us to be avoided. And I did like Uncle Ambrose,' she added inconsequentially.

'Good. Well, Bonnie's going to miss the fun again. Although she and I went over everything last night. She had some good ideas.'

'She always does,' said Simmy warmly.

'So I'll see you about eleven, then?' He paused. 'Why is the baby clinic traumatic?'

'Don't worry about it. I couldn't possibly explain. It'll be our first one, so I really don't know what'll happen. Just fear of the unknown, I expect.' But she knew there would be talk of vaccinations and contraception and sleeping arrangements and the ever-daunting business of the infant's weight. None of it appealed to her in the slightest.

'Is it compulsory?' Ben wondered.

'Probably,' she said miserably.

Robin was sleepily unco-operative when she tried to give him a feed before setting out for Bowness. Then, when she strapped him into his car seat, he woke up and complained vociferously. 'Stop it,' she told him. 'You had your chance.' An automatic calculation told her he had taken almost no sustenance for over five hours. 'Just let's get to Ben's, okay? Shouldn't be long.'

It was twenty-five minutes in total, the baby screaming the entire way. There was a bottleneck on the road into Windermere for no obvious reason, and again on the final stretch before turning into Helm Road where the Harknesses lived. Even two minutes in a stationary car with a howling baby was a whole new kind of torture, Simmy discovered.

The only parking space she could find was a hundred yards further down the road. Without bothering to release the seat, she unbuckled the baby and cantered up to Ben's front door with Robin under her arm. 'Sorry,' she panted, when Ben appeared. 'I'll have to feed him before anything else.'

'No problem,' he said calmly. 'I can see I'll soon be getting used to this.'

Robin quickly redeemed himself, feeding composedly while Simmy tried to relax. 'It's a complete tyranny,' she said, 'I never properly realised that before. He has all the power. If I dared to try to cross him, I'd definitely get the worst of it.'

'Survival,' nodded Ben. 'Stands to reason when you think about it.'

'Well, it's quite a shock to the system, I can tell you.' She exhaled exaggeratedly. 'So let's get down to business.'

'Yes, let's. Just look what I found!' He laid out a page of notes and another covered with one of his typical diagrams. 'Aunt Hilda was quite a girl.'

Simmy made no attempt to decipher the handwriting. 'Just tell me,' she ordered.

'Okay. Well, in 1962, when she was in her thirties, she made a paternity claim against the son of a very famous man. A member of a political dynasty, if you like. Her story was that over a decade earlier, when she was only twenty she had given birth to a child that was fathered by this person during an important conference at Chequers. You know what Chequers is, don't you?'

'I do,' she said. 'Of course. What was she doing there?'

'Working as a secretary. Anyway, the whole thing seems to have been politically motivated, trying to wreck careers and so forth.'

'What happened to the baby? Who was the man? Stop being so mysterious.'

'Don't know for sure, but the strong hint is that it was most likely Randolph Churchill. He was quite a womaniser and was out of parliament because he lost his seat in 1945. I could go on. I read up on him – he was handsome and keen on drink, and constantly in trouble.'

'Was he married?'

'He was between wives. He married for the second time at the end of that year, but it sounds as if he was perfectly capable of seducing a secretary and fathering her child in the meantime.'

Simmy didn't know what to make of this discovery. 'Petrock mentioned some newspaper scandal,' she remembered. 'He said it was spurious.'

'So it might well have been. But all that came ages later, in the 1960s. The odd thing is that Hilda deliberately set it going. She went to the papers and claimed to want the whole thing exposed to view.'

'Did she want money? What happened to the *child*?' Simmy burst out.

'You already asked me that. I couldn't find any answer. Adopted, presumably.'

'But how much of a scandal would that really have been?' Simmy wondered.

'You need to understand how hypocritical they were in those days. Being born out of wedlock was a hugely shameful thing. People didn't tell their kids they were adopted. The chances of the man who brought you up being your biological father were surprisingly small. I mean – not *small*, but probably only about seventy per cent. Before DNA, there was much less chance of being found out. All I could discover was a potential scandal that was quickly hushed up, with no harm done. Hilda said there were letters that could prove her story, but they were never produced. And they wouldn't have been hard proof anyway.'

'So she definitely didn't keep the baby? If there was one? Are we sure about that?'

'No, not entirely, although the papers reported the story as if there certainly was a child. They insisted she had it fostered out, but nobody knew where. The investigative journalists tried to track down any adoption records but came up with nothing. Only one – at the *Daily Herald* – kept trying to get to the bottom of the story. They were the Labour Party's mouthpiece, essentially, and the man Hilda was trying to damage was a Tory. Hilda had gone to them originally. But she wouldn't provide any real evidence and, in the end, it looks as if they concluded she was inventing the whole thing.'

'So what do we know for certain?'

'Almost nothing. Reading between the lines, I think there must have been a real child. My hunch is that the famous politician paid her off – because she was suddenly in a position to buy a decent house and set herself up in business. It's very unclear where the money for that came from.'

'You told me about that on Tuesday,' she nodded. 'Supplying good quality food to airlines.'

'No – that was much later. Through the sixties and much of the seventies, she was in the hotel business. Not running them, exactly, but offering a sort of time and motion service. Efficiencies of scale, innovations in the kitchens, promotions and publicity. She put herself about as a consultant, and apparently offered them a payment system dependent on results. Clever stuff. I found a little website all about it. She really was a pioneer.'

'Sounds as if there's plenty of material for Petrock's book. She must have been an absolute dynamo.'

'What we really need is some sort of link to Josephine Trubshaw, if we're thinking this is all relevant to her murder.'

'And you haven't found one?'

'Only the vaguest hints. Hilda liked collecting things and so did Josephine. These people all knew each other, and most of them are related. The timing seems too close to be coincidental – Fabian showing up the day before the murder. What's his agenda, anyway? What does he really *want*?'

'He said yesterday that they all want justice for Josephine, because she was a good friend and they are appalled that someone would kill her.'

'But no sign of Uncle Richmond?'

'No. Did I tell you that Oliver told us that Richmond wanted to marry Josephine? For a minute that seemed to explain the whole story. He'd gone mad with frustration and rage at being rejected, and gone round to her house and stabbed her.'

'If that's what killed her. We still don't know for sure.'

'I think it must have been. Oliver said there was a lot of blood.'

Ben shrugged. 'Doesn't really matter. Tell me more about Richmond.'

'They said he'd accepted that Josephine was never going to marry him, years ago, and it was very old news.'

'Who said that?'

'Fabian and his cousins. They're Richmond's sons.'

'Yes, I've got all that. What did they tell you that was new?' He tore the diagram page off his notepad and started a fresh sheet.

Simmy complied as best she could but couldn't dredge up any helpful details. 'It was a real invasion – outrageous when you think about it, turning up in force like that. But Uncle Ambrose was sweet,' she added with a smile.

'Yes, you said. He's probably the killer, then.'

'No, he's far too insubstantial. I really can't think why they dragged him along.'

'Did he appear to go willingly?'

'Oh yes, I suppose so. He was Hilda's brother, after all. She was a lot older than her siblings, wasn't she? Did you get all their dates of birth when you were doing your googling or whatever it was?'

'Oh yes. They're very widely spaced. Ambrose comes next after her. He's mid eighties. Then I think Richmond is a good ten years younger again. And Fabian's mother fits in between somewhere. I can't find where I wrote it all down now. Is it important?'

'Probably not. Did they all have the same parents?'

'I don't know.' Ben shook his head irritably, and Robin chose that moment to emit a plaintive cry, as if something had severely disappointed him. Simmy peered into his face and asked him what the problem was. Ben waited patiently. 'He's been very peculiar the last day or so,' Simmy said.

'Ask my mum for advice. She knows all there is to know about babies.'

Simmy's instant reaction was to resist asking anyone for help, including Ben's mother. Helen Harkness had admittedly produced five healthy babies, while maintaining her place in the competitive world of architecture. Simmy had unconsciously assumed that she'd had nannies and home helps and done a minimal amount of the dirty work herself. Although she had shown gratifying enthusiasm for Robin on Tuesday, she had not made any of the usual enquiries that one mother made to another. Sleepless nights, nappy rash, sore nipples. It was as if none of that side of baby care was relevant.

'We need to know why now,' said Ben, taking up the thread again, in a new place. 'That's always relevant. Why did Fabian show up when he did? The obvious answer has to be Hilda's death. And something about Josephine inheriting the house. Houses are always relevant, aren't they?'

'We thought the one in Grasmere was,' Simmy agreed. 'Old ladies and houses obviously go together.'

'This one's a lot more than just a house though. Family. History. Money. All good motives for murder.'

'We don't seem to be getting anywhere,' Simmy complained. 'At first I was blaming Christopher for making that promise ten years ago, but since Josephine was killed, that doesn't seem so relevant. We'd have been involved anyway.'

'Would you, though? You'd have the excuse of the baby, and you hardly knew the woman. It was only because of Fabian that you felt a connection. It's quite flimsy, when you think about it.'

'I should never have gone to Keswick yesterday. That made it worse – I mean, that pulled me in even further. I got to know some of the auction people and can see how they're all knocked sideways. Oliver's trying to keep calm about it, but it's sure to have interrupted his retirement plans.'

'Is it? How?'

'Well – I suppose he thinks he'll have to train up her

replacement and be there more than he really wants. He was there yesterday when I got the impression he wouldn't have been normally.'

'He'll be worried about their reputation,' said Ben, tapping his teeth with his pen. 'Although a bit of scandal's often good for business.'

'It's a murder, not a scandal. Not like the thing with Hilda and her baby.'

'I'm not sure they're so different.' He tapped faster. 'There *is* a connection somewhere, I know there is.'

'It's such a long time ago, Ben. How can a baby born seventy-odd years ago have anything to do with Josephine being killed? It would make a lot more sense if *Hilda* had been the victim, but she just died of old age.'

'Did she? Are we sure?'

'Come on! Don't start that. From what Fabian says, nobody's benefited from Josephine's death. If anything, it's caused extra trouble for them all.'

'Can we go and look at Hilda's house? We can assume there's nobody living in it. Don't ask me what we'd be looking for, but it can't hurt to see it.' He tapped his screen and came up with an address in seconds. Then he tapped again and got Google Earth to show the handsome building overlooking Ullswater. 'Very nice,' he sighed. 'Very nice indeed. That's got to be causing untold ructions, if they can't decide who gets it now. There could be a clause somewhere that says it reverts to the Armitages in the event of Josephine's death.'

Simmy gave him a look. 'Really? That sounds highly unlikely to me. And wouldn't it incriminate them totally when Josie was murdered?'

Robin had fallen asleep, milky dribble running down his chin, his head flopped back. There was a new rash of pink spots across his nose, which Simmy told herself was entirely normal. Some gobbledygook about the bloodstream flushing out unwanted substances floated around her head. The mysteries of neonatal biochemistry were well beyond her knowledge or interest. Half of it sounded too unlikely to take seriously, anyway.

'We need to go and look at it,' Ben remarked carelessly. 'We could go now, I suppose.'

'No, Ben. I want to go to Beck View for lunch and pop in to have a chat with Bonnie.'

'You did all that two days ago.' His tone was too close to a whine to be taken seriously. 'We're stuck until we make something happen somehow. The police are going to be miles ahead of us at this rate.'

'I didn't know it was a competition,' she said. 'We ought to be pleased if that happens.'

'Oh, well – I don't actually expect it will. Have they even interviewed all those Armitages yet?'

'I assume that happened yesterday – Fabian, anyway. Why would they want to question Uncle Ambrose? Nobody's said anything about him knowing Josephine.'

'Ah – but do they know about Uncle Richmond and Josephine? Who apart from Christopher would have told them the man even exists? Which way are they taking the investigation, I wonder?'

'Good question.'

'Where's Helen?' Simmy asked suddenly. The silence in

200

the house made her think they were the only two in it. 'Is she out?'

'What? Oh, yeah. She had to go to Kendal or somewhere to look at an RSJ. Whether it's big enough to hold up a whole second storey or something. Happens all the time. I keep telling her they could send a picture on Skype and she needn't go out. It hurts her knee to drive now.' He grimaced, having finally come to understand how Helen's incapacity would affect the whole family. 'She's going to be in and out of hospital for years at this rate.'

'No, she won't. People are running around in no time, after these operations. It's miraculous.'

'Sometimes it is, and sometimes it goes wrong,' he said darkly.

'Well, I can't stay much longer. I suppose I should volunteer to drive up to Aunt Hilda's house when I go home, and just get an idea of what might be happening. Though I doubt it would be any use, and I don't actually want to. Even if I took you with me up there, we're not likely to find anything just by looking at it, are we?' She nibbled her lip and then grinned. 'I would like to know which one it is, though. Can you explain it to me exactly? It wasn't clear on the computer screen how far along the lakeside it is.'

He sighed and pulled an Ordnance Survey map off a shelf and opened it up. 'This must be it, look.' He put his finger on a tiny outlined rectangle. 'Opposite that pathway that goes down to the lake. As we saw on Google.' His exaggerated patience made it very clear that he thought she should have worked that out for herself. 'It's big enough to get its own place on the map. Much too big for one old lady to live in by herself.'

'We don't know that she did – do we?'

Ben blinked at her. 'But . . . surely? Fabian would have said if there was somebody still living there.'

'You'd think so, yes. But he's not a reliable informant. I really do think there's something wrong with him. Much of what he says is either hot air or hard to believe.'

'Unless that's all part of the act,' said Ben.

Nothing more was deemed relevant after that, and Simmy bundled up her infant ready to be carried back to the car. She had brought no equipment with her to the house. No nappies or wet wipes or plastic bags. All her life she had listened to her mother condemning the way women with babies took vast quantities of paraphernalia everywhere they went, as if one small child was a whole army of helpless creatures. 'I only ever took a spare nappy and some water,' Angie would boast repeatedly. Simmy had unthinkingly absorbed this doctrine and was automatically living by its tenets. So far, it had worked well enough. And she really did hate the infuriating all-purpose seat that the child was supposed to spend most of his day in.

'What about going to Ullswater now?' Ben persisted. 'I really do think it might help.'

'Do we have to? It's at least three miles past Hartsop, and there's never anywhere to park on that stretch. I know I'm being a wimp, but I don't want to do more driving than I have to. Robin doesn't like it.'

'I thought all babies loved cars. Aren't you meant to

drive them round to get them to sleep?'

'Not in this case. Maybe when he's a bit older.'

'And you've got the clinic tomorrow,' he remembered.

'So I have. Thanks for reminding me.' The sarcasm was muted, because she really had forgotten all about it. 'That makes it even more impossible for you to get to see the house, unless we go now.'

'If we did that, you'd have to bring me all the way home again, which I agree is too much to ask. I could probably get myself there on the bike, today or tomorrow.'

Simmy understood without asking that to cycle from Bowness to Hartsop, over the Kirkstone Pass, was not a trip to be undertaken lightly. 'Listen,' she said. 'If you can get as far as Troutbeck tomorrow morning, I'll collect you from there. It'll have to be before the clinic.' Ten minutes in the car was not a lot to ask, she conceded.

Ben gave it some thought. 'Maybe it's a daft idea anyway. I can't actually see how the house would fit the story, at least as far as we've got with it. But I like looking at houses. Must be my mother's influence.'

'We should have gone up there on Saturday with my father. I could have inspected the house then, if I'd known about it.'

'Can't be helped.' There was resignation in his tone as well as his words. 'We're stuck, let's face it. You might well have overlooked something that Fabian or a cousin said, which would set things moving again, but I don't expect you to repeat every word. I have a feeling I've let that family get in the way of following up more on the victim. I hardly know anything about her, which is ridiculous. I can't even remember what she looks like – assuming I saw her at the auction house that time.' He and Simmy had gone to watch Christopher in action, some month ago.

'She was at the reception desk when we first arrived, I think. Plump, with frizzy fair hair. Fairly obviously in charge of everything.'

Ben shook his head. 'Nope – not ringing any bells. It's far too long ago now.'

'You're right that we still don't know very much about her. She doesn't seem to have *done* anything in her life. Just worked at the same place, learning all about antiques and computers, and adoring whichever man was in charge. First Oliver, then Christopher. All a bit immature, but harmless surely?'

'I think there has to be more to it than that. It raises a whole lot of possible issues. Office politics. Female rivalry. What if one of the pretty young workers there made a mockery of Josephine? Undercurrents of real hatred and spitefulness. You know what women are like,' he finished with a grin.

'Wouldn't that make Josie the killer, not the victim?'

'Could be that was the intention,' he said obscurely.

'Well, I think she was just a natural assistant – she'd have made some important politician a wonderful secretary. Clever, but self-effacing. Never speaking out of turn, but more than capable of keeping the lesser minions on their toes. She did keep a close eye on everything during an auction.'

'Bit of a stereotype, then,' said Ben absently.

'I'm afraid so. Except that she was linked to the Armitage

family, to the extent that one of them wanted to marry her and another one left her a very valuable house. Along with four filing cabinets full of papers. I did tell you about that, didn't I?'

Bun was spluttering. 'I think this is what they call *l'esprit d'escalier*,' he said. 'We are literally standing on the doorstep – admittedly not a staircase, but the meaning's the same.'

'What are you talking about?'

'What you just said – a vital detail that you almost forgot to mention. How can we find out what was in them? The filing cabinets, I mean.' He shook his head in a mixture of excitement and frustration.

'We can't,' Simmy said firmly. 'And we're not even going to try.'

Chapter Fourteen

Lunch at Beck View was brief to the point of rudeness. Angie was knee-deep in crumpled sheets and Russell had been given the task of replacing all the cloths on the dining-room tables. The dog was lurking in his basket by the Rayburn.

'There isn't any lunch *per se*,' said Russell. 'You can dig around for some cheese and there might be a tin of soup somewhere. We had a bit of trouble with a tricky family this morning. It's put us all at odds with the world and each other.'

'Bread? There's got to be bread,' said Simmy. 'I need nourishment. You said yourself that I'm eating for two.'

'Of course there's bread,' Angie shouted down from the top of the stairs. 'There's all sorts of stuff in the pantry. Help yourself. How's the baby?'

Simmy went out into the hallway, where she could at least see her mother. 'He's fine. Fast asleep. I really hate that seat thing, though. It's ridiculously heavy and awkward.'

'Not much choice about that, as I understand it.' Angie was breathless, her hair disarrayed and her cheeks flushed. 'Honestly, those people! They didn't go until after eleven, and all they did was complain. Said the road was too noisy and they couldn't sleep. I ask you! We hardly get any night-time traffic past here.'

'Where do they live? Somewhere deadly quiet, I suppose.'

'That's what's so silly. They're from Swindon, of all places. But apparently it's a cul-de-sac on a big estate and never gets passing traffic.'

Russell drifted out of the kitchen, holding a somnolent Robin against his chest. 'I got him out of that seat thing,' he said proudly. 'But you'd need a degree in engineering to put him back again. Don't ever leave me in charge of doing that, will you?'

Simmy laughed. The buckle device on the contraption was indeed mind-boggling. Small plastic shapes had to be fitted together in exact formation before the catch would click into place. With a floppy, sleepy baby, or a rigid screaming one, it was a major exercise to get him into it. 'I know,' she said. 'Christopher's only just got the hang of it.'

'Does he need a feed?' asked Russell. 'Shall I try to wake him up?'

'Don't you dare. He should last till about two – I'm going to see if I can get home in time. I appear to just be in the way here today.'

'Well . . .' said Angie, never one to tell a needless lie. 'As you can see, it is a bit fraught.'

'You could leave him with us while you pop to the shops or something,' said Russell hopefully. 'I'll amuse him if he wakes up.'

Simmy hesitated. She would like to see Bonnie again, but there was no pressing reason to do so. It was a five-minute walk from Beck View, but it involved crossing one busy road and other smaller streets, and the possibility of being knocked down and rendered incapable of returning to her dependent offspring was suddenly terrifying. 'Better not,' she said. 'I do need a bit of shopping but nothing I can get round here. I thought I'd call in on the one in Troutbeck, on the way home. I can park right outside and do it in no time. There'll be enough fruit and veg and biscuits to keep us going for a bit. We've still got one or two bits of meat in the freezer.'

'Take some mushrooms. We've got far too many,' panted Angie. She had turned back to her large pile of bedsheets, preparing to carry them downstairs.

'Thanks, I will. Do be careful on the stairs,' she added. 'Why don't you just throw the whole lot down? That's what you used to do.'

'I was going to.' And she plonked the bundle on the top stair and gave it a hearty kick. It stopped halfway down, and she followed it, kicking it again. 'This is fun,' she said. 'I can pretend it's that awful man's head.'

Simmy and Russell both laughed. Simmy experienced a surge of optimism for a future containing these two in their role as Robin's only surviving grandparents. They would make life fun for him, with their cavalier approach to the world and its restrictions. They would show him how to be brave and independent and argumentative. Something that Simmy felt that she herself really was not.

She stayed for half an hour, and then bundled Robin, still fast asleep, back yet again into the despised seat. The familiarity of the road up to Troutbeck made her feel sentimental and nostalgic. So much had changed in the past year, shifting her out of the comfortable single life and detaching her from the almost incredible scenery that had been right outside her door. Such drama was missing from Hartsop and Patterdale, despite the proximity of Ullswater. And the roads up there were even worse. However many times she drove over the Kirkstone Pass, she was intimidated yet again by the sheer insanity of the endless kinks in the road that went on for three miles or so, forcing a total concentration and making any decent speed unthinkable. The walls felt as if they were alive and far from benign. There had been moments when she could swear they shifted in the night, making sharper bends than ever.

Robin obligingly remained asleep while she dashed around the village shop in Troutbeck. It was also a tea room, much valued by walkers, with the grocery side of things intended purely as a stopgap for essentials. Self-catering visitors bought their bread and milk there but were disappointed if they wanted fresh fruit and vegetables, or even any meat. Simmy grabbed necessities for that evening and next day's breakfast and resolved to send Christopher out to a bigger shop at the first opportunity. His promise to go out to a supermarket on Tuesday had been thwarted by Fabian's appearance, as he eventually admitted.

As she opened the passenger door of her car to sling her purchases onto the seat, a man cleared his throat behind her. Without looking, she said, 'I'll be gone in a minute. Am I in your way?'

'Mrs Brown, it's me.'

She turned, already half aware of his identity. 'DI

Moxon!' she greeted him with a beaming smile of genuine pleasure. 'I haven't seen you for ages.'

'It's pure coincidence that you see me now – although I was thinking we would probably have to have a little talk one day soon.'

'About the murder in Keswick,' she nodded. 'Out of your area, again, I assume?' The occurrence in Grasmere the previous year had also technically not involved the detective from Windermere, but in the event, he had been drawn into it as it neared its conclusion.

'And I wanted to see your little one.' As Pattie had done the day before, Moxon peered into the shadows of the rear seat. 'Boy or girl?'

'Boy. Robin. All very straightforward, when it came to the crunch. He's three weeks and two days old.' DI Moxon knew most of the story of little stillborn Edith and Simmy's subsequent divorce. He had shown a finely balanced sympathy and understanding, and endeared himself to her accordingly. His exasperation with the persistent involvement of young Ben and Bonnie in murder investigations had mellowed into a grudging admiration, and a rare acceptance of a participation that most police detectives in his position would regard as blatant and outrageous interference.

'And here you are, out and about just as always.'

'Yes, well, that's how it is these days. I didn't actually go anywhere for the first week, but since then . . . well, as you see. What're you doing in Troutbeck?'

'Bit of trouble at the tourist village. Car had its tyres slashed, would you believe. Not very nice, I must say.'

'Appalling,' she agreed. 'So, you've made the connection between me and the Keswick murder.'

'It wasn't very difficult,' he said with a twinkle. 'Very bad luck for your . . . partner.'

'Fiancé,' she corrected. 'We're getting married in a little while. It's all decided.' She wondered whether he would expect an invitation and was half inclined to issue one there and then. 'In fact, I was meaning to go and talk to them at the pub this afternoon. I'd forgotten until now. We might have the party there. What my granny would have called the wedding breakfast, I suppose.'

'Congratulations,' he said as if he meant it. He threw another look at Robin, which clearly said, *A child's parents really ought to be married*, even though he knew better than to say it aloud.

'Ben Harkness is on the case of the murder, needless to say,' she told the detective. 'He'll be delighted that I've seen you.'

'You mean, so that I can disclose confidential details about the investigation, I suppose.'

'Something like that. He needs an excuse not to go back to Newcastle, I suspect. He's changing his course and there are ructions. The truth is, he really doesn't like it there, which is a real shame.'

'Changing his course? Whatever for? I don't think I've ever met such a dedicated student of his subject. What happened? Why would he do that?' The man was clearly shaken.

'I know. I was shocked as well. But I suppose after two terms, he's given it time enough. I don't think anything happened, exactly – he's just not suited to it, somehow. He says the syllabus is too narrow and ignores too much of the bigger picture. Something like that. He wants to do history instead. I get the impression it's turning out to be less simple than he thought.'

'Good Lord,' said Moxon helplessly. 'I'm gobsmacked.'

Simmy giggled. 'Anyway, we've just been going over bits of the Armitage family history, to see if we can find any meaningful links to Josephine.'

'Oh?' He blinked two or three times. 'Explain.' When she gave him an old-fashioned look, cocking her head teasingly, he went on, 'You're right that I'm not directly involved in the investigation. You are quite likely to know more than I do – which you're free to disclose to me here and now. I can then pass it to the proper quarters. Anything I can contribute will be gratefully received, I promise you. Or has Christopher already told them everything they should know?'

'They interviewed him on Tuesday, and we went to Keswick yesterday and met up with some of the people who worked with Josephine. I don't know any of them very well. We've mostly been talking to the Armitages. Hilda Armitage left Josephine her house. She's known them all for decades. One of them wanted to marry her. Did you hear about the filing cabinets?'

Moxon made slowing-down motions with his hands. 'All this and a new baby too,' he said, sounding oddly reproachful.

'Who sleeps a lot of the time. Although I will admit he doesn't much like it in the car.'

'Looks contented enough now.'

Robin was still asleep, but his posture yet again caused Simmy some concern. The seat held his body more or less straight, but his head flopped down on his chest at an angle that would give anybody neck ache. 'It's not good for him,' she said. 'All screwed up like that.'

'Filing cabinets,' he said.

'She was killed beside them, apparently. They're full of letters and things from Aunt Hilda's house. Ben thinks somebody should have a good look through them.'

'How many filing cabinets?'

'Four.'

He whistled. 'That's a lot of papers.'

'I know.'

'I have no knowledge of their contents – or even their existence. What I have been party to is a statement from a certain Mrs Harriman, who lives a couple of doors down from Miss Trubshaw's house in Keswick,' he said. 'The closest thing she had to a best friend, it seems. It so happened that I was available at the right moment and had the pleasure of interviewing her.'

'Never heard of her,' said Simmy. 'And I don't think Christopher has either. Why is she relevant?'

'You didn't get this from me, okay? But it seemed to me she might be quite usefully forthcoming if you could manage a little chat with her. I didn't get very far, but I have a strong suspicion that there's more she could tell a patient listener.'

'Oh?' This was a whole new situation. Previously the detective had done his best to prevent unofficial approaches to potential witnesses. 'Gosh! Tell me more.'

'She's in her sixties and spends all day minding her small grandchildren and one or two others, I suspect. She seemed a bit nervous about that, so she's probably unregistered as a childminder, but does it anyway in a small way. There's a big garden, from which she can see into Miss Trubshaw's. I gather the staff at the auction house had regular weekdays off in lieu of the Saturdays they had to work, and the two women had got into the habit of meeting up and taking the kids out somewhere when Miss Trubshaw was free. Mrs Harriman is extremely upset about the violent killing of her friend, as you'd expect but she can offer no hint as to precisely what might have happened.'

'I see,' said Simmy, following all this closely. They were still standing beside her car, which was parked so that anything large trying to get through the village would be impeded. There were very few wide stretches of road in Troutbeck, and even fewer straight ones. Fortunately, nothing had so far required her to move.

'There could be some backstory,' Moxon explained. 'The sort of thing a woman would tell another woman in conversation that just wouldn't crop up in a police interview. It's one of the great frustrations of this job, as I might have mentioned before. We start off in complete ignorance of all the undercurrents and background history, and it takes a lot of time and patience to ferret it out. Quite often that never happens at all, of course.'

'You're telling me it wasn't just a burglary that went wrong, then.'

'Did you ever think it was?'

'I did hope it might be. That would be so much less *malicious*, somehow. And if she knew the person who killed her, that must be a dreadful final thought. The betrayal, the bewilderment. It breaks my heart to think of it.' She cocked her head again. 'But what about the Armitages? Fabian and Richmond and Aunt Hilda and the cousins? They all knew Josephine, and they're all involved somehow. But Ben and I couldn't find a concrete connection that might account for her being murdered. Just a few random theories is all we could manage.'

'That sounds very much like undercurrents to me.'

Then a large van approached, and Simmy heaved a sigh. At the same time, she saw Robin jerk himself awake. 'I'll have to go,' she said. 'What's this woman's address?'

Quickly Moxon fished out a notebook and after a moment consulting a page, he copied down the details and gave Simmy the sheet he'd written on. 'Just turn up with your little one, and I'm sure everything will fall into place quite naturally,' he said blithely.

'I'm not making any promises,' she warned him. 'This really isn't the sort of thing I do. You'd probably glean just as much from Ben. He's made an in-depth study of Aunt Hilda, for a start. She was quite famous at one point.'

The van tooted, and Moxon waved at it to be patient. He gave Simmy one of his kindly, probing looks, and said, 'Well – that's it for now. We'll speak again in a day or two.'

'Right. It was lovely to see you – I'm going now.' And she got into the car, throwing a soothing word at Robin, and drove off.

Hilda had a secret love child – this idea revolved in her

215

head. Or perhaps it would be truer to say she had been forced to swallow a secret that she was keen to reveal. She had done her best to make it public, all those years ago, and the forces of respectability or political discretion or whatever had pushed it out of sight again. There was no DNA testing in those days. As Ben had observed, proving paternity had until recently been a very inexact science.

Weren't secrets often at the root of violent deaths? Ben had apparently unearthed something shameful – although Hilda herself didn't sound as if she'd been ashamed. The claim against the putative father had been made, the fact of a child exposed to public gaze and then seemingly forgotten, with no apparent harm done. So was there something else, more recent? Something entirely unconnected to the mysterious child who would now be over seventy years old? Even perhaps dead.

The drive, as always, required concentration. Again, the grey stone walls tormented her, twisting ahead, bordering a road that belonged in a fairy tale. In the distance she could see Brothers Water glistening, marking a return to more reasonable driving conditions. Before she could reach it, she had to crawl past two vans and a Range Rover, all of them forcing her to cringe into the grass, millimetres away from the wall. There was an obvious beauty to the landscape on all sides, anyone would agree, but for the practical exercise of getting from one point to another, it was completely unfit.

But the seven miles from Troutbeck to Hartsop still only occupied a scant twenty minutes. In the straighter final section, Simmy entertained a host of swirling ideas about families, and how a woman could be fertile for thirty years or so, but seldom more than that. You could in theory have a full sibling thirty years older than yourself, although she had never encountered an instance and they were likely to become even more rare now that teenagers had stopped having babies. Twenty-five years was a lot easier to credit, although even that must be unusual. Quite why she was following this line of conjecture she could not have explained. It had just begun to flow into thoughts of Bonnie Lawson and how Simmy could very easily be her mother, when she reached her new home. 'Here we are!' she sang to her baby, as she parked beside the house that was still not much more than a barn. Humphrey's van was there and she could hear him whistling at the top of the stairs. It was twenty minutes past two.

By three o'clock, Robin had been fed, changed and played with. His temper seemed to be set fair and the weather outside likewise. Humphrey and his mate were fully engaged with creating a third bedroom out of a large empty space – a project that would take at least another two weeks. The controversial door had been changed and Humphrey's spirits were back to their usual buoyant state. 'Going like clockwork,' he reported.

'Let's go for a walk,' Simmy said to her son. 'We haven't had any exercise today. We might get as far as Patterdale.' She tied him onto her front in the complicated contraption that made her feel like something between a Welsh woman and a Native American. At least it left both hands free and the sensation of the warm little body against her chest was delicious. She set out down the small road that led northwards, following the stream that fed into Ullswater. There were gates and stiles and stony outcrops to be navigated, but none of them presented any real difficulties. The exercise was palpably beneficial. She could feel her muscles and bloodstream responding. What very strange cultural attitudes there were to new mothers, she reflected. Although thankfully almost all those which ordained forty days of postnatal passivity seemed to be out of fashion.

She knew she ought to be going up the road to look for Aunt Hilda's house. But that was much too far to walk, and no way was she bundling poor Robin back into the car. Instead, she would methodically go over again everything she had learnt about Fabian and his family, and try to formulate a coherent narrative out of it. It would be a useful mental workout if nothing else.

But she was repeatedly distracted by the bustle of nature all around her. Birds were scurrying to and fro with their beaks full of either nesting materials or food for babies, Simmy supposed, unsure of quite where spring had got to in that respect. It sounded fanciful even in her own mind, but she did suspect that she had a deeper understanding and empathy for the busy little homemakers now that she was a mother herself.

And then, under a tall tree she saw movement. Bending awkwardly, she found a scrap of grey fur that twitched when she nudged it. A baby squirrel, she realised, looking up to see if there was a visible nest. What did a squirrel nest look like anyway? What ought she to do about it? Any small furry mammal would soften a maternal heart, and this one was characteristically cute. Its eyes were open, and it seemed to be unharmed. Inevitably she picked it up for a closer look. And equally inevitably, she decided to adopt it and give it a decent chance of life.

But – oh God! – It was a *grey* squirrel! A child of Satan, a loathsome piece of vermin to be stamped into oblivion by the self-appointed guardians of Lake District fauna. There were actually laws about them, although Simmy did not know the details. Genocide, ethnic cleansing – as Russell Straw would say. She ought to throw it into the river and forget she ever saw it. Instead she tucked it into a fold of Robin's sling, keeping some fabric between child and animal, just in case it might try to bite him. And she gave up any idea of walking to Patterdale, after all.

Chapter Fifteen

Christopher came home to find Simmy leaning over a cardboard box filled with a mixture of newspaper and grass, with a bundle of grey fur curled up in one corner. 'Good God, what's that?' he demanded, like any outraged patriarch coming home to find an intruder.

'Sshh!' she told him. 'I don't want the builders to know about it. They probably belong to some outfit that protects red squirrels.'

'Uh-oh,' said Christopher, looking more closely. 'Tell me that's not—'

Again, she hushed him. 'I found it on the ground. It's almost old enough to survive on its own, I think. I couldn't just *leave* him, could I? He probably only needs a week or so of help.'

'And then what? Isn't there a pogrom out against them?'

She gave him a tragic look. 'That's exactly the word for it. I've been getting all overwrought and emotional about the whole business. It feels so *fascist*, don't you think? Favouring one species over another and talking about foreign invaders that have to be exterminated. It's impossible not to make comparisons with places like Rwanda and Nazi Germany. It's a horrible thing to do. It's bad enough that they wage war on random plants like Himalayan balsam or giant hogweed, but when it comes to animals, I can't bear it.'

'They're convinced they've got right on their side. I heard they're thinking of introducing lots of pine martens because they eat grey squirrels but not red ones. It's bound to end in a whole lot of unforeseen consequences. Like cane toads,' he added with a grin.

'Why am I not surprised?'

'Well, don't let it upset you. You've probably been unduly influenced by your parents, who can be very . . . *contrary* about this sort of thing. Hasn't your mother deliberately scattered giant hogweed seeds at the end of their garden?'

'And good luck to her,' said Simmy fiercely.

'In any case, I'm pretty sure this little thing will die. One of its legs looks funny – did you notice? It's probably been deliberately rejected by its parents as a misfit.'

Simmy inspected the leg. The lower part of the limb was undoubtedly set at an odd angle. 'No, I didn't see that,' she admitted in a small voice. 'I expect I've interfered with nature, then.' And she turned a mournful face on her fiancé. 'That just compounds the moral dilemma.'

'You're talking with your hormones,' he concluded. 'I've heard about this sort of thing. Moral dilemmas and the cruelty of the world. It's all down to bringing a new life into being and worrying about the responsibility of it all.'

'Don't you feel it as well, then? You brought the life into existence as well as me.'

'I do a bit,' he laughed. 'But in my case, it seems to be focused more on worrying about why a perfectly harmless middle-aged woman should be slaughtered in her own home.'

Simmy's laugh was breathless with relief. 'Well, then – we're both as bad as each other, and that makes everything all right.'

'Good,' he said and gave her a warm hug.

'Why are you back so early?' she asked him, a little while later. 'It's not even four o'clock yet.'

'They didn't need me. Now Fiona and Pattie are jostling for Josephine's job they're both straining every nerve to show how competent they are. It's quite funny, actually. They're grabbing new deliveries the minute they come in, ordering poor Jack about and arguing about whether the old system could be improved. Imagine that! Pattie did have quite a good idea, that I'll have to run past Oliver and think more about. And we need another pair of hands, at least . . .' He tailed off, aware that Simmy's attention was wandering.

When he fell silent, she gave herself a little shake. 'I've got two things to tell you. At least.'

'Can we have some tea first? I know you're the one who's always meant to be thirsty, but I'm parched.'

'I bought a few things in Troutbeck. Custard creams, for one.'

'Goody.' He busied himself with kettle and mugs, and cut two large slices of Corinne's very stodgy cake, which was all the tastier for its maturity. 'Can we have this instead of your biscuits?' he asked.

'Of course we can. Hasn't it always been a rule to eat

222

things in rotation – I mean, according to their age? It's wasteful otherwise.'

They sat at the table, with Robin on his father's lap, waving his hands in front of his face and following their movements with absorption. 'Fire away, then,' he invited.

'First – Ben thinks he's found something momentous about Aunt Hilda's past.' And she repeated the tale of the mysterious baby born over seventy years ago and somehow lost. 'That is, Ben can't find any trace. We don't even know if it was a he or a she. It was a brief scandal that somehow never really went anywhere. Something else must have been in the news at the time that people thought more interesting.'

'Not exactly a secret, then, if it was in the papers.'

'There could have been much more to it. Something about the child that had to be hushed up. Not just its father.' She eyed her orphan squirrel thoughtfully. 'Maybe it had a wonky leg, like little Nutkin here.'

'Nutkin?'

'From Beatrix Potter. You remember.'

'I remember the cover of the book, and I could swear that was a squirrel of a different colour.'

'So perhaps *that* was the real scandal about Hilda's baby then – it came out the wrong colour. People were horribly prejudiced in those days.'

'Not if its father was a prominent politician. I don't think there were any black ones in those days. Though there might have been a few Asians. Possibly in the Midlands.'

'I was joking.'

'Oh. Right. Well, the Churchill theory does sound very

223

persuasive. That would have made real headlines. But why didn't she just name him? What sense was there in telling only half the story?'

'She must have been blackmailing him. Demanding money for her silence. Isn't that the obvious explanation?'

'Guesswork. As Ben probably already said, where's the evidence?'

'He would say that,' she agreed. 'But I bet you I'm right,' she insisted. 'I wonder if we'll ever know.'

'She hasn't been dead very long. Sooner or later secrets float to the surface, once a person dies. Probably something incriminating in one of those filing cabinets that have found their way to Josephine's house – which I think is really a bit weird. Not that it matters much what's inside them now. So what was the other thing you had to tell me?'

'What? Oh – yes. I met Moxon just now in Troutbeck. Outside the shop. He's not directly part of the Keswick investigation – but like last time, he gets to see the notes and do some of the peripheral stuff. They got him to do an interview, I suppose on Tuesday when it was all very busy.'

'And that's you, is it? Peripheral stuff?'

'Potentially,' she said, with a sniff. 'Why wouldn't I be? And he was very nice about Robin, and very upset about Ben going off university. He feels quite paternal towards him, you know. I realised that during that awful thing in Hawkshead.'

'Who does he think killed Josie, then?'

'Come on – you know better than to ask me that. He wants me to go and talk to a woman who lived in the same street, informally. See if I can ferret out any clues that she wouldn't tell the police.'

'You're joking! Didn't he notice you'd got a new baby?'

'He probably thinks the baby would make a good introduction. A talking point. The woman looks after small children.'

Christopher leant back and clasped Robin to his chest with both hands. 'That's disgusting,' he said, making a poor show of flippancy. Simmy could see that he was serious.

'I don't see why. He can't come to any harm.'

'It's immoral. Not just exploiting you, but an innocent child as well. Turning you into some sort of undercover informant, because the police haven't the wits to do the job themselves.'

'It's not like that at all. There's no way the police could ever solve this sort of murder without the co-operation of people who know the background and the history and how everything connects up. They're always working in the dark, completely dependent on what people tell them. And if there's no goodwill towards them and people won't open up, they can't function. I thought you understood all that.'

'I told them about Fabian,' he said defensively.

'Bully for you. Anyway, I'm going to do what he asks, whatever you say.'

Christopher took a deep breath and rubbed the baby's head with his chin. 'Okay. I overreacted. I still haven't caught up with the way you and that detective are with each other. But I don't get how this could work. What are you going to do? Knock on some strange woman's door with Robin under your arm, and say, "Look at my lovely baby. Can I come in so you can admire him?" Or what?

How can you even *think* that would work?'

'I haven't thought it through yet.'

'Well, I can't see any choice but to use subterfuge. You'll be deceiving this poor woman, whoever she is, into being all friendly and chatty, when all the time you're storing up everything she says to tell the police. It's immoral,' he repeated 'Whichever way you look at it. And it's pretty silly, if you think about it.'

Simmy had to admit he had a point. 'I expect I'll lose her address if I'm not careful. He jotted it on a flimsy bit of paper.' She pulled it out of her pocket. 'Harriman's her name.'

Christopher stared at her, as if she'd just told an outrageous joke that he was struggling to find funny. 'You're not serious? You don't mean *Chrissie* Harriman, do you?'

'I haven't got a first name for her. Why?'

'She's only one of our most regular vendors. It's a rare sale that doesn't have ten or twenty lots from her. Cameras and binoculars mainly. We never can understand where she gets them all from.'

'Can't be the same woman. This one's a grandmother who spends all her time minding small children. How old is your Chrissie?'

'Sixty or thereabouts, I'd say. Very active, dashing all over the country. So no, it can't be her. Very likely related, all the same.'

'Husband's sister, at a guess. I suppose the connection might be helpful. I could pretend I wanted Chrissie but went to the wrong house. Moxon said I should just show up and get chatting. It sounded quite easy, the way he said it.' She pulled a rueful face.

'Drop it, Sim. Don't let him drag you into it. He's got no right.'

'I never actually said I'd do it. But if she *does* know things about Josephine that would get the investigation on the right track, then I really ought to have a go. That's what Ben would say.'

'Then let Ben do it,' Christopher snapped.

'That's probably a very good idea,' said Simmy placidly.

The afternoon ended with no firm plans made, and no real disagreements hovering over them. The builders went home, Robin enjoyed a lengthy feed and Christopher actually spent some time out in the garden, pulling out young buttercups and thistles, which Simmy conceded were unambiguously weeds and definitely undesirable. She lay back on the sofa and gave herself permission to go blank, merely gazing rapturously at her baby's face. She had forgotten the appointment at the clinic next day and the fact that she was soon getting married. Ben and Moxon and Oliver and her parents all faded into the background for a whole blissful hour. This was all perfectly acceptable, because she was a new mother, and nothing was more important than that.

But it was only sustainable for an hour. Her brain came awake again in spite of itself. Questions were swirling and ideas about the Armitages and how they were the only credible suspects for the murder. Just as she was musing yet again on Uncle Richmond, the landline summoned their attention.

Christopher had just come in, and he answered it, but his monosyllabic responses left Simmy no wiser as to what the call was about. He did say, 'No, no, we'll come there. We might be a while,' at one point. And 'I hope he's not causing you any bother?'

Could it be Ben, she wondered. Or, more likely, Fabian Crick. Impatiently she waited for enlightenment.

It came soon enough. 'A man called Richmond Armitage is at the pub in Patterdale, asking how to find us. Luckily the landlady didn't much like the look of him, so said she'd phone us. Can't imagine how she found the number. I said we – or I if you don't want to – would meet him there.'

'Yes, I heard that bit. I gave her our number last week because she offered to put me in touch with a woman at Glenridding with a baby, who might like to go for walks or something. And yes, I'm coming. Robin can lie on my lap in the car just for that little way.'

'No, he can't,' said Christopher with uncharacteristic firmness. 'That's just the sort of thinking that leads to disaster. If he's coming, he's got to go in his seat properly.'

'You're right,' she conceded. 'But you can strap him in, because he's going to hate the person who does it.'

'This is very weird,' she continued a moment later. 'It can only have been Fabian or Richmond's sons who told his uncle about us, so why not give out our address as well? Did the pub lady say what he looked like?'

'No, but I got the impression she was nervous of him.'

'He must have been standing right there while she was talking. She could have just given him the number. That in itself suggests she didn't trust him. How nice of her to protect us like that.'

Christopher straightened up, the baby and his seat in one hand. 'We wouldn't be so hard to find, once anyone knew we lived around here. But I agree I'm more comfortable meeting him on neutral territory.'

'You still feel responsible,' she realised. 'This is still the result of that undertaking you made to Fabian. Honestly, love, I don't think you need reproach yourself about it any more.'

'It's more a sense of drowning in a bog of Armitage and Crick business. As soon as I think I've got myself out of it, I'm dragged down again. I'm hoping we can give this bloke what he wants and that'll be an end to it.'

'Optimistic,' she murmured. 'Could it be that he got wind of Ben's researches somehow and doesn't like it?'

'Don't see how. Come on, anyway, and let's get it over with.'

'Let me put my shoes on, and I'm ready. I hope the squirrel will be all right. Thank goodness we haven't got a dog.'

'A dog would have finished it off before you even noticed it,' said Christopher sourly.

The man at the pub was recognisably the father of Petrock, the aspiring writer. The same features looked up at the little family, merely grooved and solidified by age. Simmy stared at him, and Christopher muttered, 'Looks like an Aztec.' They stood just inside the door, uncertain of the next move. There were only three other people in the bar.

'Mr Armitage?' said Christopher, too loudly. 'I understand you wanted to talk to us.'

The man did not get up but waved at the window seat facing him across the table. He had a pint of beer in front of him. Simmy shuffled along the seat, taking Robin in his little chair and leaving space for Christopher. She was trying to give all her attention to the matter in hand, dredging up the scattered details she'd gleaned about Richmond. For the first time she wondered about his wife, mother of the two grown sons. She can't have lasted long, if Richmond had been proposing to Josephine for so many years.

'I've had the police after me,' he said without preamble. 'And I'm told that's down to you two.'

'Er . . .' said Christopher. 'I don't think . . .' He looked to Simmy for help.

'Who told you that?' she demanded.

'My relatives. According to them, you've got us all mixed up with this bugger of a murder, when it's got nothing whatever to do with us. Josie was our *friend*. Why d'you think we'd kill her? What's that about?'

'We've never said anything to suggest otherwise,' said Simmy, her thoughts assembling themselves with very little effort. 'But you should understand that Fabian came to us on Sunday, asking us to find you for him and see if we could somehow bring you back together. Sort of go-betweens. Since then, we've realised that this was just some kind of ruse, but we don't understand what it's all about. I mean – *obviously* he knew where you were all along. Because here you are,' she finished with a hint of triumph.

'You don't get it at all, do you?' He seemed genuinely

230

confounded by their stupidity. 'You're talking as if my brothers and nephew and sons are all of a package. I can tell you, that's not the way it is, not at all.'

He then lifted the tankard to his lips with his left hand. His right arm did not move, and Simmy suddenly understood that it stopped well above the elbow. The man only had one arm. By a leap of association, she connected this fact to her rescued squirrel and its wonky leg. A great wave of pity and concern swept through her, exacerbated, she supposed, by maternal hormones. From one irrational moment to the next, she found herself unalterably on Uncle Richmond's side.

But Christopher was far from sharing her reaction. 'You said "relatives" just now, as if you see them as a package yourself,' he accused. 'We can't hope to understand if nobody tells us, can we? You've dragged us up here for some unknown reason, which is pretty much the same as the way Fabian's been behaving. We'd really prefer it if you all just left us alone. As you see, we've got enough on our plate as it is.' He indicated the sleeping baby. 'If you've got us here to tell us to back off, then that's absolutely fine with us.'

'No,' said Richmond Armitage tiredly. 'I wanted to tell you the exact opposite of that.'

Robin was remarkably docile throughout the hour-long session with Richmond. Beer was consumed, along with a bar meal when they realised how late it was getting. Questions were raised and answered, details filled in and affection established. This was a nice man, Simmy concluded, in spite of his somewhat sinister appearance. But she still regarded the rest of the family as being at best self-serving and argumentative. 'I really don't feel very warm towards any of them,' said Richmond.

'Even your sons? Even poor old Ambrose?' Simmy asked.

'Ambrose doesn't really count. He opted out decades ago.'

'And yet he came to see us yesterday,' said Christopher. 'And he seemed to know pretty well what was what.'

'You surprise me. I suppose Fabian felt there would be strength in numbers.'

'Is it a fight, then?' Simmy wondered.

'In a subtle sort of way, I imagine it is. Fabian's panicked about poor Josie, and my sons are squabbling over Hilda's life history.'

'It all comes down to her, doesn't it?' said Simmy. 'That's why Fabian's dragged Christopher into it.'

Richmond was clearly puzzled by this. 'How d'you mean?'

'Well, you might not know that he made a promise ten years ago, when he thought Fabian was dying. He was supposed to go to Hilda and give her a message – tell her how she was in Fabian's thoughts to the end. But he never did, so now he feels bad and Fabian's latched onto that.' She patted her fiancé's leg reassuringly. 'He just forgot about it by the time he was back in England.'

'You've lost me. I should tell you that Fabian and I have no truck with each other, never have. My boys have kept up with him, on and off, since they were all living close to each other, but I never had any time for him. Sneaky little beast he was, always causing trouble. Made my life a lot harder than it might have been.'

'Aren't your boys much younger than Fabian? Why would they have been so close?'

'Fabian's fifty-six. Petrock's forty-eight. Keith's forty-six. They worshipped him when they were small. My wife went off with them, back to Keswick, when Keith was barely three. Fabian's dad was good to them all. They were thrown together.' He shrugged. 'I was the one left out in the cold.'

'Fabian asked me to find you,' Christopher reminded him.

'Yes – you said. And you're right, it was all a game, to keep you dancing to his tune. That promise you made, whatever it was, he must be rubbing his hands to think he can tweak your conscience any time he likes.' He puffed out his cheeks. 'I mean – nobody keeps a promise to a dead man, do they? If you thought he was dead, why go to the trouble?'

'I did mean to,' said Christopher feebly. 'At the time. We were in Africa and he had sleeping sickness. Everyone was sure he was dying.'

'Take a lot to kill the little rat. My wife used to say he was just like his mother, when she first knew him.'

Simmy sat up straighter. Here was a gap she'd hoped would be filled. 'Did she?' she said.

Richmond sighed. 'Her and Fabian's mum were cousins, funnily enough. Very alike in their characters. And they died within six months of each other. There's a genetic thing they'd both inherited. Don't ask me for details. Seems none of the boys have got it, luckily.'

'And you've known Josephine a long time,' Simmy pressed on, making the inevitable connection.

The man nodded miserably. 'The best woman in the world, bar none. How some evil swine could kill her I shall never know. There's nothing she could ever have done to deserve that.'

'Nobody deserves to be murdered,' said Simmy, with a determined glance at her little son. How he came into it she could not have explained, but he did.

'We've been thinking a lot about that,' said Christopher. 'We've got this young friend, you see, who's a bit of an amateur detective. He and Simmy have been quite closely involved in a number of murders over the past couple of years, and this boy—'

'Ben Harkness, right,' nodded Richmond carelessly. 'We all know about him.'

'He found your address,' said Simmy defensively. 'Took him two minutes. And he unearthed Hilda's secret. There's nothing he can't ferret out on the Internet. It's like magic.'

'Hilda's secret? What's that then?' The man seemed determined not to appear interested. 'You don't want to believe everything on the Internet, you know.'

Something about his tone gave Simmy pause, and with another warning pat on Christopher's leg, she just shrugged. 'Well, it's probably not what Fabian was talking about anyway. What do you think of Petrock writing her life story? Is it going to be a bestseller? She does seem to have done a lot of remarkable things through the years.'

'Don't ask me. I never even met the woman.' Again, he spoke with a studied nonchalance that was not convincing.

'What? How is that even possible when she was your

big sister? And you must have lived in Keswick if your boys went to school there. Just a few miles away.' She frowned. 'What happened?' she asked simply.

'Long story.' He brandished his stumpy arm. 'Has to do with this. And don't you get that Harkness kid onto investigating it, because he won't find anything.'

Embarrassment silenced both Simmy and Christopher for half a minute, before Simmy's curiosity broke through. 'You don't wear a prosthesis, then? No bionic hand or anything?'

'Tried it for a bit when I was younger. Never got on with it. People stared at that even more than they did at the stump, and asked the same questions a million times. You can go off people very quickly, you know.' He smiled tightly, and tucked the arm back where it had been before.

'At the risk of asking one of those annoying questions – were you born with it like that?' asked Christopher.

Simmy did a rapid calculation, thinking Richmond must be too old to have been a thalidomide baby. Could you be born with a truncated limb like that? She doubted it.

'Hospital error. I was a C-section delivery, as they call it now, big emergency, and the surgeon's knife slipped. Severed blood vessels and tendons and they couldn't save the arm. So, yes, in a manner of speaking, I was born with it.'

'That's terrible!' Simmy declared, thinking of how her mother would react to such a tale. It took very little to enrage Angie Straw against the health service, for her usual perverse reasons. It was certainly true that when they did make mistakes, they made them on a grand scale.

'I don't want to go into it. It's not relevant to anything, except to say that it meant I never grew up as part of the family. I had a good foster mother from the start, and never realised she wasn't my real mum until I was about ten. I had the Armitage surname, and she was called Forrest and eventually I asked her why that was.'

'Did she have a husband?'

'Actually, yes. Angus. He worked away a lot and never seemed to take much notice of me. I called him Dad and he did take me fishing now and then, and rowing on Derwentwater once or twice. A harmless sort of chap.'

'So – do you know who your biological parents were?' asked Simmy directly.

'Oh yes,' he nodded with a stony expression. 'I got most of the story when I was twelve. That's when it was in the papers. But we're not going to get into that now. It has nothing to do with you.'

Simmy found herself unable to agree with this. 'It seems to me that it might have quite a lot of relevance,' she said, without quite knowing her reasons. She could feel Ben at her shoulder, urging her to stick to the subject. 'You're not Hilda's brother, then? Or Ambrose's?'

'Leave it,' said Richmond tightly, and Christopher muttered something similar.

'Yes, but—' Simmy persisted. 'I'm sorry, but it leaves so much unexplained. And where does Josephine fit into it?'

'Yes, that's the nub, isn't it? That's what we're doing here. Which of the accursed Armitages stabbed her to death in her own home – and why? You'll be thinking it was me, due to being rejected by her, as I'm sure you'll have discovered by now. And I'm thinking that weaselly Fabian's capable of anything. And Petrock's all excited because he thinks it'll make his book sell better if there's a nice murder all tied up with his old auntie.'

'And Keith?' prompted Christopher, with a smile of pure enjoyment on his face. Simmy could see that he felt justified in relishing the situation, given Richmond's straight talking.

'Who knows what Keith is thinking?' said his father. 'Never was any good at explaining himself. But there's no way he'd kill anyone. He hasn't got the spirit for it.'

'It's often the quiet ones,' said Christopher.

'My son is no killer,' Richmond repeated firmly. 'Not either of my sons, in fact. Petrock's a selfish swine at times, but he wouldn't take the risk. He knows he'd never get away with it. Besides, neither of them would have the slightest reason to do such a thing.'

Simmy glanced anxiously at Robin, who should be having his bath and bedtime feed by now, but he appeared to be sleeping soundly. *Forget the routine*, she silently adjured herself. *This is too interesting to stop now.* Christopher evidently felt the same. 'It would make more sense to kill Aunt Hilda,' he said. 'Except she died anyway.'

'And left the house to Josephine, which was a surprise, I admit – but a nice one. Showed the rest of them up. Sloppy of them to let that happen. Funny, when you think about it. Nice house, so they tell me.'

Christopher stared. 'It's barely half a mile from here. You can't seriously tell us you've never seen it.'

'I live in Workington, nearly an hour's drive away. Until

today I hadn't left the farm for months. The Land Rover's not even taxed, so I have to hope I don't get stopped going home.'

Simmy giggled, suddenly thinking that her mother would share her liking for this unusual man. She savoured various images of him working on his farm, throwing hay bales around or even driving a tractor, with only one arm.

'You're not dairy, then,' said Christopher. 'Otherwise you'd be doing the milking now.'

'It's not that sort of farm,' said Richmond stiffly. 'More a matter of polytunnels and packing sheds. Tomatoes, peppers and so forth and a few acres of soft fruit. Blackcurrants mostly.'

'I see,' Christopher nodded, with the subtlest suggestion of scorn. 'A sort of market garden, then.'

'Do you grow flowers?' Simmy asked, mindful of her role as a florist. Richmond shook his head. From one moment to the next it had become clear to them all that the conversation was over. Even Robin – who was learning quickly – picked up the atmosphere and began to whimper.

'Better get this young man home to bed,' said Christopher, squaring his shoulders. 'I'm not sure what we've accomplished, but it was good to meet you.'

'And you,' said Richmond with a straight look. 'I mean that. It's not often you meet a decent little family like you. I know I don't cut much of a figure, and you had no reason to trust me or listen to me, but you've been good enough to hear me out, and I'm grateful. We're in a pickle, between us, and you ought never to have been dragged into it, but there it is. It's good to talk to someone who knew Josie and will miss her as much as I do – or very nearly.' The little speech seemed to embarrass the speaker more than the listeners. His eyes grew shiny.

Simmy was increasingly sleepy; the task of maintaining a hold on any logical thread was proving difficult by that point. She had tried listing headings that she could report to Ben, but everything seemed to fly around in disconnected shreds, with nothing remotely resembling a clue to Josephine's murder to be glimpsed. And yet, there had to be something. Every instinct insisted this was so.

The next hour was devoted to Robin's needs, and then Simmy fell asleep over his feed. Christopher found them on the bed in a heap together and heartlessly woke them up. 'Put him down, and come and talk to me for a bit,' he ordered.

But Robin had other ideas. His day had been spent almost entirely asleep and now he wanted to be sociable. 'You can play with him while I have another nap,' said Simmy. 'Come back in half an hour.'

Grumbling about the loss of an evening and the whole idea of a routine going out of the window, he did as he was ordered. It was nearly nine when he came back with a docile baby and dragged Simmy downstairs. 'We'll have to talk it through now,' he insisted. 'There won't be another chance until this time tomorrow.'

With a muzzy head and a guilty sense that Christopher was right about the routine, she followed him into the kitchen where he gave her a mug of coffee and yet more cake – this time small pieces of the one Angie had donated. 'This is the last of it,' he said. 'It'll be biscuits from here on.'

'That's a shame,' said Simmy.

'So – what do we make of Richmond?' he asked in a determined tone.

'He's nicer than his relations. But I didn't follow a lot of his story. What happened after he was born? Who was his mother? Why is he so against Hilda? There's a great big gap somewhere. I'm sure we've been told everything we need to fill it, but I'm too tired to figure it out.'

'I expect Ben can fill the gap for us. I admit my attention wandered during some of that family stuff. My mind doesn't work like Ben's. I can never put myself into people's heads like he seems to. That man doesn't like Fabian much, does he?'

Simmy shrugged as if to say *Who does?* 'Ben has a special knack. I hope I remember everything I need to tell him. Poor Richmond – what a terrible start in life. Caesareans were pretty unusual back then, so something must have gone wrong to need one. A massive emergency, in fact, which is why they sliced his arm off by mistake. Think how ghastly that must have been! And if he was an afterthought, following three or four others, they might not have wanted him anyway.' She was obsessing over the details, imagining the cold, bright room, the blood and the horror. It inevitably took her back to her own first experience of childbirth and the way everything could go so terribly wrong.

'Don't dwell,' said Christopher briskly, seeing the way her thoughts were going.

'No – I won't. We really do need Ben, though. All the facts will be recorded somewhere and he's the man to find them.'

'You make it sound pathetically simple.'

'It probably isn't. Why do I feel so *busy* all of a sudden, when it's practically bedtime, and there'll probably be two night feeds, and it's the clinic tomorrow.' She sighed heavily.

'Not to mention an adopted baby squirrel,' he reminded her.

'Aaghh. I had forgotten all about that. What shall I feed it? Nuts? Worms?'

'Don't ask me. All I can think of is wholemeal bread, which seems to be good for most creatures.'

'There must be a website about it. At least it seems to be old enough to need solids. I might have to breastfeed it otherwise.' She hauled herself over to her laptop and searched for information. 'Kale and fruit,' she summarised. 'I guess cabbage and apple will do, then. I've got both those. And it should have milk, apparently. Well, maybe water with just a bit of milk mixed in will do.'

'This is very silly, you know. You should have left it where it was. It says here,' he pointed over her shoulder, 'that the mother is usually close by.'

'Too late now.' She found a quarter of white cabbage and a bright red apple, and cut them up. The squirrel was curled in the nest she'd made for it and showed no interest.

'It'll be dead by morning, I expect,' Christopher predicted.

Privately, Simmy thought he was probably right. Nevertheless, she wanted to do her best for the little thing. When she'd finished she collapsed exhaustedly back onto the sofa and directed her thoughts to the following day. 'I'm actually scared of the clinic, would you believe? It makes me all fluttery to think about it.'

'Do you want me to come as well? What time is it? They won't give him any injections, will they?'

'It's two o'clock in Ambleside. They do the injections terribly young now, but I think it's six weeks, not three. I'm going to be in a seriously awful state for that. You don't really need to come tomorrow. I don't think they encourage fathers. Your work was done once he'd been delivered, as far as the medical people are concerned.'

'I'll definitely come for the injections. You hear such awful stories.'

'Stop it! You sound like my father. And mother, come to that.'

'Sorry. But you should hear Hannah and Lynne on the subject. They both went to some monstrous place in Penrith, where the woman was a certifiable sadist. Like something from the Spanish Inquisition, apparently.'

'That was years ago. Didn't one of them complain?'

'Hannah did, yes. No wonder there's such a persistent movement against vaccination, the way some people administer them. Torturing innocent babies for fun.'

'I'm sure it's better now,' said Simmy firmly.

Chapter Sixteen

They were in bed by ten. Robin demanded sustenance at eleven-thirty and four-thirty, which was reasonable enough from his point of view, but resulted in sleep deprivation for both parents. In Simmy's case it was made worse by swirling thoughts of murder and medical accidents and a driving sense of urgency that she could not properly account for. She slept fitfully and was bleary with Christopher when he brought tea at eight next morning.

'Friday today,' he said, and then gave his customary report, having gained an advantage over her by being downstairs already. 'Your squirrel is still alive, and it's eaten some apple. I didn't interfere with it at all. I'm leaving it all down to you. I've had some toast and I'm off in five minutes' time. There shouldn't be much doing at work. I don't suppose there'll be any news about Josephine's funeral.' He paused and scratched his head. 'Who'll be arranging that, I wonder? She's even shorter on family than you are.'

'Not possible,' said Simmy. 'Except that now I've got you and Robin to bury me, I suppose.'

'Josie knew a lot of people, but I don't recall a single relative. Her father died ten years ago, and I don't remember any mention of a mother.'

'Oliver will know. Maybe he'll have to do it himself.'

'Serve him right if he does.'

'Why?'

'Oh, I don't know. After that lunch on Wednesday I've seen a different side of him. He didn't come near the place yesterday, you know. Got some consultancy thing down south, apparently. That's pretty much all he does these days.'

'Consultancy on what?'

'I told you that. He's an expert at assessing the authenticity of old objects. He's got a pretty big reputation by now.'

'Lucrative as well, do you think?'

'Only some of the time. People running museums and archives never seem to have much cash. He's not short of a penny, anyway. Nobody who knows as much as he does about antiques could fail to be nicely off.'

'Oh good,' said Simmy sleepily. 'That'll be you, then, in a few years' time.'

'We can always dream. Anyway, the point is, I won't be late home. Most likely I'll be back soon after you, depending on how long you take at the clinic. Then we can have a lovely, lazy weekend. The forecast is almost too good to be true. Blue skies, no wind. Perfect for a stroll round a lake with a baby. All we need to make it perfect is a dog.'

'Go away,' said Simmy.

There had been a note left on the kitchen table from Humphrey saying: *See you on Monday. Starting on the back bedroom. Will need to turn electrics off at some point, if Elliott shows up.* Simmy had rapidly learnt that there was no such thing as an all-purpose builder any more. You had to have separate specialists for plumbing, wiring, plastering, roofing. Humphrey did carpentry, stonework, floors and walls and would paint his woodwork if requested. He attached skirting boards and created windows. Elliott had installed essential wiring before Simmy and Christopher had moved in, but there were many more details to be finished off. Sockets for televisions and computers, a smoke alarm and numerous complexities that were apparently necessary for modern living. 'Even if you don't use them, the house should have them,' Humphrey had insisted. 'There are all kinds of regulations. You'd never be able to sell the place if you weren't compliant.' In vain did Simmy assure him she was never going to want to sell it. He merely raised an eyebrow as such unwarranted certainty.

For the moment, however, she had the house to herself. No need to get dressed all morning, if she didn't feel like it. Except – what had happened to that sense of being uncomfortably busy? Were there not a dozen things she was supposed to be doing? People to talk to, questions to ask, mysteries to solve. Ben would be expecting her to phone, as would Bonnie, and probably her parents. There was nothing to actually *do* in the house, other than stuff a number of little outfits into the washing machine and then hang them out to dry. Christopher had left the kitchen impressively clean and tidy. Except the squirrel! She had forgotten it yet again. Christopher had said it was alive, and therefore she had a duty to attend to it. The box it was in was no good as a permanent home. It should perhaps have a little enclosure in the small garden shed. The website she had consulted had been stern about the keeping of wild animals as pets, so she ought to give it freedom as soon as it was safe to do so. With the wonky leg it might never cope, though.

She went for a look. The little thing was actually sitting up in a corner of its box looking a lot brighter than the day before. The water level in the little glass pot had gone down and there were scraps of chewed apple strewn about. 'Well done!' she applauded. 'What a clever boy!'

She supplied dried raisins and a small nut from the muesli box for its breakfast and promised fresh quarters before long. The shed – which had been originally used as a small shelter for distressed sheep – was cobwebby and cluttered. The task of finding a habitable corner felt too much just at the moment.

She realised she had been foolish to tell Ben there wouldn't be time to take him to see Aunt Hilda's house. The suggestion of cycling to Troutbeck and being collected from there would have been entirely feasible, after all. And still was, of course. She had until half past one entirely free, and anything to distract her from the terrors of the baby clinic would be welcome. The thought of it had been so dominant that she had somehow assumed the whole day would be taken up with it – which she now realised was ridiculous. She had imagined herself getting Robin immaculately presentable for the nurse person, fed and clean and smiling.

She would make a few notes about their routine and how he was at night and then ask a few bland questions about his spots. But none of that seemed rational now. It would probably cause tension between herself and the baby, which she was learning could be disastrous. She should carry on as normal all morning, doing what she wanted to do, letting Robin fit into her activities as best he could. That was the healthy way, she told herself. Like a mother cat or dog, she would be there to keep him warm and safe and fed, while she attended to her own requirements as well.

So, feeling gratifyingly grown-up and sensible, she texted Ben to say she could spare him some time after all if he still wanted to come and see the Ullswater house. He replied ninety seconds later to say of course he did and would be at Troutbeck by ten, waiting outside the Mortal Man. *Okay*, Simmy texted back.

Then she phoned Bonnie to check that all was well at the shop. 'I'll try to come in tomorrow,' she said. 'Will Tanya be there?'

'Oh yes,' said Bonnie fervently. 'She'd better be. I need a break from Verity. Although she hasn't arrived yet – it's not like her to be late.' The temporary stand-in would only undertake to work Monday to Friday, with Ben's sister taking her place on Saturdays. The relief this brought the stoical Bonnie was palpable.

Simmy laughed. 'It's only quarter past nine. She probably thinks you can manage for a bit without her.'

'She probably guesses I prefer it this way.'

'You're a hero,' Simmy said. 'Will you be able to bear it for a few more months?'

'How many months?'

'Well, I don't know exactly. But I'm sure it'll get better. It's only been a few weeks after all. You're still getting to know each other.'

'The more I know, the worse it gets,' said Bonnie darkly. 'I actually liked her at first. But luckily there are plenty of orders, so she's out half the time.'

'Well, hang in there. If business keeps up, you might even get a rise.'

'And if Ben doesn't go back to uni this term, I'll have him as compensation,' said the girl cheerfully.

Simmy said nothing about the morning she was about to spend with Bonnie's beloved. She didn't have time to describe the events of the previous evening, and she was diverted by the thought of Ben losing an entire term of study. That felt ominously risky, despite his youthful confidence that it would all work out somehow. The prospect of starting again in the autumn, with three more undergraduate years ahead of him, did not appear to worry him.

'I'll call you again this evening, maybe,' she said. 'You'll want to catch up with everything. I can't stop now.'

'Nor can I. There's a customer,' said Bonnie.

On the road down to Troutbeck she was quickly aware that the tourist season was really getting into its stride. Not just cars and caravans, but cyclists and even a coach full of pensioners all competed for space on the small winding highway. Kirkstone Pass, as always, gave Simmy a little shiver. She had seen it in all seasons now, and still could not bring herself to like it. The bare, windswept fells on every side made her feel small and vulnerable. There was a weight of history pressing down on the place, with tales of frozen bodies missing for weeks until the snows thawed. Mostly sheep, admittedly, but enough humans to cast a blight. There was no rest for the eye, no hopeful point to aim for, where warmth and food might be available. Except for the pub, of course, which called itself an inn and which had a handy car park. It attracted tourists effortlessly, but Simmy had never been inside.

She would have to come this away again to get to the clinic at Ambleside, but instead of carrying on down the relatively civilised A592 to Troutbeck, she would turn right and plunge down the steep road known as 'The Struggle'. Going down was worse than coming up, she had decided. There was no reason to doubt the efficacy of her brakes, but you could never be sure of other vehicles. Big old vans or trucks losing control and crashing into her from behind was one of her persistent imaginings. The road was not especially narrow, but it had sturdy stone walls on either side, and there would be no escape. With a helpless baby on the back seat, the whole thing readily became nightmarish.

The landscape was not as nature intended. There was a big slate quarry, for one thing. And there was a growing conviction that there ought to be trees covering the fells right to the top. Once this idea took hold, the very bareness of the slopes looked wrong. Simmy was mildly inclined to support calls to remove all sheep from at least some areas, and then stand back to see what happened.

It was only a few miles to her rendezvous with Ben. When she found him, he said he would leave his bike at the Mortal Man and walk back from Hartsop for it later. They had both realised it would not fit in the car as well as Robin's buggy. 'I'm coming back this way anyway, later on,' Simmy told him. 'So you don't need to do such a long walk. At least I can drop you at the turnoff to Ambleside, if you want the exercise. It's not far from there.'

'We're going up to Ullswater now, are we?' he asked.

'Might as well.' She inspected her baby. 'He seems okay for a bit.'

Ben gave the infant a cursory examination. 'He looks bigger,' he said.

'No, he doesn't. He looks exactly the same as he did yesterday. You just think that's something I want to hear. People keep doing that.'

'Suit yourself,' said Ben easily.

He, unlike Simmy, remembered the precise location of Aunt Hilda's house, and directed her to its door. It was at least a mile further north than she had visualised, on the left-hand side of the A592, overlooking the placid expanse of Ullswater, with a patch of woodland rising behind it. 'Gosh, we're almost at the Dockray road,' said Simmy. 'Lucky I didn't try to walk here. I'd never have made it from Hartsop.'

'It is quite a way,' Ben agreed. 'You can park here, at a squeeze.'

Parking was such a perpetual challenge, an issue that never went away and was never fully resolved, that Simmy did not demur at the proposal that she drive onto a patch

250

of ground that was obviously private. 'Does it belong to Hilda's house, do you think?' she asked hopefully.

'The next one, I guess. The one we want has its gate round the side, look.' He pointed out a small track with a gate opening onto it. The gateway was just wide enough to admit a car. 'Where did she park, I wonder? What if she had visitors?'

'Maybe somewhere further along the track,' Simmy suggested. 'But this will have to do for now.'

It was mid morning on a Friday in springtime. Visitors were thronging the whole area, wedging their cars into any available cranny and getting told off as a result. But it was mild with a hazy sunshine and for the moment nobody wanted to stop to admire this particular stretch of lake. The famous Aira Force was half a mile further along the same road, with its own expensive car park and a spectacular waterfall. Wordsworth's daffodils were there too. 'We'll be fine here,' said Ben, getting out of the car.

The house was large and handsome but not unduly special. Made of the usual dark grey stone, it had double gables, with a front door symmetrically central. Ben pushed through the closed gate and headed along the path. The only non-symmetrical quirk was the fact that the path had to turn at ninety degrees to bring you from gate to door.

'Has it been cleared of furniture?' Ben asked. 'There are still curtains at the window. I wonder what Josephine intended to do with it.'

251

Simmy was dithering as to whether or not to leave Robin in the car, instinctively weighing up relative risks. A large lorry could smash into the car, which was not completely off the road. Getting the buggy out of the boot and fitting the baby seat to it would be awkward but not dangerous. Having him to consider would make exploring the house more difficult. Then she shook herself. 'We won't be able to get in, will we?' She realised she had imagined them just walking through the front door and making free with the uninhabited building.

'Not unless we break a window,' quipped Ben. 'Maybe at the back . . .'

'We're trespassing, aren't we? What if someone next door sees us?'

'If we look purposeful they'll think we're here with permission. That one's sure to be a holiday house, anyway.'

'It is interesting to see it, I admit.' She was still standing beside the car, trying to assess the danger of passing traffic to her baby. Finally she decided he was fine where he was for a few minutes. There didn't seem to be many large lorries on the road that morning anyway and the car was visible for at least a hundred yards.

'Come on then.' He headed for a stone path that led to the back of the house, on the side further from next door. 'I can see a shed.'

It turned out that there was a good-sized garden behind the house, with a wide gate opening onto the track, which dwindled to nothing only a few yards on. The shed proved to be a garage. 'Why don't I drive up here?' Simmy said. 'That would be safer for Robin.'

'Feel free. You'll have to reverse out again, though. This gate's chained shut, so you'll never manage to turn round.'

'I can do reversing,' she assured him, and fetched the car.

Ben was at the further end of the garden when she joined him again, looking up at the house. 'No curtains this side,' he noted. 'And I can't see any pictures on the walls. I think someone's taken everything out. It's just an empty shell now. Did Josephine cram it all into her house in Keswick – or sell it at the auction house?'

'I keep wondering who gets it now? We still have to consider it as a possible motive for killing her.'

'I did have a quick look online last night, but trying to identify a person's relatives isn't at all straightforward, if you've nothing to go on. You don't know where to start.'

'I suppose we'd know by now if she'd left it to Christopher,' Simmy said with a laugh. 'She *was* awfully fond of him.'

'Dream on. The chances are she didn't leave it to anybody. Not many people make wills at her age – especially if there's no immediate family.' He was staring up at the house. 'Don't you think it has a *relaxed* kind of atmosphere? There's no hint that anybody's fighting over it.'

'It's neglected and sad,' Simmy judged. 'And that could be because there don't seem to be any women in the picture any more. It's been owned by one woman after another, and now they've gone, it's lost its soul. Nobody to keep it nice and put its best face on. They won't get its proper value, looking like this.' She waved at the straggly garden and the blank walls of the house. 'Josephine can't have had time to do anything with it.'

'Let's have a look at the garage,' Ben suggested. When he tried the small door in the side wall, it opened easily. 'Hey!' he gasped. 'Didn't expect that.'

Simmy followed him in and waited for her eyes to adapt to the gloom. There was no window. A small stack of cardboard trays, the sort used by market traders to carry vegetables and other goods, was against the back wall. A scatter of dusty old magazines was in the top one. She flipped through them, watchful for spiders. Then a sticky label on the edge of the box caught her eye. 'Oh, it came from Christopher's saleroom, look. That's a lot number sticker. It's got the date on.'

Ben bent over it. 'Two years ago. What would have been in it, then? Not these boring magazines, surely?'

'Have a look at the one underneath.'

The second box had the same lot number written on it with a marker pen and contained nothing more than a few sheets of newspaper. 'Not interesting,' said Ben. 'But you know what – Josephine probably left these here.' He tapped the sticker thoughtfully. 'There'll be a record of what this lot was and who it came from – won't there? It'll be in an archive on the work computer.'

'You think?'

'Unless they delete them after a year, which is unlikely. We need to ask Christopher to have a look. He might not want to tell us who the vendor was, but I expect you can persuade him.' He took a picture of the sticker and another of the boxes. 'This is really quite exciting,' he enthused.

Simmy was standing by the door, where she could see her car. Suddenly it felt irresponsible and risky to leave Robin all by himself out there. Somebody might steal him. Or he could get himself all twisted and choke somehow. 'I'm not sure I see why it's anything to get excited about,' she said. 'Josephine probably used them to carry stuff, and then just left them here. Now I've got to get back to the baby,' she added. 'He might be crying.'

'No problem. I've got all I need. And we are trespassing, technically. Better not to get caught.' He sounded almost giddy with good cheer at the apparent success of their mission. 'This is brilliant,' he said, just to ensure that Simmy knew how happy he was. 'I can't explain why, but it feels as if things just got connected up at last.'

'You just like snooping round old sheds,' she accused him.

'Can we go to Keswick now?' he asked next. 'If we don't do it today, we'll have to wait till Monday. There's no sale this weekend, is there? There's still plenty of time, and who knows when there'll be another chance?'

Simmy felt a powerful mixture of reactions. A wish to co-operate and drive anywhere Ben wanted to go fought against an instinct to stay secure and snug somewhere with her baby. 'I'll have to go home and get spare nappies, and have a drink first,' she prevaricated. 'But I suppose it's possible. Not that I see much point in it, I have to say.'

'Come on then,' he urged, seizing the moment. 'Do you want me to wave you out?' He was offering to check for oncoming traffic as she reversed onto the main road.

'No, it'll be all right,' she decided. The manoeuvre really wasn't so hazardous, after all. 'Just keep an eye out for anything coming on your side.'

It was accomplished with only a minor bump as Simmy drove over a stone on the corner, and they were quickly back in Hartsop. Robin woke when they came to a stop and began to wail. 'I'd better feed and change him,' she said. 'And he might need a jacket.' She tried to think through the requirements for taking a young child out in a car for an unspecified length of time. 'This is still all very new to me,' she whined. 'I know I'll forget something.'

'I can't see that much can go wrong,' said Ben blithely. 'So long as I can get back to my bike at some point.'

It was half past eleven before they were heading northwards again, this time to turn off the road and cut through Dockray before reaching the A66. Simmy's mind was far from clear, and she repeatedly asked herself what she thought she was doing. Ben's insistence that it was vitally relevant was a familiar force that she had often failed to resist. Generally it had turned out to be based on sound sense, with favourable outcomes. But not always. 'Are you sure this is a good idea?' she asked him, twice. 'It all feels really flimsy to me. Those boxes were obviously just handy when Josie wanted them to take junk to the tip or something. I can't believe there's anything interesting about them.'

'I admit that's possible, but on the other hand it could be a brilliant clue.'

'I'm sure there are things I ought to be telling you. For a start, I saw Moxon yesterday. He's seen at least some of the file on Josephine, but isn't directly involved in the investigation. Oh – and he wants me to try and talk to a neighbour. Gosh, I forgot that, as well.'

'As well as what?'

'Whatever baby equipment I'm sure I need to have with me. You see women with these enormous bags of stuff, and all I've got is a spare nappy and my purse.'

'Who's this neighbour woman, then? Can we see her now?'

'What? Oh! Well, Christopher thinks it's daft. He more or less talked me out of it. I can't even remember why Moxon thought it might help.'

'Neighbours see things. They get a feeling for what's going on beneath the surface. They watch each other. What's her name?'

'Mrs Harriman. Christopher knows someone with that name, but thinks it's a different person.'

'We should give it a try. What's the address?'

'He wrote it down. I think it's in my bag.' She indicated the shoulder bag she'd slung on the back seat next to Robin. 'I can't imagine how we could do it. Just knock on the door and say we knew Josie? Which we didn't. The woman's a sort of childminder, according to Moxon. She'll be knee-deep in toddlers.'

'Perfect! You can say you're looking for somebody to mind your Robin.'

The thought sent a sharp pang through Simmy's heart. How anyone could even contemplate leaving their baby with someone other than close family was entirely beyond her. But it seemed to be a viable plan, looked at from Ben's perspective. 'So who do we say you are, then?'

'Why say anything? You can tell her I'm a hitchhiker you just picked up, for all it matters.'

'If you were a hitchhiker, you'd stay in the car and let me go in by myself. Instead, you can do all the talking. And we don't want to tell any lies. That always ends badly.'

'It wouldn't be a lie to say you were going to need a minder, would it? Or is your mother taking him on full time?'

'He's three weeks old, Ben. He's not going anywhere.'

Ben sighed and shook his head at her obstinacy. 'I don't know why we're arguing about it. I'll be your stepson then, if I have to be anything.'

'I can't see why you need to explain yourself.'

'You never know. People can be suspicious. I can say I'm worried about my dad because he was terribly upset about Josephine. That might be enough to get her going.'

Simmy was thoroughly unconvinced. 'I don't understand how we get from knocking on her door to talking about your dad – who you'd have to say is Christopher, and that's a lie that could very easily come back to bite us. Everybody knows him.'

'Let's just do it, okay? It might turn out to be really easy.'

Ben had found the address, and asked his phone to direct them to the house. They drove to it without difficulty, only to see a middle-aged woman escorting two children out of the front gate. 'There!' said Ben. 'Couldn't be simpler. Park up the road a bit, and we can get out and go to meet her. How long does it take to get Robin into his buggy?'

'Ages. Christopher says it's like a Transformer he had as a child. All the baby stuff's like that.'

258

'Keep going to the end of the road then, to give us a bit of time.'

'Honestly, Ben, this is ridiculous.' But she parked alongside the pavement as instructed.

'It's not, though. Leave it to me. You'll see this is going to work perfectly.'

He sauntered ahead of her, leaving her to assemble Robin's transport. The baby took exception to being disturbed and protested vigorously. Ben turned back and gave a discreet thumb's up sign, as if to suggest that Simmy had deliberately upset her child in order to attract the attention they wanted. Outrage at this idea combined with resentment at the complexity of the buggy's mechanism to effectively increase Robin's distress. With a final bad-tempered thrust of the seat into the wheeled frame, Simmy got the flanges and sprockets to click as they were intended, and began to follow Ben. Robin's cries filled the air.

'Oh, that poor baby! What's the matter with him?' cried the woman they hoped was Mrs Harriman. 'Are they with you?' she asked Ben. 'Why aren't you helping your mother? See what a pickle she's in. That blanket's going to catch in the wheels, look.'

Without another word, she bent over the buggy, straightening the covering and cooing over the furious infant. 'Would you mind terribly if I got him out?' she asked Simmy. 'I am very good with babies. Stay there, you two,' she ordered the toddlers in her charge. 'Don't go into the road.'

Everyone was quickly organised with military precision,

and Robin subsided gratefully onto his new friend's shoulder. 'Thanks,' said Simmy on his behalf. 'He didn't like being woken up, that's all.'

The two small children edged closer for a look at the baby. Simmy smiled at them. 'He's called Robin,' she said.

'That's a bird,' said the older child. 'Like Lark. She's called Lark.' He indicated his little companion. 'She's my sister. I'm three and she's two. This is our nanna. We come here because Mummy goes to work.'

'Lark,' breathed Simmy. 'Gosh!' Names never ceased to fascinate her, given how original her own was.

'They must be a handful,' said Ben to the woman. 'Do you have them every day?'

'Not quite,' came the brusque reply. It appeared that questions from young men were regarded as impertinence.

'Well, thanks for sorting the baby out,' said Simmy, reaching out to take him back. Seeing him on a strange person's shoulder was unsettling. 'We should get on.' Ignoring Ben's small hiss of protest, she retrieved Robin, and began to settle him back into his buggy.

'How old is he?' asked the woman.

'Three and a half weeks. I feel as if I've had him for ever.'

'You're doing well. Nice and confident. Seems as if you're enjoying it, unlike most.' She sighed and glanced at her grandchildren. 'For myself, I can't get enough of them. I had five, you know.' She smiled proudly.

'Like my mum, then,' said Ben, unthinkingly. Simmy gave him a wide-eyed look of reproach.

'Oh?' The woman looked from face to face. 'Robin's your fifth, is he?'

It was tempting to let the assumption lie uncorrected. But that carried too much risk. 'No. It's a bit complicated. He's my second, actually, but the first one died.' It was the first time she had given this information to a casual stranger, and it gave rise to a tidal wave of emotion that came quite out of the blue. 'She was stillborn,' she added, wanting to give Edith a clearer identity. 'Quite a few years ago now.'

'That's very sad,' said Mrs Harriman in a tone that struck precisely the right unsentimental note. 'Lucky this one's a boy,' she added without further explanation. Ben made a sound expressing confusion, but Simmy understood.

Then, as if Providence felt the need to move things along, a big square van pulled up outside a house further down the street. 'Oh, Lord – more police people,' said the woman. 'There's no end to it.'

'Is that where someone was murdered?' Simmy asked quickly. 'I knew her slightly. Terrible business.'

'You knew Josephine?' Suspicion was plain on her face. 'Is that why you came here?'

'Er . . .' said Simmy. Where had she gone wrong, she asked herself. If there had been a cover story planned, she'd forgotten it.

'Yes,' said Ben boldly. 'It's awful of us, I know. But sometimes you just can't resist. We were going into Keswick for some shopping and decided to take a detour to look at the house. It's funny, isn't it – the way we all criticise the public for gawping at accidents or murder scenes, and then we do it ourselves. Nobody's exempt from the herd, when it comes to it.'

'Um . . .' said Mrs Harriman. 'Well . . .'

Lark and her brother were getting restive, hopping around each other and looking quite likely to run off in another few moments.

'Did you know her?' Ben asked.

'Of course. She came and helped me with these two, once in a while. Told me a lot about herself, as it happens.' Again, a look of complacent pride. 'Quite a clever lady, as I expect you know. Up half the night with her researches. I could see her computer screen flickering from my bedroom. Kept me awake a few times, though I never complained. My own fault for liking to keep the curtains open.'

'She was clever,' said Simmy. 'A real expert, in fact.'

'What was she researching?' asked Ben, with another of his annoying direct questions. It occurred to Simmy that his interview technique was sorely lacking in finesse.

'Don't ask me. History, I think. Something about the war and the people around Churchill. She never gave me any details. Struck me as a bit dry, to be honest. And then all those filing cabinets arrived. Whatever's going to happen to all that stuff now, I wonder?'

'Was she writing a book or something?' asked Ben.

'That's what I presumed, but she never said so exactly. All I can say is she enjoyed a walk with the kiddies, and she was very good with them for a maiden lady. Told them little stories and made up games.' Her eyes suddenly turned pink around the rims. 'And to think some monster killed her! It's beyond all belief. It's given me a real turn, I can tell you. Can't settle in my own house for thinking about it. That's why we're off again now. Taking them to the cafe down the road for some lunch. I'm not a gawper, like you,' she concluded crossly. 'All I want is to get away from the whole horrible business.'

It was all they could hope for. 'Well, nice talking to you,' said Ben, holding out his hand. 'My name's Ben, by the way.' He looked down at the children. 'And I won't forget that I met a little girl called Lark.'

'And I'm Chrissie Harriman,' said the woman.

They drove to the auction house in a state of some excitement. In the back, Robin was whimpering softly, as if trying to decide on which mood to opt for.

'That was Chrissie Harriman,' said Simmy, more than once, still not quite able to believe it. 'Christopher knows her. She's a regular at the auction. He said this person couldn't be her.'

'So what?'

'It closes the circle. Or at least makes the whole circle smaller. Everyone's more tightly connected than we thought. I'm glad I didn't tell her who I was. That might have got seriously complicated.'

'It went well, though,' said Ben with satisfaction. 'Even talking about Churchill! She's probably got Winston and Randolph confused, but that doesn't matter. Just the fact that Josephine mentioned the name clinches it – I must have been right about the politician in the scandal. Amazing, the way we got all the questions answered so easily – in about four minutes. Fancy calling that poor child "Lark". I wonder what the boy's called.'

'I'm hungry,' she realised. 'Do you think we could find some food? A garden with a pub would be nice.' She laughed. 'I mean a pub with a garden. What's happening to my brain? I could probably feed Robin at the same time.'

'Does that child never stop eating?'

'Don't say things like that,' she flashed at him. 'I'm warning you. If you can't say something positive, don't say anything at all.'

Suddenly he was no longer the schoolboy she still assumed him to be. He had turned into a man when she wasn't looking – albeit a man who appeared young enough to be her son, in the eyes of passing strangers. Now he gave her the same look that men everywhere gave when a woman stepped over a line. The subtlest automatic glance of offended superiority. Even now, after decades of female aggression, it lurked deep inside. Even when their own powerful mothers did it, they reacted like this. Ben sniffed and muttered 'Okay, then,' before changing the subject. 'There's a pub along here, I think.'

They found a table in the agreeable spring sunshine and Simmy gave Ben money to go and order food and drink. 'Something with plenty of carbs,' she said. 'A ploughman's would be perfect.'

'Ham or cheese?'

'Both, if they'll do that.'

He was soon back, carrying two pint glasses of beer. Here was further evidence of his maturity. The Ben she thought she knew had been wary of alcohol. Student life had done its usual trick, she supposed. 'Food won't be long,' he said.

As she suckled her infant, with a modest cardigan thrown over her nakedness, she tried to analyse the fresh information concerning Josephine. 'I'm sure Christopher didn't know anything at all about that researching or whatever it was,' she said. 'He never mentioned it.'

'I got the impression it was kept very separate from her day job.'

'Mm.' She found herself feeling very sleepy again. It had been a short and broken night and a busy morning. The beer wasn't helping. 'Gosh, I'm dozing off here,' she said. 'Do something to wake me up.'

'Like what?'

'Go over all the connections between Fabian's family and Josephine, and see if we've missed something. There's a whole lot I haven't told you about Richmond yet. Did I say he's only got one arm?'

They were interrupted by the arrival of their food, the man bringing it showing extreme alarm at the nursing mother in front of him. Ben and Simmy merely smiled their thanks and quickly started to eat.

Ben spoke with his mouth full. 'You've barely said a word about Richmond so far. We dashed up to Hilda's house without any proper debriefing. Not that it matters. We can do it now.'

But they were interrupted after two or three minutes by Ben's imperious phone, playing a tune that Simmy didn't recognise. After only a few seconds he handed it to Simmy, saying, 'Bonnie wants you.'

'I knew he was with you,' the girl explained. 'You're not answering your own phone. I've tried about ten times.'

'I'm not even sure I brought it with me,' Simmy confessed. 'We left in a bit of a rush. What's the matter?'

'The thing is, Verity's had to go home, so I'm here all on

my own and it's quite busy. She only stayed about an hour and then dashed off. What do you want me to do? There are three deliveries booked for this afternoon, which I can't possibly do.'

'What's the matter with Verity?'

'It's not her. It's her mother. She fell downstairs or something and they think she might die. It's all rather a drama.' Bonnie's tone was commendably calm and Simmy felt a matching absence of panic. 'There's not much point trying to get Tanya – she can't do deliveries, either. I was wondering if your mum . . .'

'No, no,' said Simmy. 'Listen – I can come in for a bit this afternoon and do the deliveries. We're having a quick lunch and then going to the auction house. We found something that Ben thinks is exciting this morning and he wants to have a look at the computer in the office there for the archives. We can tell you all about it when we see you.'

'That's great! You sound quite fired up. How's the baby?'

'He's behaving beautifully, even though Ben seems to think he has too many feeds.' His remark was still rankling, she discovered, to her own shame.

'What does Ben know?' said Bonnie supportively. 'He's only a man.'

'Anyway, give us a couple of hours at most. Ben's bike is in Troutbeck, which will mean a bit of a detour. There'll be awful traffic, as well. Where are the deliveries to go to? Did Verity put fuel in the van this week?'

Bonnie filled her in on the details, and Simmy ended the call on a surprising high. It was deeply satisfying to be needed by her assistant, to be reassured that the shop was still hers, and there were times when only she could deal with its needs. Her identity as a businesswoman and a florist was still intact, just beneath the new role as mother. She bounced Robin on her arm, as if encouraging him to share her foolish elation.

Ben had gleaned almost everything, including the reference to his tactless comment about the feeding of babies. 'We're going back to Windermere, then?' he said.

'After we've looked at Christopher's computer, yes. And after I've taken you to collect your bike.'

'So what about the baby clinic?' he asked.

Chapter Seventeen

'I forgot all about it,' she said, with an embarrassed giggle. 'Never gave it a thought. What time is it now?'

'Twenty past twelve. You'd have had a rush anyway, without having to rescue Bonnie. I was just going to mention it when the phone went.'

'I'll go next week instead. I can send a text or something. There's no way I'm leaving Bonnie to struggle on her own. And the deliveries have to be made, come what may. I'll lose business if I let three lots of people down. It's unthinkable.'

'If you're sure,' he said, with a concerned glance at Robin. Again, there was that annoying male assumption that without some official medical surveillance the child might be at risk.

'Of course I'm sure. They only want to interfere anyway and upset us both. I never thought I'd feel like this, but I'm very happy indeed to find I'm more than merely a mother. It won't hurt him to come down to the shop. I might even pop into Beck View while I'm there.'

'You'll have to leave him somewhere, if you're using

the van,' Ben pointed out. 'I don't imagine there's a baby seat in it.'

'Never mind all that. Let's go to the saleroom. Finish that pasta thing and we can get going. I'll tell you the rest of the Richmond story in the car. I'll just take Robin into the ladies' and give him a new nappy.'

She managed to convey everything she could recall of the conversation with Richmond the previous evening, in the five minutes it took to reach the auction house. 'That's it,' she concluded. 'He was nice. And I'm assuming that the lack of an arm would make stabbing a fit and healthy woman quite difficult.'

'It definitely was a stabbing, you know,' Ben said. 'It was in the latest news report last night.'

'Oh. I'd been assuming it was, ever since Oliver said there was a lot of blood. Not that I really want to know that sort of detail.'

'It would be very difficult for Richmond to have done it, I agree,' Ben said. 'But the backstory could be crucial, all the same. There's obviously something murky.' He went quiet, before bursting out, 'What if he's the mystery baby that Hilda said she'd had? Isn't that what he was trying to tell you? That Hilda was his mother, not his sister?'

Simmy forced herself to stay focused on the road, despite the buzzing in her head that this idea caused. 'What? Good Lord, Ben – isn't that a pretty big leap? If it's true, why didn't he just say it directly? I actually asked him who his parents were and he dodged the question.'

'I don't think it's a leap at all. I think it's crystal clear. The main question is why – if she'd dumped him on a foster mother at birth – did she then make the whole thing public umpteen years later?'

'Circumstances change. I can think of all sorts of reasons.' Despite herself, she was fitting the known facts into Ben's hypothesis and finding it was not entirely ludicrous after all. 'But where did that idea even come from?'

'Where any ideas come from, I suppose,' he shrugged. 'Of course, the other massive question then is, how does it link up with Josephine?'

'Remind me why we need to find out what that auction lot in the garage was. It was just a box, after all.'

'Two boxes,' he corrected her. 'But I do admit there's only the slightest cause to think they're important. The honest truth is that I thought it would be an excuse to see how the auction database works, and how much information they keep about every item sold. If we could persuade Christopher to let us rummage around in it, we might come up with all kinds of useful stuff.'

'Us,' Simmy sighed. 'It's all hugely confidential, I expect. And it would take hours to have a proper look through the whole thing.'

'Days,' he said happily. 'I wonder how hackable it is.'

'Don't you dare! Christopher would never speak to you again. Oliver would probably give him the sack. You won't, will you?'

'Don't panic. Even if I did, nobody would ever know.'

'We're here now. Just behave yourself,' she ordered, still hankering for the schoolboy he had been half an hour ago.

Christopher met them at the entrance to the reception area, looking tired and worried. Simmy initially took his concern to be about her and the baby, but she was soon disabused. 'We're having a rather fractious meeting,' he said. 'I saw you out of the window and came to head you off. Why are you here?'

'Ben had an idea and wants to look something up on your database. A sale two years ago. Is that allowed?'

'I guess that depends on what he plans to do with the information.' He rubbed his face. 'Honestly, Sim, it's not a very good time. Aren't you supposed to be at the baby clinic?'

'I'm putting it off till next week. This is more interesting.'

He gave a sceptical laugh. 'How can anything be more interesting than our baby?'

'I didn't mean it like that. Is everybody at your meeting? Isn't there a girl somewhere who'd like to do a bit of dandling?'

Christopher looked at Robin, who was already in his buggy. 'We won't be much longer. Have a look round while you wait. There's some really nice Moorcroft just in. Even you can recognise Moorcroft, can't you? Just don't break it.' He looked at his son again. 'You won't turn up with him like this when he's three, will you? He'll be in full vandalism mode by then.'

He then hurried back to the meeting and Simmy turned to Ben. 'Looks as if we've got to wait,' she said.

'I know. I heard. Let's check out that Moorcroft, then. You know it's the single most consistently sought-after china there is, don't you? People never seem to get tired of it.'

'I expect some real antique snobs look down on it, for that very reason.'

'Possibly,' said Ben dubiously.

They went into the big saleroom and started to look around. 'That must be the Moorcroft over there.' Ben pointed to a shelf.

They found a group of three slender vases, all the same shape but with very different decoration. 'They're so *elegant*,' breathed Simmy. 'Nothing bulbous or fiddly. The more you look at them, the more gorgeous they are.'

'A triumph of form,' nodded Ben. He then looked around at the large area that was the main saleroom. 'Where do they put the memorabilia?'

'It hasn't been sorted yet. There aren't any lot numbers on anything. These stickers are the vendor numbers.'

'Hey – get you!' he said. 'You're picking it all up, aren't you?'

'Only the basics,' she admitted. 'I'll never work out the system they use for deciding on the lot numbers. Apparently it used to be alphabetical by vendor, but there were complaints because the same people always came last, when most buyers had gone home.'

They wandered aimlessly around the disorganised-looking tables, the buggy barely squeezing between the rows in some places. Large items of furniture were lined up against the back wall, with rolled-up carpets and rugs leaning against some of them. 'It's all rather magical,' said Ben. 'I can see how people could get addicted.'

Then a woman approached them, and their wait was over. 'Fiona,' said Simmy. 'I'm sorry if we're a bother.'

Suddenly their intrusion felt embarrassing and foolish. She and Ben would have to be careful not to say too much. Any mention of the Armitage family would be ill-advised, for a start. 'Do you think we could check out a sale you had here two years ago on your computer? We've already asked Christopher about it.'

Fiona looked very pale and droopy. Simmy remembered that there was potential rivalry between her and Pattie for Josephine's job. Perhaps the meeting had decided in favour of Pattie, leaving Fiona to sulk. Except this looked more like grief than resentment. 'Are you all right?' Simmy asked.

'More or less. Everything's changing, and we're all in a muddle.' She waved a hand at the piles of objects. 'We're at least a day behind with all this, and then Oliver calls a meeting that puts things back even further.'

'Oliver's here, is he?'

Fiona nodded. 'We don't seem to be able to manage without him.'

Before any more could be said, Christopher appeared, followed by Pattie, Oliver and a woman Simmy didn't recognise. 'Come on then,' Christopher said to Ben impatiently. 'Let's get it over with. Everyone's going for lunch now, so we've got a bit of time.' The whole group seemed jaded and discordant. Only Pattie acknowledged the presence of baby Robin, and she was nowhere near as enthusiastic as she'd been two days before. 'He's looking very contented,' was all she said.

Christopher led them into the small office, where the buggy was very much in the way. He sat Ben at the computer and, leaning over him, tapped a few keys. 'What date was it?' he asked.

Ben extracted his phone and showed his picture of the auction house label. Christopher copied the date and lot number and then stepped back. 'There it is,' he said, without giving the result a proper look.

'"Two boxes of papers and letters from the 1940s",' read Ben. 'Hammer price six pounds. Right. Seems like a bargain.'

'Does that leave you any the wiser?' asked Christopher.

'Can we see who sold them and who bought them?'

'It's all there. Scroll down a bit.'

With a surprised glance from Simmy to Christopher and back, Ben did as advised. 'Vendor was somebody called W. J. Bolt, and buyer was a person called H. M. Armitage. Right. As we expected, really. Any idea who the Bolt character is?'

'Um . . . wait a minute. That date. Just over two years ago. I think that was my very first time as auctioneer. The date is engraved on my heart. I made a right mess of the whole thing. I was so slow we didn't finish until gone seven o'clock. It was pouring with rain and there was a big football match on, so there were very few buyers, either here or online.'

'Do you remember this lot, by any chance?'

Christopher read the description for himself. 'Oh God,' he said, turning a nasty shade of grey. 'I do. It got me into trouble with Oliver. That and a few other bloopers. Gosh – it's all coming back to me now. That wretched old woman – she came up to me later, when she was collecting the boxes at the end. Full of herself, she was, smiling from ear to ear. "You don't know what you've just let go for peanuts," she gloated. I tried not to take any notice, but a few days later, Oliver gave me a bollocking because the vendor had complained that we didn't list it properly. I was only doing it because he'd been off sick and there wasn't anyone else. Everyone could see I wasn't ready to be dropped in the deep end like that.' He stared at Ben. 'Why, out of all the thousands of lots I've sold since then, did you have to choose this one?'

'That woman was Aunt Hilda,' said Simmy slowly. 'The very one you promised Fabian you'd go and see. We found boxes with this lot number on them in her garage.'

'Oh,' said Christopher. 'Then I can only assume it must be karma, chasing me up because I didn't do what I promised Fabian.'

'That'll be it,' said Ben. 'Who's the Bolt person?'

'The name rings a bell, but I don't think I ever met him. He's in London, deals in memorabilia.'

'So what was in the boxes that was worth more than six pounds?'

'I have no idea. I never even looked properly. The woman held up a bundle of letters and waved them in my face. They didn't look like anything special to me – not even in envelopes with stamps on. Sometimes that's the only reason people buy that sort of stuff. She must have had a good look at them at the viewing the previous day, and spotted something. But there was no reserve, so there was nothing to stop her buying them for a few quid. Actually, I think if she'd waited, I'd have dropped down even lower.'

'Nobody else bidded for them?'

Christopher shook his head.

'Well, it's a fascinating insight into how it all works,' said Ben happily. 'Even though it might not be relevant to anything. The 1940s was a long time ago.'

Simmy was only half listening to the conversation, as she bent over Robin and tried to interest him in a plastic toy attached to the buggy. His jerky, swiping motions persuaded her that he was trying to grab for it, and that made her proud of his obvious intelligence. 'If the vendor knew he was selling something valuable, he'd have made a point of it, wouldn't he? I mean, you wouldn't just bung an original letter from Hitler or someone in a job lot without a reserve, would you?' said Ben.

'Exactly what I said to Oliver,' Christopher agreed. 'I assumed the vendor was just disappointed in a general sort of way. He apologised eventually and said there was no real harm done. Turned out the buyer was a better friend than the vendor. So at least she was happy with us.'

'Did Oliver see the letters?' asked Simmy. 'Isn't he interested in that sort of thing?'

Christopher groaned helplessly. 'I really don't know. And I'd much prefer it if you didn't ask him. It took him quite a while to get over being cross with me for being so sloppy. Josephine tried to defend me, I remember. Told him that none of it was my fault.'

'And she would have known who the woman was, because of her friendship with that family,' Simmy noted.

'It does all connect,' said Ben, obviously thinking hard. 'Papers, letters, history. And that nephew trying to write

Hilda's life story. She was probably co-operating with him and feeding him information, with hard evidence to back it all up. You know something? We might yet find some real evidence concerning her baby. The date's about right, after all.'

Christopher had transferred much of his attention to his son. The word 'baby' could only refer to Robin – but that was puzzling. He frowned. 'What baby?'

'Hilda claimed she had a baby out of wedlock somewhere late in the 1940s. I'm sure I told you. It was in the papers,' said Simmy. 'Not at the time, but years later, when she tried to sue the father, or something.'

'Old history,' Christopher said. 'Why does it matter now?'

'It might well matter if the father was somebody important, as seems very likely. And now we're wondering whether that baby might possibly have been Richmond – abandoned because of his missing arm. People didn't like defects in those days.'

'And Hilda *really* didn't like them. Fabian told us that,' Christopher added thoughtfully. 'Do the dates fit?'

'Looks like it.'

'Which somehow seems to bring us back to Hitler,' said Christopher, with another frown, this time a more playful one. 'Please don't tell me that Richmond Armitage is Hitler's lost love child.'

'No – because Hitler died three years before the child was born,' said Simmy irritably.

Ben was still scrolling up and down the auction house database. Suddenly he took out a notebook and pencil and jotted something down. 'What's that?' demanded Christopher.

'Just the basics. Simmy's going to want to go in a minute and I don't want to keep her waiting. Bonnie needs her at the shop.'

'Annoyingly, this young man has just filled his nappy,' said Simmy. 'It was only on for five minutes, too. I'll do it in the loo, if you like. Lucky I put two spares in the bag.'

Christopher groaned again and rubbed the top of his head. 'Do it anywhere you want. I'm really not enjoying today,' he complained. 'Nobody's telling me anything. Even Oliver's gone all tight-lipped. He's upset the girls, and as for Jack – I think he's weeping in a corner somewhere. He was very attached to Josephine, apparently, although I can't say I ever noticed.'

'It's all here,' said Ben obscurely. 'It just needs to be figured out.'

'You need to do an algorithm,' teased Simmy over her shoulder, as she headed for the toilet.

'I do,' he agreed with perfect seriousness.

'We forgot to tell him about Chrissie Harriman,' said Simmy in the car. 'I keep forgetting to tell people things. I should phone Moxon and update him, I suppose.'

'You'll get at least two Brownie points.'

'What did you write in the notebook?'

'Just the Bolt person's email address,' he said airily. 'That can't hurt anything, can it?'

'I don't know. It's probably breaking data protection laws – as you jolly well ought to know.'

'That's why I didn't tell Christopher what I was doing. Nobody's ever going to know. It's a good database, though. Beautifully organised.'

'Josephine must have been very capable.'

'I shouldn't think she could take much credit for it. The software comes already packaged – you just have to put the information in.'

'Even so,' Simmy argued, 'I imagine plenty of people make a mess of doing that.'

'It must be a nice one to work with – I mean, there's something very straightforward about it all, and yet there's so much variety in the things they sell. I never wondered about the descriptions, until now. Everything hinges on that, when you think about it.'

The conversation was disjointed, as Simmy drove southwards to Windermere. They passed the outskirts of Grasmere and Banerigg where Simmy had been handed a small baby, just at the very start of her pregnancy. Superstitiously, she credited that infant with the successful implantation of the fertilised egg that became Robin. A surge of hormones just at the right moment seemed to her a perfectly rational assumption. Then they were into Ambleside, which had numerous associations with murder and malice. Having Ben as a passenger heightened and focused the memories. There had also been Hawkshead and Coniston and Staveley, all of them bringing her and Ben together in the contemplation of violent crime.

'Bonnie must be feeling a bit left out,' Simmy said. 'Stuck there in the shop all the time with only Verity to talk to.'

'Yeah, she does. Don't forget my bike,' he warned, as

they approached the first of three possible turnings up to Troutbeck. 'This is the quickest way.'

More reminiscences gripped Simmy as she did as directed. She had lived in Troutbeck since moving up to the Lakes, and selling her cottage there had been a wrench. It had not been given enough time to fully adopt her personality, the garden still a long way from perfect, and she felt an occasional foolish shame for abandoning it as she did. Christopher and Robin had diverted her expected trajectory, to the point where she had almost forgotten the Troutbeck interlude. The sudden appearance of Moxon the day before had swamped similar feelings of nostalgia.

The road was steep and well filled with tourist traffic. 'What are you going to do next?' she asked.

'Go home and start that algorithm. I'll need to ask you more questions, I expect. The Petrock chap, for example. Quite a lot keeps coming back to him. I'll do a bit more googling, see if I can unearth any more about Hilda and her family. Today's moving too fast – we're dropping things that we should be thinking about. There's a whole *armful* of clues, if we just slow down and really look at it intelligently.'

'Right,' said Simmy, hoping she was being sufficiently intelligent for his purposes. 'So I guess you're on your own for the rest of the afternoon. I'll be out delivering flowers until half past three or so, and then I expect I'll go to Beck View and give my poor baby some attention. Thank goodness we're not trying to stick to any sort of schedule. All that seems to have gone out of the window.'

'My mother always says they thrive on neglect.'

'She's probably right, but maybe it's just slightly too soon to experiment. If he has even the mildest mental health issues in later life, I'm going to blame myself for neglecting him when he was tiny.'

'Phooey to that,' said Ben.

Chapter Eighteen

Bonnie was being stoical in the face of adversity when Simmy finally reached the shop, having weaved the baby buggy in and out of groups of tourists who were looking for something to do in Windermere. *Just go down to Bowness, why don't you?* she silently shouted at them. For many of them, this was the last day of their holiday, and they were probably checking out Windermere just in case they'd missed something.

There were three customers waiting for Bonnie's attention, presumably wanting flowers for the weekend. Simmy experienced a strong sense of déjà vu. 'Haven't you got any irises?' the one at the head of the queue was demanding. 'What about freesias?'

'Irises no, freesias yes,' said Bonnie patiently. 'And scented roses that came in this morning.'

'You can't put roses with freesias,' said the woman, as if this was one of the Ten Commandments.

Simmy pushed forward, and addressed the second person in the line. 'Can I help you?'

'I just wanted this,' said the meek, middle-aged woman, who had the air of spending most of her life waiting in a queue. She proffered a large fern in a pot. 'I've been looking for one like it for a long time now.'

'It's lovely, isn't it. Where will you put it?'

'In the bathroom. They like moist air, don't they?'

'They do,' Simmy confirmed. She then had to wait for Bonnie to finish at the till before she could take the customer's money. She sometimes wondered why it was that people buying flowers so often paid with cash, rather than a card. Were they embarrassed at having the purchase show up on their statements – or what?

The third person waiting was suddenly receiving double attention, as the way cleared. Simmy automatically waved him forward, before catching herself and looking at Bonnie. 'All yours,' she said.

The man was straightforward, wanting a nice colourful bunch for his wife and paying shamelessly with a card. Simmy and Bonnie both knew him as a regular. 'Sorry you had to wait,' said Bonnie.

'No problem. I'm earlier than usual. We've got a new thing at work, where we can knock off at three on a Friday. It's meant to help us get ahead of the rush, but if anything it's worse.'

'You've got all the school people as well,' smiled Bonnie.

'Right.' The man was in his late fifties and had probably forgotten all about school schedules.

At last the shop was empty. 'Phew!' gasped Bonnie. 'It's no fun trying to do this on your own. Am I minding Robin while you do the deliveries?' She looked worried.

'Well . . . that was the idea. But he's going to get hungry soon. It's been a very weird day, from his point of view.

Lots of driving, which he didn't seem to mind, luckily. But rather snatched feeds at random times. And now he's fast asleep, look.'

'Go now,' Bonnie urged. 'You'll only be forty minutes or so – unless the traffic gets really bad. There's Newby Bridge, then Blackwell, then someone just round the corner from Ben's house. I've got all the postcodes for you – shall I put them in the phone?'

'All the way to Newby Bridge?' Simmy sighed.

''Fraid so. It sounds quite easy – you've been there before, I think. The flowers are all done, anyway. I'll go and put them in the van.'

Despite her earlier relief at still being needed at the shop, it caused Simmy a certain degree of distress to abandon Robin and return to her old routine of flower delivery. 'It's not even a month yet,' she whined to herself. 'And here I am back at work, just as I vowed not to be. I'm a mess of contradictions, let's face it.' She could hear, in her mind's ear, the baby's howls of hunger and abandonment. How could she – and not even leave him a dummy for comfort? Angie had threatened to disown her if she ever used a dummy.

The traffic was mercifully co-operative, until the final few minutes, when trying to get back onto the main road after the last delivery proved almost impossible. In the end, she simply pushed out in front of an elderly woman driving an elderly car, waving a thanks that would have gone unseen through the solid sides of the van. She threaded it through the narrow alley that led to the back of the shop and rushed to her baby's rescue, terrified of the implications of what she'd done.

'He hasn't moved a muscle,' said Bonnie complacently. 'I parked him in the back room and forgot all about him.'

Simmy's next horrified thought was that he must therefore be dead. She almost shook him in her efforts to check for a breath. 'Calm down,' said Bonnie. 'He's absolutely fine.'

Which he was. 'I'd better get off to Beck View, then,' said Simmy. 'I can feed him there, if he ever wakes up.'

Bonnie's forlorn expression gave her pause. 'Oh Lord, you poor thing,' said Simmy. 'I'm really sorry you got landed with it all. When's Verity likely to be back?'

'She didn't say. It'll be all right for a few days now, anyway. If Tanya comes in tomorrow, and if Monday's as quiet as it usually is, we needn't worry till Tuesday. Maybe you could call her and make her say what she's doing.'

'Ben and I need to talk to you about things. It's been a very productive day. He's gone home to do an algorithm and work out who's the chief suspect. We had to go to Keswick.'

'Yes, I know. He's been texting me about it.'

'Has he? That's good.'

'I don't really understand it, though. There's no way he can tell me everything until I see him. I'm going down there this evening, to see if I can catch up.'

'I'm supposed to be phoning Moxon. He asked me to talk to a neighbour of Josephine's and we met her in the street. Christopher knows her. What she told us was interesting. In fact, the whole day has been extremely interesting, one way and another. I think we sort of know the whole thing, if we can just put it all together.'

'It's half past four, Sim. You'd better get going. Maybe we can get together on Sunday, like last week, and sort it all out then.'

Sunday still felt quite a long way off to Simmy, as she walked her somnolent infant back to Beck View, where she had left her car. Her main concern was a sudden raging thirst, due to having nothing to drink since the pub lunch. She began to walk faster, which had the useful effect of lulling Robin into yet more sleep.

Her parents were in receptive mode, settling her on the sofa, bringing a large mug of tea and inviting her to talk to them. 'We heard about the woman at Christopher's workplace,' said Angie. 'You never told us.'

'Didn't I? I can tell you now, if you like. Dad met her last year – the woman in the office, sitting at the computer.'

'Don't remember,' said Russell.

'Ben and I have been doing detective work all day. It's been fun, mostly. Robin was incredibly co-operative. He doesn't mind the car any more. Christopher's in a tizzy, obviously. Not just because they've lost Josephine so horribly, but because there's this man called Fabian Crick, who knew Josephine and has a whole lot of relations called Armitage.'

Russell's eyes went wide and his head jerked forward. 'Is one of them called Petrock?' he asked.

'Actually, yes. He's a cousin. The person at the centre of it all is their Aunt Hilda. She died not long ago, and Petrock's writing her biography. She did a lot of remarkable things, apparently.'

Russell laughed. 'He's been saying he'd write it for years. I doubt if he ever will. Though it'll help that she's dead. You can't libel the dead.'

'You know him?' It was his wife who spoke. 'How?'

'He was in that little writing group I used to go to in Ambleside. When I was trying to collect local anecdotes for a booklet – remember? We were all decades older than him, and I suspect we patronised him rather. He didn't stay very long. I remember him mainly for his wonderful name. We all thought he was rather a fantasist, I'm afraid, dreaming of revealing some shocking incident from his aunt's early life. We warned him about libel and so forth, I remember, but he said it would all be true and he was determined to prove it. Some documents he said would confirm the whole thing.'

'He's written most of it,' Simmy said. 'I saw the manuscript. He even read some of it to me and Christopher. And Ben found some newspaper reports about Hilda in the 1960s. It looks as if things have moved on since you knew him.'

'Made more progress than you did with your booklet, then,' said Angie rather unkindly.

Simmy briefly told them the main points concerning Ben's discovery of a mysterious baby and the apparent links to Josephine, which were tantalisingly difficult to pin down in any detail. 'We still think one of them must have killed her. When we tell Ben that you knew Petrock, he'll be thrilled. I have a feeling he thinks that he's the most likely suspect.'

'No, no,' said Russell firmly. 'That man could never kill anyone. He's much too dithery for that.'

'He's young and strong and didn't seem a bit dithery to

me. His brother's more so. And as for Uncle Ambrose . . .' she giggled. 'He's the very epitome of ditheriness. He's an archivist and spends all his time with musty old books.'

Russell gave her a severe look. 'That's a very inaccurate stereotype, if I may say so. Archivists are the sharpest people of all. They never miss a detail or fail to spot a connection. They can read handwriting from the sixteenth century that's totally illegible to anybody else. I often wish I'd been one,' he finished wistfully.

'I stand corrected,' smiled Simmy. 'He should be working for Oliver, by the sound of it. I never realised that his speciality is authenticating old bits of ivory and documents – and Josephine seems to have been doing something interesting with old documents as well. Her neighbour told us today that she used to sit up half the night poring over papers or letters or suchlike. She collected that sort of stuff, apparently.'

'What sort of stuff?'

Simmy didn't answer for a moment, as she shifted Robin to the other side, and asked her mother if there was any more tea on offer. 'There's some sort of thread running through all this,' she said slowly, more to herself than to Russell. 'Something about letters from the 1940s. It's all gradually coming clearer. I wish I could go to Ben's now and talk it through with him.'

'But you've got responsibilities,' said Russell, eyeing the baby.

By a quirk of mental association Simmy suddenly remembered another dependent creature. 'The squirrel!' she yelped. 'I forgot all about the squirrel! It will have died of hunger by now. I've been out all day.'

'Have you changed that baby's nappy lately?' Angie asked, coming back with the second mug of tea. 'There's a bit of a whiff.'

'I haven't got any left. I put the last one on when we were in Keswick. He seems to be a right little poo machine today. I didn't think I'd be out this long when I left home this morning. Have you got any here?' She did not expect an affirmative answer, but Angie Straw was nothing if not resourceful. As the owner of a busy B&B, it was, Simmy supposed, hardly surprising that such emergency items should be kept available for feckless guests.

'Of course I have,' she said. 'But mostly in larger sizes than you need.' She went off to rummage in the appropriate drawer.

'Squirrel?' Russell prompted. Simmy explained. 'A *grey* squirrel?' He was delighted, to the point of gently clapping his hands. 'You devil. Although, did I tell you I heard on *QI* this week that the reds are in fact more recently introduced than the greys? Can you believe that? It's a bit of a semantic game, but all the reds were totally wiped out centuries ago – presumably by human beings – and quite a while later they imported replacements from Scandinavia, much more recently than the greys got here from America. And now they're exterminating them. Doesn't that create some sort of moral quagmire, don't you think?'

'I thought so already,' said Simmy, feeling idiotically distressed about her neglected little pet. 'Will it have died, do you think?'

'Not from hunger. Did it have water?'

'A bit. I'll have to go. Christopher's going to be there before me as it is. What a bad wife I'm going to make.' She paused. 'And that's another thing. The wedding. I can't imagine how we're going to get everything ready in time. Even keeping it simple, there's a horribly long list of things to do. I haven't thought about it at all today.'

'Wedding schmedding,' said Russell, apparently thinking he was being hilarious.

Driving home, Simmy felt painfully torn in a number of directions. Only hours ago she had been congratulating herself on managing to be a fully functioning person, engaged in another unofficial murder investigation with Ben, while at the same time being a more than adequate mother to Robin. It struck her now that Christopher had not featured at all in this self-congratulatory thinking. How was it that she so often found herself secondary to someone else's needs, stressing about who came first and what she might best do for them? It had to be, she supposed, that this was how she liked it. If pressed, she could not have identified any other course than this. There was nothing she actively wanted to do differently. She loved the shop and the autonomy it brought her. There at least she was only answerable to herself. But she was loving the new house and the new baby just as much.

And, to her horror, she realised she very much loved the intellectual games with Ben, solving the mysteries of the criminal mind, plunging into the labyrinth of brutal murder with Ben and Bonnie and earning the approval of DI Moxon. She wanted it all, she concluded – and that probably made her a very greedy person.

She had texted Christopher with an update, apologising for failing to be at home to greet him and asking him if he would please feed the squirrel. 'I just got carried away,' she said at the end.

Kirkstone Pass was cluttered with tourist traffic, some of it evidently eager to watch the sunset from such a good vantage point. Mindful of the baby in the back, Simmy slowed down and kept a careful watch for any careless drivers or panicked sheep that could require a sudden application of the brakes.

She got back at five forty-five, to find Christopher frying sausages while the deep fat fryer sizzled with chips. 'Ooh, calories!' she rejoiced. 'Wonderful!'

Robin sat in his little chair while they ate. 'He's been in that thing all day,' Simmy worried. 'Do you think it'll damage his posture?'

'Probably not. I fed the squirrel for you. It was very grateful. We won't have any muesli left at this rate. Apparently it doesn't like carrots, though.'

'Thanks. Maybe it'll be ready to go back into the wild in a few days.'

'The sooner the better. We haven't space in our lives for another baby just at the moment.'

'I thought we were getting a puppy this summer.'

He looked up in surprise. 'Oh? I thought you were still vetoing that idea.'

'I thought perhaps a golden retriever . . .' she said shyly. 'It'd be nice for Robin. It could be my wedding present to you.'

'Hallelujah!' he cried. Then he said, 'I've earned it, actually. After you'd gone today I had a look at the database, checking to see what else Hilda Armitage had bought, before and after those papers. She wasn't anything like a regular at the auctions, but she did get hold of another couple of collections, like the one you found. I asked Jack if he remembered her. He's very sharp, you know, in spite of seeming so inconspicuous. He knows everybody, and remembers most of what they buy – and sell. He had a think and said he'd seen Oliver and Hilda in a huddle over old papers and stuff, quite a few times. And he told me that Oliver went to Hilda's funeral, but Josephine didn't, which seems a bit odd, given that she left Josie the house.'

'It's new information. Were all three of them working on some sort of historical project, do you think? Maybe Petrock as well. So – could they have fallen out somehow and divided into two camps?' She shook her head. 'That doesn't seem to work, does it? Or if it does, we need a lot more to go on.'

Christopher plucked the baby from his bondage and lifted him high in the air. Robin blinked. Simmy bit back the urge to tell Chris to be careful. 'I still can't quite believe he's real,' the new father marvelled. 'And now I can have a dog as well. It's a miracle.'

Simmy just smiled, then remembered to say, 'My father knows Petrock. Says he'd never be capable of killing anyone.'

He shifted the baby so he was lying along his father's forearm, and then gently rocked him as the conversation went on. 'Really? I'd have said of all the Armitages, he's probably the most likely.'

She sighed. 'We're still just guessing. So why were you all so boot-faced after that meeting today? I've never seen such a glum lot. Was it just about Josephine, or what?'

'Mostly that, but Fiona said something that annoyed Oliver, and when Jack stuck up for her, he got a bollocking as well. Pattie said the atmosphere was so horrible she was considering looking for another job, and I got caught in the crossfire.'

'What did Fiona say?'

'I didn't catch all of it, but she seemed to be suggesting that Josephine had brought it on herself somehow. I think she said something like, "You'd think getting that house would have been enough for her." Oliver went very red and told her she ought to know better. Then she started accusing him of cowardice in sending her to Josie's house instead of going himself. Oliver said that had been me, not him, but I wasn't standing for that. He'd told us what to do, over the phone. There was almost a suggestion in Fiona's mind, apparently, that he knew what she would find.'

'I suppose that isn't too surprising. I mean – not that Josie had been murdered, but that there was something wrong.'

'It was all pretty toxic for a few minutes. I felt much the same as Pattie about it.'

She switched subjects yet again. 'Why do you think Petrock's the chief suspect?'

'How about this: if Hilda had a big secret – as we know she did – then him writing her life story is going to unearth it, right? And probably make a big deal of it. Maybe somebody's very worried about that and wants to stop him. And knowing that, he takes pre-emptive action and silences that person – who might very well have been Josephine. Do you follow?'

'Gosh!' she sat back, full of admiration for his lucidity. 'Put like that, it all seems to slot into a perfectly credible picture. I expect Ben's got there already and has it all mapped out on a flowchart. Even so – I'm impressed.' Christopher smirked, and Simmy went on, 'But why would Josephine be worried about the secret?'

'Good question. Something to do with Richmond, maybe? He might have a whole lot of seething resentment that she could have helped him deal with. She might even have been helping him get some kind of revenge.'

She was struck by a thought. 'Something Ben said a day or two ago – whether it's the opposite of what we're all assuming. Maybe Josephine was making threats to someone, not just by knowing a secret, but by actively making it dangerous for them in some way. She might have been seen as a real risk to their well-being – reputation, finances, whatever. What if she knew Petrock was going to deliberately lie in his book and told him she'd expose the truth? That would fit.'

It was exhilarating, she discovered, airing bold theories like this to a partner who knew the characters involved and was fully engaged with the whole story. 'Wow!' she breathed. 'I'd forgotten what fun this can be.'

'Fun?' He cocked an eyebrow at her. 'Wasn't it you I heard telling Ben and Bonnie that it really wasn't a game – I think when my father was killed.'

'I expect it was. And I do feel awful about poor Josephine, but not awful enough to crush the excitement of working out what happened. The two aren't incompatible, after all.'

They were interrupted at this point by Robin's demands, which both parents devoted all their energy to satisfying. 'I have to say I'm enjoying this a lot more than I thought I would,' said Christopher, as he lifted his little son out of the bath and wrapped him in a towel. 'I mean – I knew I wanted children, but I expected to have to wait a year or two before they . . . I don't know . . . became real to me, I suppose.'

'He is very real, isn't he,' Simmy agreed. 'A proper little person.' Which little Edith had never been, she sadly admitted to herself. A stillborn baby had no chance of overcoming the fantasies and dreams of its parents, never asserting its own personality.

An hour later, just as Simmy was rehearsing what she would say in an overdue phone call to Moxon, she saw a figure passing the kitchen window. 'Damn it,' she said. 'Not again. That looks horribly like Fabian.'

Chapter Nineteen

And it was. 'Quick – don't let him in,' Simmy hissed, already knowing that such a move was impossible. 'At least tell him to go away. Doesn't that damned scooter ever run out of battery? He must be breaking all records, the way he's up and down the road all the time.'

But Christopher was incapable of telling anyone to go away. 'Thank goodness it's only him this time,' he muttered, before opening the door. 'Fabian,' he said flatly. 'Fancy seeing you again.'

'Sorry, sorry.' The man came in, left shoulder first, appearing to have shrunk and somehow twisted since they'd last seen him. Simmy was put in mind of Derek Jacobi in the part of Claudius on the TV series she had watched on video with her father in her teens.

'Are you ill?' she asked him with a frown.

'No more than usual. Stress doesn't help. You've got to do something.' He looked from face to face, mutating from Claudius into Uriah Heap. 'It's all wrong. And – sorry to say it – but it's all your fault. Yes, it is, very much so. I can't stand another day like this.' His twitch added to the figure of pathos that he presented.

'Explain,' said Christopher, waving him in and closing the door behind him. 'What on earth do you think we can do?'

'Find out who killed Josie, of course. You and that boy in Bowness. The police are practically camping on my doorstep, watching everything I do. And it's the same for the others – Petrock and Keith anyway. It's not right. We never touched her. We all *loved* her.'

Simmy forced herself to relax, refusing to accept the burden that Fabian was trying to unload. This was what he did, she thought. He used other people, made them give assurances and undertakings that they never wanted to. 'I suppose they're just following the evidence,' she said calmly.

'What evidence?' Fabian shot back. 'There can't *be* any evidence. It's all wrong, I tell you.'

'Don't get upset,' said Christopher. 'Have a drink and then go back home. You've probably been overreacting.'

'Home!' said the man bitterly. 'A mean little room that costs more than you'd believe. I'm at the end of my rope, I can tell you. I'd be better off in gaol, and that's the truth. Maybe I'll go out and stab someone, just so's I can get a free bed.'

Neither of his listeners responded to that. *Not our problem*, Simmy repeated silently. She had learnt some time ago that you couldn't rescue people from their own bad choices or character defects. Fabian apparently thought otherwise. He had said it was their fault, and in a small annoying way he was probably right. Christopher had given Fabian's name to the police, as well as failing in his mission to go and see Aunt Hilda. It was not entirely unreasonable to feel affronted by both those details, she supposed.

'What am I meant to do?' Fabian whined on. 'How can any of us carry on as normal with all this suspicion hanging over us? You've got everything upside down, making things hard for us without any grounds for it. No *evidence* as you call it. And you won't listen when we tell you to look somewhere else for her killer.'

'If you know who it was, why don't you just tell us? Or the police? Why are we having all these games?'

'You think they'd believe us? We hoped you two and your little friends would get to the truth and make sure we were off the hook. Instead, you've done the opposite. We're all feeling the stress, wondering if one of us might be next.'

This was a whole new idea, and Simmy stared at him. 'That's ridiculous,' she decided. 'You're just being dramatic for the sake of it.'

'And you're not?' he flashed back, suddenly savage. 'All you had to do was *listen*, and instead you go charging around with that boy, upsetting everything.'

'Listen to what? If you've been dropping subtle hints, I'm afraid we've missed them. You'll have to be a lot more plain-spoken. Let me say it again – if you know who killed Josephine, just tell us. Simple as that. No messing about. No more games.'

'I don't *know*,' he admitted. 'But I've a very good idea.' He twitched for a full fifteen seconds, and then said, 'We're not stupid enough to just give you a name. Anybody knows that's the quickest way to disaster.'

None of them had moved to sit down, but stood uncomfortably in the big main room. Simmy was moving around the room, talking and thinking and feeling a rising anger. 'So let's cut through some of this nonsense,' she said, looking at Christopher, who appeared to be following some very absorbing chain of thought. 'Ben thought Richmond might have been Hilda's child, given away because of his arm. Is that true?' She knew she was crossing a line, but all her patience had evaporated. She could see no reason to hold back, having got this far.

'That's no secret,' said Fabian, astonishingly. 'They told him the full story when he was eighteen, but he never wanted to have anything to do with her. They both agreed that things should stay as they were, once he'd been told the truth.' He shrugged. 'That's got nothing to do with anything now.'

'Yes, but—' Simmy wrestled her thoughts into some kind of order. 'You all call him "Uncle". He's got your surname.'

'So what? All that was long before my time,' he said irritably. 'And I'm telling you – it's got nothing to do with what we're talking about.'

'Of course it has,' interrupted Christopher, who had finally gone to sit on the sofa, leaving Simmy to handle the conversation. 'It's the whole reason for everything.'

Fabian almost choked and Simmy belatedly pointed him to the armchair by the sofa. 'What?' he gasped.

'Who was his father? Isn't that where all this leads?'

Simmy closed her eyes, rerunning all the talk she'd had with Ben and Christopher and the Armitage family. She could not recall her fiancé paying much attention to Ben's

299

findings about Hilda's child. When she opened her eyes again, both men were looking at her.

Fabian gave a croaking sort of laugh. 'You need to ask Petrock about that, as well as your boss, bloody Oliver West, who's meant to be such an expert on everything. Giving poor old Josie the runaround, making life hell for Richmond, always looking for the main chance. That girl – Fiona – she'll tell you.'

Again, there was astonishment. But neither Simmy nor Christopher could face listening to yet more of Fabian's utterances. 'I guess that's for another day,' said Christopher stiffly. 'Now, could you please leave? And don't come here again. We've had a long day, and there's nothing more to be gained now. Remember – you came to us in the first place, and every time since. We've been very patient, but enough's enough. As I see it, you're nothing more than a mischief-maker with too much time on your hands. And none of it is our problem.'

Fabian's mouth opened and closed, but no words came out. Simmy struggled against a surge of pity for him. 'Go home,' she said quietly. 'And we'll see you at Josephine's funeral.'

'Point taken,' said Fabian nastily. 'Sorry to waste your time.'

'Just go, will you?' said Christopher. 'You've had your say, and we admit we haven't been very helpful where the police are concerned. But if it's true that none of you Armitages have anything to feel guilty about, then it'll be over soon enough. It's always like this when they're investigating a murder. People feel insecure, anxious, even offended. Their lives are picked apart and nasty stuff gets exposed to the light of day. Believe me, I know what it's like. I dare say it'll only be a few more days now.'

Fabian went meekly and with very few more words. Simmy noted that his expression was very thoughtful as he turned to go. Some new idea appeared to be preoccupying him – as it was her. Faint flutterings began in her stomach. There were inescapable connections to be made, if only she could stay awake to make them. But she was hopelessly tired, it was dark outside, and she and Christopher had a long list of things to talk about. So did she and Ben. And she and Moxon. Fabian had told them something crucial and all they'd done was send him home without properly listening.

'Errghh,' she groaned, when Fabian had finally gone. 'This is too much. I don't want to do it any more. I'm so tired I don't even care who killed who or why.'

Her fiancé wrapped an arm around her shoulders. 'Leave it till the morning. Nothing's going to happen tonight. Fabian's a real case, isn't he. I thought he'd totally lost the plot when he started on poor old Oliver. Why drag him into it?'

Simmy only yawned.

Saturday morning dawned as usual with Robin wanting his early feed to coincide with the rising of the sun. The two events really did coincide this time, as the feed was nearly an hour later than usual and the sunrise was getting slightly earlier every day. Simmy sat watching it and thinking about the previous day. From the moment she and Ben had found the boxes in Hilda's garage, there had been clues falling like ripe peaches into her lap. Odd remarks, sudden connections, database revelations – she knew that the whole picture was concealed amongst them somehow – probably not even very hard to find, if she just applied herself.

Her first duty was to call Moxon and claim his approval for going to see Mrs Harriman as requested. Whether or not she would have anything fresh to tell him remained to be seen. It was entirely likely that the police already knew at least as much as Simmy and Ben did. More, in fact. They could have identified other areas of Josephine's life that caused her to be a murder victim. Or they could have established beyond doubt that she had been killed by a manic burglar, panicked by her unexpected presence as he stuffed her collection of china and porcelain into his bag.

As usual, she went back to bed after the feed, with Robin cuddled close, drifting in and out of sleep until past eight o'clock. 'Are you sure it's all right to do that?' Christopher asked her, when he brought the morning tea. 'I get the impression it's virtually illegal.'

'Are you going to report me?'

'Only if you don't let me have a turn sometimes. It looks blissful.'

'It is. And unless you weigh twenty stone or are dead drunk, there's absolutely no danger whatsoever. At least, there's probably the same danger as dropping him out of a window or falling downstairs carrying him. Things happen, but that's no reason to live like the Murdstones.'

'Well said.' At the age of fourteen, Simmy and Christopher had simultaneously read *David Copperfield* and quoted it to each other for years afterwards. They had delightedly gone back to doing so now, when they discovered they could still recall the whole story. 'Although I worry a bit that Agnes wouldn't have had her babies in bed with her.'

'Oh, she did. She wouldn't be at all risk-averse.'

'And she'd never get drunk.'

'Definitely not.'

'In fact, you can probably tell the quality of a person's character by just that – how much cuddle they give their babies. And, of course, it would explain a lot about how the babies themselves turned out.'

Christopher smiled, but let the banter drop at that point. 'By the way, your squirrel is demanding to speak to his solicitor about unfair imprisonment. I think we need to let him go, and pretend we never met him.'

'Another law we'd be breaking.'

'I don't suppose I'm the first to observe that the law can very often be an ass.'

'You're not. Mr Bumble said it – though I think the exact words are "the law is a ass".'

'So – what are we going to do today, then?' he asked. Because he only had alternate Saturdays at home, they acquired added value. 'It's not raining.'

'I've got to phone Moxon and Ben, for a start. And I need to be available if Bonnie wants me at the shop. I think we also said we'd try to get together tomorrow.'

'You won't go down there, will you? Not after yesterday?' Simmy had told him of her emergency deliveries, driving down to Newby Bridge in the van without Robin. He had been careful not to criticise, but

303

she could see he hadn't liked it.

'Not if I can help it. My time is yours, Bonnie permitting. I doubt if she'll summon me today, anyway. I don't think any of us can say for sure what could happen tomorrow.'

'And that's the nearest I'll get to a promise, is it?'

'I promise I won't go anywhere today without you,' she prevaricated. 'We might have to go places together. You won't mind that, will you?'

He laughed. 'Why would I? The fact is, you've got me well and truly sucked into this murder malarky. I keep thinking of poor Josephine and how harmless she was. And the effect it's had on everybody at work is tragic. The place is in meltdown, and I'm furious with whoever made that happen.' He hesitated. 'Did you get the impression that Fabian virtually told us, last night? Or was I imagining it?'

'The only impression I ever get from Fabian is that he's auditioning for the part of Uriah Heep. I don't think his mind works well enough for anything he says to be credible.'

'All the same—'

'What?'

'I'm finding myself worryingly keen to get to the bottom of it. I seem to have caught the sleuthing bug from you and Ben, because I can hardly think about anything else.'

'Good,' said Simmy.

Moxon was evidently delighted to get her call and even more delighted to hear what she had to say. 'You really did it?' he repeated. 'I wasn't sure you would.'

'It was quite a lot to ask,' she reminded him. 'But it turned out to be all very easy. Christopher knows her, as it happens. Did she tell you about Josephine doing some sort of research? Have the police taken her computer – because it must all be on there.'

'They have. That's all I know.'

'I think she must have been working on something with Hilda Armitage. They were buying up old papers at the auction.' A thought struck her. 'I wonder if Josephine tipped Hilda off about what was coming up for sale. She might even have arranged for it to go cheap, if she somehow managed to hide the best stuff. There was a bit of trouble, when Christopher first started doing the actual auctioning.'

'Slow down. You've lost me.'

'It's only speculation, anyway. The real point is that Chrissie Harriman told us that Josephine was very much into this project, whatever it was. She stayed up late every night working on it.'

'But isn't Hilda Armitage dead?'

'Quite recently, yes. But her whole family was close to Josephine—'

'Right,' he interrupted. 'Which is why they're persons of interest and are being kept under close scrutiny.'

'And they don't like it. Fabian came here last night again complaining about it.'

'Was he harassing you?' His tone had become suddenly sharp.

'Oh, no – not really. He's too pathetic for that. I don't think there's any real harm in him.'

'Not a killer, then?'

She laughed. 'I'm sure you're not supposed to ask me that. Aren't there laws against slander?'

He returned her laugh, and after a few more questions, he concluded the call with sincere thanks for her help. 'Call again any time,' he said in conclusion.

Christopher had been listening, his expression very thoughtful. 'Fabian is harmless, isn't he?' he said, as soon as she'd finished the call. 'And I'm pretty close to believing him when he says none of his family are killers. Which doesn't leave many suspects, does it?'

'As far as we know, it would focus everything onto the auction house,' she agreed sadly. 'It must have been someone she knew, if she let them in – as it seems she did.'

'Not necessarily. All kinds of criminals con people into letting them in.

'And if it wasn't one of her own knives, then they'd have come prepared. Premeditated. I keep coming back to the same thought,' said Christopher miserably. 'I was awake half the night trying to work round it, but it won't go away.'

'I think I might know what it is. And I think there's a chance that Ben will have arrived at the same one. But we probably shouldn't say it out loud, in case we influence each other. Is that silly?'

'A bit. I mean – what happens now?'

'I'll phone Ben.'

But Ben got there first, with dramatic news. 'I've had a letter from Richmond,' he said. 'I haven't read it all yet, but I think it explains the whole thing.'

Simmy mind clogged up. 'What? Why you? He's never even met you.'

'Says I'm the only independent party he can think of. He thinks you and Christopher might have vested interests. And I guess he doesn't know your exact address.'

'What a cheek!'

'He says it's all in Josephine's filing cabinets – unless the murderer took it. Which is possible. But he's sent copies. It *was* Randolph Churchill all along.'

'Hang on.' Her brain was still barely functioning. 'Isn't he dead by now?'

'Letters, Sim. Five highly incriminating letters from him, saying he took no responsibility for her child and no attempt to blackmail him would have a hope of succeeding. Richmond made copies of them. He was helping Josephine. It's all here – but I still haven't had a chance to read it properly.'

'We'll have to come down,' she realised. 'None of it makes sense over the phone. Do you want me to tell Moxon? Should he be there as well?'

'Not yet. Help me figure out the implications first.'

'Right.' She looked at Christopher, who was listening to her end of the conversation with eyebrows firmly raised. 'We'll be there in about an hour.'

The eyebrows dropped and a long breath was exhaled. Simmy thought she detected an encouraging level of excitement along with the more obvious signs of resignation.

Chapter Twenty

Simmy bundled her unprotesting infant into his car seat, and waited impatiently for Christopher to lock the house and join her in the passenger seat. 'Why are you driving?' he said.

'Because I know the road better than you.'

He started to question her about the phone call, but she said, 'Don't talk. We need to keep open minds until we see these letters. Richmond thinks we're biased.'

'Against who?'

'Whom,' she said, in honour of her father. 'I don't know. Possibly in favour of somebody.'

'Can I talk a bit? I keep remembering more to tell you.'

'If you must.'

'For a start, when I checked the computer yesterday I finally remembered a bit more about that sale where I had to deputise for Oliver. I remember Oliver arguing with Josephine about it, and not having any idea what was going on. All I could glean was that there was potential trouble over the description of the lot.'

'Yes, you told me that already,' said Simmy.

'I didn't tell you all of it,' he persisted. 'You know there's a disclaimer, and we make it clear we can't confirm what the vendor claims about provenance and authenticity and all that. But we're still expected to get it right as far as we possibly can. It was a few months later, when some more papers came in from the Bolt person. Oliver was quite excited and insisted the stuff was genuine, and put a high reserve on it. I remember him saying "We don't want a repeat of last time, when Henderson let it go for peanuts." I was a bit wounded by that, I remember.'

'What did Josephine say?'

'I'm not sure, but she wasn't happy about it. But Oliver was the boss, and I assume they did as he wanted.'

'How much did it sell for, then?'

'Nine hundred pounds. For one letter. Hilda Armitage bought it. She had plenty of money, it seems.'

'That's a lot. But not exactly enough to justify a murder, surely?' She realised that Christopher was working on a different level from her and Ben. Obsessing about one small detail, when they were trying to get a hold of a far bigger picture. She wasn't even certain she was following his logic.

'I think it must have been one of a string of similar transactions. I didn't get a chance to go through the whole file – it's enormous, and I never was much good at finding things on a computer. I was rather hoping that Ben might have managed to hack it, after all.' He smiled ruefully. 'That would get me off the hook.'

'He didn't.'

'Pity.'

'So . . . ?' she prompted, not quite believing that he was on the verge of taking control of the whole matter. On other occasions she had either left him out completely or chivvied him into taking an interest when he clearly hadn't wanted to.

'So I'm not saying any more, because we agreed last night not to make guesses that could influence each other. And you need to concentrate on this ridiculous road.'

Which she did, ignoring with great difficulty the squawks from the back seat as Robin registered the outrageous fact that his mid-morning feed was imminently due and here he was in a pesky car again.

Helen Harkness opened the door to them with an expression that clearly said, 'Here we go again.' Somehow it often seemed that the final stages of understanding a crime were conducted in her dining room. Simmy was impressed by her tolerance and nervous of taking it for granted.

'Sorry,' she said. 'This must seem a bit awful to you.'

'No worse than usual. Although I would have preferred it if Ben had gone back to Newcastle two days ago, as planned.'

That was another unresolved issue, Simmy realised, hoping that Helen didn't hold her responsible for it. 'Let's hope it won't take long, then,' she said. 'It must feel a bit like an invasion.'

'He's in the dining room,' said Helen, with a shrug that said it all.

Ben had papers spread out across the table and a pad of A4 paper in front of him. 'I think I've got it,' he said. 'Come and see.'

'Let's park Robin somewhere first,' said Simmy. 'I hardly dare mention it, but he's going to be hungry any minute now.'

Ben waved this away as irrelevant, and hastened to show them the five letters, signed in a scrawl that only gradually came into focus as R. Churchill. Simmy and Christopher each took one and forgot everything else as they deciphered the handwriting. They were stiff in tone, and repetitive. Their dates covered a period of three weeks in September 1962. There was no letterhead or address – just a date. 'Richmond's letter explains nearly everything,' said Ben. 'Do you want me to summarise?'

Christopher had turned to another of the letters. 'Did we sell these to Hilda Armitage?' he asked. 'If so, they're dynamite.'

'Why would she buy them, when they're addressed to her?' Simmy asked. 'She'd have had them all along.'

'Ah!' said Christopher, going pink. 'Silly me.'

'She wanted to sell them, actually,' said Ben. 'Oliver West told her they'd raise a fortune, with the provenance and so forth. But Richmond heard about it and tried to stop her.'

Simmy and Christopher could find nothing to say. The questions were tumbling over each other so fast that words couldn't keep pace. She spluttered slightly, before waving at Ben to continue.

'Then Richmond's son Petrock got involved. Obviously it would be a great coup for his book if he could quote actual letters. He probably fancied the idea that he was Winston Churchill's great-grandson.'

'Wouldn't anyone?' said Christopher.

'Listen,' said Ben, holding Richmond's letter, which seemed to run to several pages. '"There I was, caught between my mother and my son, both of them impatient to make the whole story public, and cast shame on the man they believed to be my father. I became obsessed with it myself, comparing my appearance with photographs of the Churchills. I insisted there should be a DNA test, but could find no way of doing it. I would need something from Randolph or one of his offspring, and that didn't seem possible. Hilda refused to see me or speak to me – as if I was a mere detail in the story. If it hadn't been for Josephine, I think I might well have murdered somebody myself."' He looked up. 'As you see, it's nowhere near as simple as you might think.'

'I didn't think it was simple,' said Simmy, feeling very churned up. 'The poor man.'

'Where does Josephine come into it?' asked Christopher, suddenly pale.

'Aha!' Ben sorted the pages of the letter, and selected another. 'It's all here. "She came to me, a year ago now, having realised what Oliver and Hilda were trying to do. Oliver was widely regarded as an expert in the authenticity of documents, and he stated with complete certainty that these letters had definitely been written by Randolph. Josephine knew Hilda, of course, and asked if she could have a look at them herself. Well, almost immediately she had doubts. The lack of an address struck her as very strange, for one thing. And the fact that there were no envelopes with them. She accused Hilda of forging them herself. Hilda denied it and begged her to keep quiet. What was there to gain from making trouble, she asked. And so much to lose. Josephine was torn – and then Hilda said she'd leave her the house if she promised not to rock the boat."'

'Blimey!' said Christopher. 'That's a bribe and a half.'

'So she did promise and did get the house,' said Simmy. 'Poor Richmond. He must have felt terribly let down.'

'They were going to get married,' said Ben, flourishing the letter. 'And then he was going to find a way of doing the DNA test and the whole thing would be set right, publicly.'

'Which wouldn't matter once Hilda was dead,' said Simmy. 'And they probably knew that nobody was ever going to take much notice of Petrock's book. It's got far too many adjectives.'

'It would matter to someone else, though,' said Christopher slowly.

Ben looked at him and nodded. Perched in his chair at the end of the table, Robin gave a little squeal.

'Oliver,' said Simmy.

'To save his reputation,' said Christopher.

'Shall I call Moxon now?' said Ben.

They all went up to the Mortal Man in Troutbeck for lunch. 'We can confirm the booking for our wedding breakfast at the same time,' said Simmy.

Bonnie was with them, having closed the shop at twelve-thirty. 'We owe you,' said Simmy. 'You've been a star.'

'Will they have arrested him yet?' asked the girl, after listening intently to three people all trying to bring her up to date.

'Unlikely,' said Christopher. 'They'll need to have a chat with Richmond, first.'

'Maybe not,' said Ben. 'They can take him in for questioning at least.'

But nobody really cared. 'Are we absolutely sure it wasn't Petrock?' Simmy worried, just before they got to the pub. 'Hasn't he got just as much of a motive?'

Ben laughed. 'Surely I told you – he's got a perfect alibi. He spent the whole of Saturday, Sunday and Monday at a writing conference in Aberdeen. There must be two hundred witnesses to vouch for him.'

'How do you know that?' Simmy wondered.

'I googled him,' said Ben, as if it was obvious. 'There's a list of people they call "attendees" which seems a weird word to use. Anyway, he *attended* it all right. I happen to know someone else on the list and I called to check.'

'Who?' asked Bonnie.

'A student at Newcastle. She's a writer – already got her first publishing contract. She was on a panel with Petrock.'

Simmy cheered. 'Ben – you're wasted on us. Honestly, I think you'll be Prime Minister one day.'

'What about Fabian?' Christopher said later, when they were all seated round a table in the pub. 'How much did he know about it all?'

'I never met him,' Ben reminded them. 'But my guess is he was completely out of his depth. He never knew Oliver and had nothing to do with Richmond. Aunt Hilda had spurned him, and the cousins probably thought he was a nuisance and an embarrassment.'

'And Josephine?' said Simmy.

'We might never know,' said Ben. 'But I can't see that he had anything at all to do with her death. Nor Uncle Ambrose. But everyone else was right in it. Two factions – Oliver, Hilda and Petrock on one side, with Josephine and Richmond on the other. Fighting over the authenticity of those letters.'

'You forgot Keith,' said Simmy.

Ben waved this aside. 'It all comes down to history, when you think about it,' he went on. 'Proper nuts and bolts, brass tacks history. I've been thinking that's the sort of thing I want to focus on. The real stuff. The papers and objects that people used and valued, that mattered in their daily lives.' He looked at Christopher. 'Do you think there might be an opening for me at your saleroom?'

Even Bonnie was silenced. Ben laughed uncomfortably, and explained. 'I'm not saying I want to become an auctioneer – but I want to learn more about things from the past. Just a summer job – okay? Checking provenance, writing catalogue descriptions, that sort of thing. And I can see a few ways your database could be smartened up.'

Christopher sighed. 'If you do that, either Pattie or Fiona will kill you.'

'Well, you're going to be the boss now. You'll have to tell them not to.'

Simmy went to talk to the pub landlord about her wedding, and Bonnie found herself with Robin on her lap. Christopher's phone tinkled and he blinked at the screen.

'It's Humphrey,' he said, to the uncomprehending

youngsters. 'He says he's found a supplier of the ideal stone for our new fireplace, and thinks it'll work well. He'll see us on Monday for the final leg of our Big Undertaking.' He showed Simmy the message when she came back.

'Great,' she said. 'But first I need you to undertake to be my lawful wedded husband.'

REBECCA TOPE is the author of three bestselling crime series, set in the Cotswolds, Lake District and West Country. She lives on a smallholding in rural Herefordshire, where she enjoys the silence and plants a lot of trees.

rebeccatope.com